All the King's Men

A KINGS OF CHARLESTON NOVEL

KAT H. CLAYTON

Dedication
In Memory of Ms. Chafin

Chapter

1

M Y HEARTBEAT PULSED UNDER MY skin, so loud and fast I could feel each thud as if it were keeping time with a race horse. I was excited, but terrified. For the first time in my life, there was no chosen path to follow, only endless possibilities.

I let down the windows and let the air rush against my hair and skin as we sped out of the Charleston city limits. I had always loved the tingly feeling of the wind on my skin. Normally, I was flying on horseback, but today a car would have to do. Either way, the wind against my face was what I thought freedom should feel like. Maybe that's why had always loved horses . . . the rush of air, the pounding of hooves, and the open space all equaled freedom. The one thing I wanted more than anything else.

I never thought finding freedom would require running away, but I hadn't known what else to do. I just hoped that one day my parents could understand why I had done it. I had always assumed that when I got older, I would become a champion jumper and go on to inherit my parents' successful thoroughbred legacy, Ghost Hill Farms. But that all changed when my parents announced—a week before the end of my junior year of high school—that we were packing up our lives in Lexington, Kentucky, to move to Charleston, South Carolina.

I would never forget the emotions I had felt that day. My world had been blown to bits, and I didn't think the pieces could ever be put back together—at least, not like they used to be. And maybe that was okay, because as terrible as the situation was, it had led me to Cal.

I looked over at Cal, who had fallen asleep in the passenger seat. His handsome face was still, and his jet-black hair was whirling in the wind, but he didn't move or wake up. I smiled to myself.

As terrifying as leaving our parents behind was, for the first time in our lives we were truly free. No more parties to appear and perform at like trained circus monkeys. No more disappointing our parents when we weren't the life of the party. I felt a pang of sadness as I thought about my dad and mother. I loved them, even though I never really understood them or felt like I belonged in their world. If only I could convince them to leave, too, and we all could live happily ever after at Ghost Hill.

I looked down at the speedometer to make sure I wasn't going too fast. I didn't need to attract the attention of the cops. I was positive by now that Tyson had called in the police to find us. We were an easy target, since we had driven away from Charleston in a black Audi clearly marked with Kythera on its wheel well and a big red "K" on the back. Now I understood why they marked their cars and tattooed their members. It made it pretty difficult to escape—but we were still going to try.

"You got an idea where we're going?" asked Cal, suddenly awake and looking around. He stretched his arms out and yawned.

"I'm not telling. You never would tell me when I would ask. What makes you think I'm not going to leave you guessing?" I said playfully, trying to lighten the mood.

I knew if I tried to be too serious, I wouldn't be able to take it and we would turn back around for Charleston.

He stared at me with his ocean-blue eyes. Those eyes were what had gotten me in this mess to begin with, but even though I had tried really hard to ignore them, I couldn't resist them. I had fallen for Cal the moment he and his parents had appeared on our doorstep our first day in Charleston. Even when I found out the real reason we had moved, it couldn't change the feelings I had for him. I was already a goner.

"You don't have a clue where we're going, do you?"

I didn't look at him, even though I could feel his eyes on me. Instead, I looked at the road sign ahead. It said "15 miles to Orangeburg," wherever that was.

"Sure I do."

"Uh-huh," said Cal, as he leaned back in his seat, putting his arms behind his head.

He knew I was bluffing, but I wasn't about to let him know that he was right. I just kept driving because that was the only thing that I could do. I needed to put as much distance as possible between myself and Charleston even if that meant driving to Canada.

A beeping noise came from the instrument panel display system. A picture of a gas pump with "low fuel" under it had taken over the screen. I hadn't even paid attention to how much gas I had before speeding out of the driveway of Cal's home. It had been the last thing on my mind, especially after the ominous text I'd received only seconds after we left that read: You can run, but you can't hide for long.

Just thinking about it gave me chills.

I had a gut feeling Tyson, Cal's dad and leader of Kythera, had sent the text, but I couldn't be sure, since neither Cal nor I recognized the number. It could've been from the person or persons trying to get rid of Kythera, too. Either way, it wasn't good.

"Hey, I need to stop for gas. Do you have any money on you?" I started scanning the side of the road for an exit with a gas station.

"I don't have cash. I only have my debit card and we can't use that. They'll track it in no time," he said, sitting up in the passenger seat, and pulling out his wallet.

I opened the middle console. There was a hundred-dollar bill. Dad always had a habit of leaving random money in our cars. He would always forget he put it there until he used that car the next time.

I waved the crisp bill at Cal. "We're good for now, but I don't know what we'll do after we've used this."

I pulled off the next exit into the nearest gas station and up to an open pump. I cut the engine off and looked around the busy station, wondering if I should have picked a more deserted place.

"We'll have to stop at an ATM somewhere and I'll have to withdraw some money. Hopefully we can get far enough away before they track us to the ATM," Cal said, as he opened the door and got out of the car.

I handed him the hundred-dollar bill and he walked into the gas station. I stared out the windshield. The sun was starting to fade into the horizon and the lights of the city up ahead were starting to flicker on. I listened to the roar of the traffic from the interstate, hoping it would drown out my loud thoughts.

Cal came back from inside the station and started pumping gas. He threw a bag of M&Ms in through the passenger window, which barely missed my nose.

"Hey! You need better aim!" I yelled across the seat in a mock-angry voice.

I crawled over into the passenger seat and craned my head out of the open window. He looked at me, his bright blue eyes twinkling mischievously. I laid my head on the door and smiled at him, unable to stop the feelings that coursed through my body. No matter what had happened, I was in love with Cal Roman—even though it was his fault that I was in this mess. He had used the powers of Kythera to get me here, and now there was no getting out, even though he had tried.

Obviously my parents' strong connections to the Queen, the Sultan of Brunei, and the like were too much for Kythera to let go, especially when my parents had no choice if they wanted to keep their money. They had finally revealed to me that we had lost most of our fortune in the stock market and that Kythera was the only thing keeping them from losing everything.

When I learned the truth, that we might lose the horses, I was willing to cooperate with Kythera—until Mr. Roman took it too far. With my classmate Jacob's blood on my hands as I knelt by his lifeless body in the Romans' library, I knew I couldn't be a part of the secrets, even if it meant my family would lose all their money and the horses that meant everything to me.

I had run from the house and got into my car, and was ready to bolt by myself—until Cal had jumped in front of my car, prepared to go with me.

"Why don't you let me drive for a while?" asked Cal, as he put the gas nozzle back on the pump with a click. I was lost in my thoughts and it took me several seconds to respond.

"But you don't know where we're going," I finally said, leaning my head on the passenger door.

"Neither do you—plus, I know the back roads. We can't be on the interstate anymore." He screwed the gas cap back on and walked over to the driver's-side door. I wanted to jump back into the driver's seat before he could open the door, but I knew he was right about the roads—and the fact I didn't know where we were going.

Cal got into the car and started the engine. I fastened my seat belt and settled into the seat, rolling the window halfway up. "I'm sorry I can't help with the money. I don't have an account on my own." I fiddled with a loose thread on my school uniform skirt.

"Don't worry about it. I'm just happy to be here with you. I don't care about the money." He reached over the middle console for my hand. I entwined my fingers with his, the sparks flying between us.

"Okay," I said, unable to keep from smiling. Regardless of the fact that we had just ticked off a lot of powerful people, Cal made me feel safe.

A few minutes later, I felt myself falling asleep. I tried my best to stay awake, but allowed my eyes to close. Seconds later, the blackness behind my lids was infiltrated by flashes of blue.

"Damn it," Cal said quietly under his breath.

I opened my eyes and instantly felt my stomach crash to the floor. There was a line of cops across the highway, their bright blue lights piercing the dark sky.

"That can't be for us, can it?"

Cal stared out the windshield, bringing the car to a complete stop. Without warning, he pushed the gas pedal and spun the car around in the other direction. I tried to brace myself, but gravity threw me into the door. I put my hands out just in time to keep my head from hitting the window. I let out a scream as the car finally started moving in a straight line again.

"Cal! Have you lost your mind!?" I said, breathing so fast that I felt like I was going to faint.

"Those cops are for us, and unless you want to go back to Charleston, we've got to get out of here."

I looked over at the speedometer as it reached one hundred and soared on toward one hundred-twenty. I couldn't say anything else. I closed my eyes, hoping that would make me feel less sick. The car swerved to the right and there was a car horn honking, but I didn't dare open my eyes. The car jolted as we obviously went off the pavement and then we went airborne for a second before slamming against the ground. I was breathing so hard that I thought I was going to hyperventilate. I tried to pretend I was on a rollercoaster at Six Flags, but I couldn't convince myself that we would exit the ride safely in the end.

Finally, the car slowed down, and I felt like we were moving at a safe speed. I opened my eyes slowly to see that we were on some two-lane road, surrounded by trees full of thick Spanish moss. I turned my head to look behind us. The cops were gone. A sense of relief swept through me and I slouched over in the seat, putting my head on my knees.

"You okay?" asked Cal.

I tried to respond, but I couldn't get the words to come out. I could only sit there, paralyzed with my head down on my knees.

After a few seconds, I was able to breathe normally and sit up. "Yeah, I think so. I guess they were for us, then."

Cal laughed. "Of course they were. How often do you see a line of cops across a highway?"

I shrugged my shoulders. "I dunno, on TV? There could be a big car chase or a fugitive on the run."

"There are a couple of fugitives on the run."

"Really?"

He laughed again, "We're the fugitives."

"Oh." I turned to look at him, totally clueless.

"You really think Kythera and my dad would just let us walk away?"

I stared out the window, the scenery now pitch-black, our headlights the only thing illuminating the road. "No, but I guess I just didn't think about them going that far with the police and everything. When I think of a fugitive, I think of murderers or armed robbers, not two teenagers."

The situation was finally starting to sink in. We were in big trouble. I had known our parents wouldn't be happy, but in that moment, I had forgotten how much power Kythera really had. Not to mention the mysterious people looking to destroy it. This was no longer a case of two teenagers running away because they disagreed with their parents, but a case of two forces fighting for power.

"We're a liability right now. We've stepped away from Kythera and they're afraid we'll spill their secrets, not to mention I've put my dad's leadership and your parents' memberships in jeopardy. Plus, whoever has been after Kythera will be desperate to get a hold of us," said Cal.

Chills formed on my arms. I closed the air vents and crossed my arms over my body for warmth. "Then what should we do? Can we really get away?"

Before Cal could answer, I saw the familiar flashing blue lights ahead. I sucked in a quick breath. How did they get in front of us so fast?

"Now what?" I asked, tightening my seat belt.

Cal slowed the car and came to a full stop a hundred feet in front of the three cop cars lining the two lanes. He threw the car into reverse and pushed the gas pedal to the floor, causing the car to violently turn in the opposite direction away from the cops. Guess that answered my question.

We were speeding in the opposite direction and I felt my stomach do a flip-flop from the sudden change in direction and bolting speed. I didn't dare speak, because I didn't want Cal to be distracted and slam us into one of the giant oak trees on the side of the road. There were more faint blue lights ahead, and I knew our run was coming to an end—unless he decided to off-road. I prayed he didn't think about that one.

As he approached the police cars ahead, he looked in the rearview mirror. The cops that we had just sped away from were now behind us. He stopped the car in the middle of the road, gripping the wheel with both hands. "I guess there isn't anything else I can do. Sorry, Casper."

"Don't apologize. I'm not sorry. We'll get out somehow." I reached over and grabbed his hand tightly. He looked at me and squeezed my hand.

The cops in front of us started walking toward our car. I didn't know what would happen next, but I knew it involved a long trip in the back of a police car. I thought I should be more terrified of being caught than I was. The little taste of freedom I had gotten only made me want to fight for it more.

I stared at the clock on the concrete block wall as we waited for our parents to come pick us up from the Charleston police station. I had smiled and waved at one of the deputies I recognized as we were marched in. He had started to wave back until another officer gave him a disapproving look. Unfortunately, the police station was becoming all too familiar.

"You've been a bad influence on me," I said to Cal, nudging him with my shoulder.

He looked up from the floor. "Yeah, and how's that? Aren't you the one who decided to run away first?"

"True," I said, forgetting the sarcastic remark I was going to make. "Sometimes you're too smart."

"Yeah, well, if I had been smarter you wouldn't be in this mess at all," he said, returning his gaze to the floor.

The double doors squeaked open and Tyson Roman walked in, with my parents following behind. I didn't see Cal's mother anywhere, but she never seemed to be involved with anything to do with Kythera.

Tyson's square jaw was tight and his cheeks were red. His eyes were trained on me and Cal—somehow at the same time. Cal didn't look much like his dad, except for that same strong square face, and they both tightened their jaws when they were angry. Cal's black, wavy hair and blue eyes were his mothers. Within seconds, Tyson was in front of us, his arms crossed over his perfectly ironed gray dress shirt. My parents stood to the left of him, with equally unhappy expressions.

"You've gone too far this time, Cal," said Tyson, as he shook his head of dirty blond hair. I usually loved his deep Southern drawl, but today it just sounded menacing.

Cal looked at the floor and nodded. Tyson turned his gaze to me. "And I don't know what we're going to do with you."

"Maybe you can do what you did to Jacob? Won't that solve everything?" I said.

His eyes widened and his face went white. "You need to learn your place. I'm in control, not you."

I just stared at him, my eyes trained on his light blue eyes. All the fear of before melted away. "For now," I hissed.

Before Tyson could throw another threat, my mother stepped toward me, nudging Cal out of the way. She was wearing a navy pantsuit, with her black hair pulled into a bun and her lips their usual deep red.

"Casper, what were you thinking?" Her eyebrows flew up her creaseless forehead. Mother always showed every emotion on her face, yet her face showed no signs of it.

I shrugged my shoulders, no longer caring what she said to me. Normally, I would have argued with her until eventually both our faces were purple. That was what we had always done in the past—but I no longer respected any of her opinions enough to argue. If she could sit by and let Kythera dictate our lives and do things that made my skin crawl, then I no longer cared what she thought about anything.

"You're grounded for the foreseeable future," she sneered, as she bent down to look me in the face. I stared at her blue-gray eyes, which were full of rage. I felt nothing.

"Let's get out of here," said Dad, as he gently pulled on Mother's arm. "We can discuss this at home." He didn't look at me as he turned for the door. He looked defeated, his shoulders slumped and his black hair flying wildly instead of the usual slicked-back style he preferred.

I reached for Cal's hand and squeezed before getting up from the bench. He looked up at me, his eyes dark and stormy, and ran a hand through his hair like he always did when he was nervous. His expression was blank, which made me feel even worse.

"Don't expect to be seeing my son anytime soon," Tyson whispered as I walked by.

I looked at him, shock written all over my face. That had never been an outcome I thought possible. We were both members and would have to be at the same functions. But could Tyson really keep us apart? For the first time, I did feel fear. I loved Cal, and he was the strength I needed to keep fighting. If we were separated I didn't know how I would ever get control of my life again. Tyson couldn't really keep us apart, could he?

Chapter

2

THE RIDE HOME FROM THE police station
was completely silent. Not one word. I
started to panic, because my parents had
never been this quiet, especially not Mother. She
always had something to say. But she sat silent,
her lips pursed and her bony cheeks sucked in.
She was not happy.

Once in the driveway, I jumped out of the car
as fast as I could and walked up the steps to our
house. The butler opened the creaky front door
and I walked into the foyer, and turned toward
the steps that spiraled up the side of the house.

"Wait right there," said Dad, his voice stern as
a drill sergeant's.

I took a deep breath before spinning around
on the wood floor to face him. His eyes were deep
green, which meant he wasn't happy. My bright

green eyes did the same thing when I was angry or sad.

Mother looked at me with her lips pursed as she walked down the hallway and disappeared behind the double doors.

"What were you thinking?" he asked, shaking his head.

I stood still for a minute, just looking at his pitiful figure. How had he become like this? My parents had always been tough as nails, but apparently the thought of poverty had made them weak.

"That I don't want anything to do with Kythera." I crossed my arms over my chest and threw my chin in the air.

"I thought we already discussed this. We need them to keep our house and the horses. Do you really want to lose Ghost Hill Farms?"

"No, but I'm not willing to give up my soul to keep them."

Dad rolled his eyes. "Don't be so dramatic. You're turning into your mother."

My eyes widened, shocked he had made the comparison. He knew how hard I worked to not be like her. I bit my lip. "I'd rather be her than what you've turned into."

He winced. "Well, I'm only trying to do what's best for this family."

"I'm so sick of that stupid line. You say that all the time." I turned around and started up the steps. I didn't want to hear the same old speech again.

"You stop right now!" he yelled, causing me to shiver.

He had never yelled at me before. I immediately turned around and went back down the stairs. He took a couple of steps forward and stood right in front of me. He was so close I had the urge to move back, but was too scared.

"I've had it with your attitude. I've always let you do whatever you want, and that has to stop. We need to be here and a part of the group if our family is to survive. This isn't some teenage drama, this is real life. Now, you're going to do as I ask and stop causing problems. If you choose to continue acting out, I'll take your away privileges at the Hunt Club. Understood?" His face was full of anger and his lips were set in a straight line.

The thought of not being able to see Wendy, my favorite horse, hit me at the core. She was my only escape in this world that felt like it had been turned upside down.

"Okay," I whispered.

"Now, give me your cell phone." He put out his hand in anticipation. I reluctantly pulled it out of my purse and placed it in his hand.

"Go upstairs and don't come back down till it's time to go to school. The driver will take you since you are not allowed to drive for six months." My mouth dropped open, but the minute I saw his stern face, I looked at the floor and then turned and went up the stairs.

I opened the door to my room and felt a sense

of defeat. I was right back where I had started, only things were worse. But I couldn't give up on the idea of getting out. I had lost the battle, but I fully intended to win the war.

———◆———

A few hours later, my alarm clock began blaring. I rolled over and put my head under the covers. I was exhausted and didn't want to go to school. I could tell them I felt sick, but I knew they wouldn't buy it today. I groaned as I removed the covers and put my feet on the soft cream rug. I dragged myself to the bathroom and turned on the shower.

I put my uniform on and brushed my hair in zombie mode, barely aware of what I was doing. I grabbed my backpack and walked down the stairs as if I were a prisoner sentenced to life without parole. I wondered if I would only get bread and water for breakfast.

As I walked into the dining room, my parents were silently sitting at one end of the table with bowls of steel cut oats and organic raisins. Bread and water would've been better. They looked up at me, but neither said anything. I took my seat at the table and Christina immediately put a bowl of steaming oatmeal in front of me. I whispered a thank you to her as she scurried out of the room before Mother could criticize her for how she had cleaned something wrong. I ignored my parents as I ate the oatmeal, blowing on each hot bite before putting it in my mouth.

Once I was done, I got up and left the room, my parents saying nothing. I walked into the front room and sat down on the couch to wait for the driver. I looked up at the stupid painting over the mantel, remembering the first day I had looked at it and wondered what it had meant. It was a pretty painting in pastels by Antoine Watteau called *Embarkation for Kythera*, and the first day in the house, I had looked at it to notice some red writing on it that said "Kythera Forever." That's where the mystery had begun.

Now, I wish I could forget it.

"The driver is outside waiting," said Dad in a matter-of-fact tone.

I looked at Mother, who was standing beside him in the doorway, but she refused to look at me. She fiddled with her huge diamond ring, twisting it around her tiny manicured finger. I picked up my backpack and went out the front door. The driver jumped out and opened the door for me. I normally would've stopped him, but I didn't care this morning.

I laid my head back in the Lincoln Town Car and closed my eyes. Nothing was going the way I had planned. Not only was my future completely altered, but now it was becoming a nightmare with no escape in sight.

But I couldn't give up on getting out. It was the only way to live the life I wanted, but I just needed to find a way to do it without angering those in control. *But how*?

"We're here, Miss," said the driver.

The driver opened the door and I stepped out. There were tons of kids going in the front doors, all dressed in navy blazers and plaid skirts or khaki pants. Several students stopped and looked at me. Melissa from Spanish class looked in my direction and immediately started whispering to her red-headed friend, Caroline. She didn't even care how obvious what she was doing was. With my head down, I walked toward the front steps. I could feel the stares coming from every angle as if they were laser guns. I practically ran into the building and made a beeline for my locker.

"Casper!" yelled a familiar voice.

I looked over my shoulder to see Marcus Gray barreling toward me with a huge grin on his face. He was the first person who looked happy to see me.

"Hey," I said as I slammed my locker shut.

"You're insane, you know that right?" he said with a wink. I stared up into his handsome face, his deep brown eyes glittering. Marcus's family had joined Kythera shortly after my family had, and we had instantly become best friends. He had always been more optimistic about our futures in Kythera, but he hadn't been able to change my mind.

I shrugged my shoulders. "Apparently."

"Don't feel bad. Insane can be a good thing when you're insanely *badass*." He nudged my shoulder with his hand.

I smiled, "You think so?"

"*Hell, yeah.* I wish I had the guts to stand up to Kythera. You're my new hero." He reached out his hand for my backpack, which I gave to him as we started walking down the crowded hall.

Everyone was still looking, but I didn't care anymore. Maybe they were like Marcus and thought I was gutsy. They were staring because they were in awe of me. Okay, who was I kidding? Even if they thought I was stupid, who cared? I had stood up to the most powerful people in Charleston and *almost* won.

"You need to include Cal in the hero category, too, especially for his amazing driving skills," I said, feeling a little better about the whole situation.

"Yeah, about that—I've got to tell you something . . ." Before Marcus could finish his sentence, I looked up to see Veronica Alamilla standing in the middle of the hallway, staring me down. Veronica was Cal's ex-girlfriend and she had made it clear that she didn't like me the moment we met. Her arms were crossed over her boobs, which were peeking out of her too-tight white button-down, and her pleated skirt grazed the top of her leg that she had stuck out to the side. Obviously she wasn't happy to see me.

"Hey, Veronica," I said sarcastically.

She didn't move out of the way, forcing us to stop in the hallway. "So, how does it feel to be the newest villain?"

"I think most people think I'm pretty gutsy. At least Cal and I stood up to them." I looked up at Marcus, who was staring at Veronica's ample assets. I hit him on the arm and he looked at me and shrugged. I guess I couldn't fault him for being a guy.

Veronica laughed her voice smoky and melodic. "You have no clue, do you?"

I raised my eyebrows, waiting for her to elaborate.

"Cal's gone, thanks to you. From the shock on your face, I guess he didn't try to say goodbye."

My eyes went straight to Marcus. I prayed Veronica was lying, but from the look on his face, I knew she wasn't. "That's what I was trying to tell you. His dad sent him to a boarding school in North Carolina. He left this morning."

"Ah, poor Casper didn't even know. What kind of boyfriend doesn't say goodbye? Oh, I know . . . one that's interested in someone else." Veronica pushed between Marcus and me as she walked down the hallway, her hourglass hips swishing back and forth.

"Why didn't you tell me!?" I felt my world continue to collapse around me.

Things couldn't be over between us, could they? Had he had enough of my attempts to get out from under Kythera? Was he tired of disappointing his parents?

"I was trying to before we saw Veronica, and I called your cell last night but you didn't answer," we continued down the hall toward my first class.

"My parents took it." My shoulders slumped as I stared at the tiled floor with each step.

"I'm sorry, Casper," Marcus said as we reached the doorway to my political science class. He handed me my backpack and took a step back before turning to go to his class.

I stood in the doorway for a couple of seconds, ignoring the chatter in the room behind me. I didn't know how much more I could take before I completely lost it. I had seriously underestimated Tyson.

"Miss Whitley, please take your seat." I jumped at the sound of Ms. Epling's voice. I whirled around and headed for my desk.

I focused on taking notes and didn't pay any attention to anyone in the class—especially Alex Alamilla, Veronica's brother, who was sitting across from me in the U Ms. Epling had the desks arranged in. Alex and I weren't exactly friends all the time. He had a crush on me and had tried to get me to leave Cal, his best friend, for him. I hadn't taken the bait—but ever since then, I couldn't tell one day from the next whether we were friends or not. The minute the bell rang, I leapt from the chair for the door.

"Casper!" shouted Alex, but I ignored him and walked faster until I was lost in the crowd of the hallway. I stopped at my locker, got my calculus book, and made my way to class.

Marcus was already at his desk. He looked

up at me and waved me over, but the minute he saw the expression on my face, he quickly put his hand down. He tapped Charlotte, in the seat behind him, facing the other direction and talking to Sarah, on the shoulder.

Charlotte Watson looked at me, her tawny eyes wide and full of surprise. "Hey! How are you? Is everything okay?" She got up from her seat and hugged me. I didn't return the hug, but stood there motionlessly. I felt so numb and broken.

Charlotte let go of me and sat back down. "Marcus tells me you didn't know Cal was sent to boarding school. I thought you knew or I would've tried to tell you."

I sat down at the desk behind her, slinging my backpack over the chair. "Yeah, well, I didn't."

She turned around to face me. "Sorry."

"Thanks," I muttered as I pulled out my notebook.

Charlotte twisted a couple of strands of her strawberry-blonde hair around her fingers. I guess she was waiting for me to say something else. She had been the first girl I had met when we moved to Charleston and—no surprise—her family were members of the mysterious Kythera. She had been so sweet to me at her family's dinner party where we met, but I knew right away she was a total gossip. She loved to play twenty questions with my social life and I usually ended up playing along, but today she was going to be disappointed.

Finally, she turned around as I pretended to take notes. I looked over at Sarah, who was staring at me. I had met Sarah—surprise! Another Kythera member—at Cal's family's Fourth of July party. She reminded me of the little ballerina who spun around in a pink music box I had as a child.

The minute she caught my eyes, she turned her graceful neck toward the teacher, who was droning on about rational functions. The hour went by so slowly; I tried to keep my mind on class, but I just couldn't. Why hadn't Cal tried to tell me goodbye? When would I see him again? And where exactly was he in North Carolina?

I started scribbling "North Carolina" over and over in the margins of the homework sheet the teacher passed out. I looked up at the clock and then at the back of Charlotte's pretty head. Why hadn't she tried to tell me? She said she thought I already knew, but that just didn't make sense. She loved any chance she could get to spread gossip, and wasn't it some kind of girl code to tell your friend that her boyfriend had been sent away?

The bell finally rung and I shot out of my seat and into the hall like a rocket. I ignored the calls from Marcus and Charlotte. I didn't want to talk to them right now. I didn't want anything to do with anyone involved with Kythera. I zoomed down the hall to my locker again, and got my books for Spanish.

I slammed my locker shut to see a guy I'd never met opening the locker next to mine, a photo of a horse taped inside the door.

"Are you new here?" I asked, assuming he was a new recruit for Kythera.

He had short black hair, deep brown eyes, and light brown skin. His blazer fit snugly around his muscular arms and he was at least six feet tall.

He looked at me and smiled. "No, my family just got back from visiting my grandparents in India, so I missed the first couple of days. I've been going to Saint Mary's until now. My names Dev Chavan. What's your name?" he asked, sticking out his hand for me to shake it.

I cautiously put my hand out and took a hold of his. I knew he wasn't a member of Kythera, because his name had never been mentioned at the meetings—and if he had gone to Saint Mary's for a long time, he wasn't a "K" recruit either.

"My name's Casper Whitley. We just moved here this past summer from Lexington, Kentucky."

"That's rough, starting your senior year at a new high school," he said, his voice pleasant and devoid of any kind of accent.

"Tell me about it," I said, half whispering.

"Do you like horses?" I asked, pointing toward the photo.

He turned and looked. "Yeah, I love riding. That's a photo of one of my horses. What about you, do you like horses?"

"Love them," I said.

He was the first person I had met in Charleston who showed any interest in horses, too. I looked up at the clock, knowing the bell was about to ring. I slammed my locker shut.

"Nice to meet you, Dev," I said, as I walked toward Spanish class.

I hated to leave like that, but I couldn't be late. I wanted to know more about his horses, but since he had a locker next to mine, I knew I would have plenty of time to ask him later.

"Yeah, you, too," he called, walking in the opposite direction.

I felt a little happiness soar through my veins at meeting not just a new person, but someone who looked like they weren't involved with Kythera in any way. I had been starting to think there wasn't anyone in Charleston who wasn't a member.

Chapter

3

THE DREADFUL SCHOOL DAY FINALLY ended and I exhaled deeply as I left the building and walked toward the parking lot. I rummaged through my backpack for my keys, but then I remembered that my parents were forcing me to use the driver. I felt so dumb sitting on the bench, waiting to be picked up in the Lincoln. From looking at the luxury car lot that was the school's parking lot, it was obvious that most of the students had money, but I still felt like a snob when I was picked up by a driver.

I watched as everyone walked to their cars and left. Marcus and Charlotte had both come over to say bye, but I had just looked at them. I'd been frosty to them since class this morning. I had eaten lunch with them, but only nodded when asked a question. They were just a reminder of everything that had gone wrong in my life and I couldn't deal with it right now.

"You need a ride?"

I looked over my shoulder to see Dev standing behind me.

I tried to think of an excuse. I couldn't think of one.

"Oh, no, thanks. I'm waiting for the driver to pick me up."

"Okay, see you tomorrow," he said, as he walked past the bench to the parking lot.

I watched him as he got into an older model Dodge truck. I couldn't help but think how it stuck out from the Mercedes, BMWs, and other luxury cars that were lined up at the exit. Suddenly, I thought of Jacob and his electric blue Ford Focus. Jacob had been given free tuition to St. Mary's in exchange for giving the unnamed group who wanted rid of Kythera information about all of us. Was Dev a spy, too? I hated how Kythera had forced me to think that way. I really doubted he was a spy, but I probably needed to stay far away from him so his blood wouldn't end up on some expensive Persian rug.

The next day, I ran into the school the minute the driver dropped me off, hoping to avoid having to talk to Charlotte or any other Kythera member. I immediately opened my locker. I put my hands on either side of the door in an effort to catch my breath. I really needed to work out more.

"Are you okay?" I looked over to see Dev staring at me with a frown on his face.

"Yeah, I'm fine. I just need to start doing my own running." I stood up straight and started pulling out my notebook and political science book.

"Okay?" he said, confusion filling his voice.

I slammed the locker shut. "Sorry, I guess I should have explained that one. I'm always riding and the horses are usually the one's doing the running."

"That makes more sense now. That's why you pointed out the photo in my locker."

"Yeah, exactly. We have a horse farm in Lexington, and I used to ride every single day." I turned to start walking down the busy hall and Dev fell in stride beside me.

"You could come out to my house sometime and go for a ride with me if you want," he said, fiddling with the strap on his backpack.

"Really? That would be awesome. You're the first person I've met that actually likes horses."

"I think it's freeing to fly on a horse across a field."

"Me, too!" I said, a little too excited.

We finally reached the door of my class, "Well, I guess I'll see you around the lockers later."

I looked up at his smiling face. He looked so relaxed and oblivious, as if he was someone who didn't have anything to worry about except homework and being late for class.

"Here." He pulled out a notebook from his

backpack and ripped out a sheet of paper. "Write down your number and I'll give you a call sometime to go riding."

I felt my cheeks turn red. Was he trying to ask me out or was he just being friendly? I thought about Cal, and although I hadn't heard from him, I was still in love with him. In my head, we were still together, even though he hadn't told me he was leaving. Would it be cheating to hang out with Dev?

I decided he was just being nice to me. I could use a friend right now. I took the piece of paper from him and wrote down my cell number and the house phone number.

"Here you go. Try the house phone first, because my parents took my cell since I got into some trouble." I handed the piece of paper back to him.

"You don't look like a troublemaker to me."

"Looks can be deceiving, can't they?"

"Yes, they can," he said with a smirk. "See you later."

He turned around and headed down the hall. Guilt flooded me again, but I quickly shifted my mind to class. I needed a happy distraction from my current circumstances, and there was nothing wrong with finding that in a new friend— emphasis on the word *friend*.

The weekend was finally here and I felt so much relief, even though I wasn't allowed to leave the house. I was tired of finding ways to ignore Marcus, Charlotte, and Alex, who all tried their hardest to talk to me at school. At least at home, I didn't have to look around every corner or hide out in the janitor's closet until the coast was clear. I knew it was stupid to go to that far to avoid my friends, but I was afraid of what I would say to them. I just wanted to be by myself—and, as bad as it sounded, I blamed them for what was happening because they were associated with Kythera.

Unfortunately, I wouldn't be able to totally disconnect since my parents were forcing me to go to a Kythera meeting this afternoon, and they would all be there.

I sat quietly in the library, reading my political science book, which was a complete bore. All I wanted to do was go for ride at the Hunt Club, but Dad had said the driver wasn't available to take me today. I was annoyed that I couldn't go riding, but happy that Dad had finally spoken to me. He hadn't said two words to me since the night at the jail, except to tell me it was time to go to school.

I stared out the French doors that overlooked our tiny backyard and dreamed of the day I could stare out at the fields of our farm. We had almost escaped. I thought about Cal, but that only made my chest hurt. He hadn't tried to contact me since he had left. Veronica had already known he was gone. Did he tell her himself, and was she the one he was interested in now? It wasn't out of the realm of possibility. Cal had dated her a couple of months before we met, and they apparently had been on and off for a couple of years. She was very pretty and she had curves in all the right places . . . the places I didn't have them.

Ugh, this wasn't making me feel any better. I decided to think positive. I knew there had to be a better explanation as to why he hadn't called me. I'm sure his dad had taken away his cell phone, and Veronica probably knew because of her brother, Alex, who was Cal's best friend. They weren't as close since I had shown up, because Alex had a crush on me. Maybe it was because Alex's dad was Mr. Roman's right hand man in Kythera. That explanation made me feel better. Plus, the boarding school could be super strict when it came to phone calls and that could explain why he hadn't tried to call me when he got there. I wasn't ready to give up on him yet.

In the meantime, I was determined to figure out a way to speak to him and get out of this mess once and for all.

"Casper, you need to get up and get ready for lunch today. We're having lunch with the Singers at the Thoroughbred Club."

I put down my book and looked up at my mother.

She was wearing a red shift dress, pearls, and her usual red lipstick. Her hair was pulled up in a bun and she looked like the perfect Stepford wife she tried so hard to be.

She frowned when I didn't get up immediately. "Seriously, we will not be late because you don't want to cooperate." She crossed her arms against her small chest and glared at me with her blue-gray eyes.

"Then you can go without me," I said, and turned back to my homework.

"I've had enough out of you. What's happened to you? I know we fight and argue, but you've never been this hard to deal with. And I never thought you would run away. Haven't we always given you everything you've wanted?" Mother's forehead creased and her pale cheeks turned bright pink.

I slammed the book shut, threw it on the coffee table with a thud, and stood up. "What's *happened* to me? I was forced to move to this place, away from the horses, which you knew meant everything to me. Then I was almost murdered in this very house. Murdered! And all because of a group called Kythera—which you seem to be convinced is the only thing that can save our money. Then someone chased me while I was at the movies, and probably was trying to kill me then, too. And if that wasn't enough, I watched one of my classmates bleed to death in front of me, all because he was giving information to someone."

I held my arms to my sides, and clenched my fists, the anger making me physically sick.

I had expected Mother to continue the

argument, but her face went white as if she had seen a ghost. Her lips parted as if she were about to speak, but the words got caught in her throat. She moved to one of the chairs and slowly sat down, touching her hand to her cheek.

"Who died in front of you?" she whispered.

"Jacob, but you already knew that. Why are you asking me?" My voice softened as I looked at her stunned face.

She turned her head and stared out the French doors. "I had no idea." She shook her head, and I could tell tears were filling her eyes. Slowly, all the anger I had built up started to melt away.

"You didn't?" It was hard for me to believe, even though I could tell from the look on her face she was telling me the truth.

"No. What happened?" She wiped away the tears with her French-manicured fingers.

"Jacob said someone had paid for his tuition to the school if he would tell them where I and some of the other members were going and what we were doing. Cal and I pleaded with his dad to let Jacob go and we thought he agreed, but after we left the library, we heard gunshots and ran back. Jacob was on the floor." I sat back down on the loveseat slowly.

Mother covered her mouth in horror. She was trying so hard not to cry, but it was no good. The tears cascaded down her cheeks, her inky mascara leaving a trail on each cheek. She finally took a deep breath and uncovered her mouth. "Did your father know?"

I couldn't bring myself to say it, but I nodded my head.

"Oh, God," she said, and her whole body started convulsing. She sucked in a breath, tears rolling down her face. I didn't know what to do. I had never seen my mother like this. She was always so strong and put-together, the perfect party host who always knew what to say and do.

I stared at the Oriental rug, examining the curved lines of the intricate green and gold pattern. I knew I wouldn't be able to keep the tears from coming if I looked at her, and I did not want to cry in front of her, even though she was my mother. I hated to cry in front of anyone. Finally, her breathing returned to normal and she sniffled a couple of times. She stood up and I finally could look at her without shedding a tear.

"I've got to go fix my makeup and change for lunch." She looked down at her dress, wet with tears. "Will you meet me in the foyer when you're ready to go?" she asked softly.

"Yes," I said, and then she walked out of the room.

I sat motionlessly, staring at the door she had just walked through. I was astonished by what had just happened. I had assumed my mother had known everything. I never thought I would feel sorry for her, but I did after that bizarre scene.

Every day seemed to bring a new revelation that had the potential to change everything I thought I already knew. When would the surprises end?

Chapter

4

FOR ONCE, I WISHED THE lunch with the Singers lasted longer. I had even tried to talk to the Singers' son William, who was in eighth grade, but all he could do was stare at me and tell me that I was pretty. I liked being told I was pretty, but it was weird coming from a thirteen-year-old who kept trying to put his hand on my leg. I had even tried to talk to him about horses, pointing to a photo of my dad and me in the winner's circle hanging on the wall behind the table. It was a photo taken after our horse, Casper's Sohini, had won the Sham Stakes, a qualifying race for the Kentucky Derby. I was about ten and my dad had me on his hip so I could put my hand on Sohini's neck. He was smiling at me, and I was laughing. Normally, I loved coming to the Thoroughbred Club and seeing all the photos of horses and their owners, but today the photos of me with Dad only made me sad. I didn't know if he would ever smile at me like that again.

I finally gave up trying to talk to William and spent my time watching the seconds tick by on the clock on the wall, each second meaning I was that much closer to having to face Tyson Roman for the first time since the day at the jail. I knew I couldn't avoid it forever, but the days had gone by too fast.

Part of me was terrified to see him, but the other part of me wanted to scream at him and demand to know where Cal was, tell him he had to bring Cal back or else. I had been brave in the past, but I had never had the guts to stand up to him when any of the other members were present. I had hated the Kythera meetings, because everyone seemed to be petrified of Tyson. Could he really be that scary? I was started to think he could.

"Are you ready?" asked Dad from the hall. I turned around to see him dressed in a dark gray suit, white shirt, and blue tie.

I got up from the couch, smoothed out my black dress, and walked toward him, my high heels clicking on the wood floor. Getting dressed up was another reason I hated the stupid meetings. Why couldn't we just wear jeans?

The car stopped in front of the fancy French restaurant downtown that had become so familiar. We were led to the kitchen, and to a back room that held the staircase to the second floor. Alex could say what he wanted, but if he thought because this was a French restaurant instead of an Italian one meant they weren't like the mob, then he was crazy.

We shuffled up the dark hallway and into a large empty ballroom, our shoes clicking across the old wooden floors. Most of the members were sitting behind long tables arranged in a semi-circle in the middle of the room. Everyone looked our way as we walked toward them. I could feel the stares and whispers. This was the first time I was appearing to all the members since my little stunt. I'm sure they weren't happy to see me.

I kept my eyes forward, avoiding direct eye contact with anyone, especially Tyson Roman, who set at a desk in front of the semi-circle of members. We took our seats silently and waited for the meeting to begin.

"Glad to see everyone this afternoon," he said in his thick Southern drawl. "We've got a lot to discuss this week. First off, as you all can tell, Cal is not with us."

I felt my heart drop at the mention of his name.

Tyson stopped and looked in my direction, but only glanced at me for a second before continuing, "He has been sent to a boarding school to finish his senior year and then he will be off to Tulane University to start college. He will be taking a less active role in our day-to-day operations for at least a year, if not longer, but I assure you, he will be back with us and participating as soon as possible."

Tyson got up from the desk and crossed his large arms over his chest as he paced behind the desk.

"Cal had a pretty big role in our organization. We'll need someone to fill his position soon if we want things to continue as usual. We need to continue to attract great families into our organization, and I know just the perfect person to take on the role."

I traced my fingers along the grain of the wood, barely paying attention to what Tyson was saying. When I finally looked up, Tyson was standing directly in front of me, a smirk on his face.

"Members, I'm pleased to introduce our new recruiter, Miss Casper Whitley."

There was an audible gasp in the room—including my own. It felt like my heart was beating so fast that it would fall out on the floor.

"What?" I said, unable to contain my shock.

"You're the perfect candidate. You have great connections and you've proved you can be influential on people, including Cal." Tyson turned around to face the other members.

"I don't know the first thing about being a recruiter—and, besides, you already know how I feel about Kythera. What makes you think I would try to bring anyone else into this horrible group?" I looked passed Tyson to see the mouths of Charlotte's parents drop open. So much for being quiet around other members.

Mother gripped my shoulder and leaned into whisper in my ear, but Tyson turned around swiftly and leaned down over the table to me before she could say anything.

"Because I know how much those stupid horses mean to you and once we take possession of them, they'll be sent to a glue factory if you don't cooperate. Do we understand each other?"

Tyson's eyes were icy and menacing. I knew if he could kill a human being, he would have no problem killing a few horses to get what he wanted.

My eyes started filling with tears at the thought of the horses being gone forever.

"Fine," I said through gritted teeth.

"Good," he said. He turned to look at the other members.

"Now, normally I would say you should go out find your own people to recruit, but I already have an easy assignment in mind for you. We've been trying to get him and his family in for a couple of years now, and I think you are the perfect person to finally get him."

"Who?" I asked, crossing my arms over my chest.

Tyson turned back around again. "Dev Chavan."

———◆———

I stared up at the ceiling of my bedroom, sprawled out on my bed. I just laid there with my eyes open, unable to do anything but stare up at the smooth white ceiling. So, the one person I had met who wasn't involved with Kythera was my first assignment in my forced role as a recruiter for Kythera. *Great.*

How was I supposed this accomplish the task without feeling like a complete hypocrite and a liar? I thought about Cal again, and how he had to live with those thoughts every day. No wonder he usually had a frown on his face. Cal had rarely looked happy, except when we were just hanging out. The minute the word Kythera came up, any trace of playfulness disappeared. Now I understood why.

I had to get past that if I wanted to not only save the horses from the auction block, but from death. Plus, if I went along with Tyson and showed that I'm willing to cooperate, he might be willing to let Cal come back. I could only hope.

I already missed him terribly. I had to figure out some way to contact him before I went crazy. I thought about sneaking around the house to find my cell phone, but who knew where my parents had put it. It could be anywhere in this humongous old house, and I didn't want to do too much snooping in a mansion from the 1700s that I was convinced had ghosts.

But they did have a landline for whatever reason, and one of the phones was in the butler pantry. I knew I would be safe to talk in there if I closed the door, since the closest my mother came to cooking was calling a caterer. I sat up straight and jumped off the bed. I ran down the long, dark hallway to the servant staircase that led directly to the kitchen. When I reached the first floor I looked around and the room was empty. I peered around the wall and into the family room, but the TV was off. I looked over to the open door of the library and my parents weren't in there either.

I crept back to the butler pantry near the stairs and pulled the door shut quietly. I dialed Cal's cell phone number, happy I could actually remember it and jumped up onto the counter. The line rang several times, and then finally went to voice mail. I was disappointed, although I should have known he wouldn't answer. He probably didn't have his cell phone, just like me.

I jumped back off the counter, hung the phone up, and opened the pantry door. As I walked out of the room, I watched as a figure stepped into the shaded back yard. I walked faster into the family room and over to the giant windows. It was my mother. She was wearing a tight red dress, white silk scarf around her head, and huge Jackie O sunglasses. She looked like she was trying to escape without being seen, but why?

Mother walked over to the garage, but took a glance back before going in the door and closing it behind her. I looked at the clock on the wall. It was almost six-thirty. We were supposed to be having dinner with some Kythera family at seven.

Maybe she just had a quick errand to run before dinner? But that still didn't explain why she looked like she was ready for a costume party.

Chapter

5

OUR FAMILY DINNER WITH THE Lautners was sleep-inducing, as usual. The Lautners didn't have any kids and all they could talk about were their prize-winning poodles. Mr. Lautner, a fuzzy, gray-haired man, droned on about the birthday party they were planning for Mr. Scribbles, their oldest "kid." Apparently, they were planning to have a magician this year instead of a clown, because Mr. Scribbles had tried to drag away the clown's enormous shoes into his doggy penthouse last year.

I drank several Cokes in an effort to keep from falling out of my chair. Normally, I wouldn't have been able to get away with drinking so much soda around my organic-loving mother, but she was uncharacteristically late for dinner and had no idea how many I had drank. She had breezed in almost forty-five minutes late, looking disheveled, and her porcelain skin bright pink. She was no longer wearing the red dress, but a more muted green sheath.

"Sorry everyone, I had an emergency Women's Club thing I had to take care of. Please, forgive me for being so late," she said hastily as she sat down.

I stared at her, my eyebrows scrunched, but she refused to look at me. I knew what she had just said was a complete lie. She wouldn't have been caught dead in such a tight dress going to one of those meetings. You could only wear stuffy pantsuits or matronly skirt suits to those things, nothing that shoved your boobs up to your chin.

I looked over at Dad, but he was busy with his iPhone, as usual. Dad couldn't have been with her wherever she went because we had come to the Lautners together. Maybe he met up with her and then came to the dinner? I tried to think about if I had seen him after the Kythera meeting and then it hit me. He had said he was up in the office all afternoon, which meant he hadn't left the house all day.

I fiddled with the cloth napkin in my lap, my mind racing at the possibilities. Either Dad was lying and they had gone somewhere together, or Mother had dressed like a vixen for someone else. I looked at Mother anxiously, grabbed the glass of water in front of me, and gulped it as fast as I could.

"Casper, have you lost all your manners?" whispered Mother in my ear.

I put my glass down, unable to say anything. I sat there quietly, as my parents chatted with the Lautners, only occasionally nodding my head or smiling when someone looked directly at me.

Was my mother having an affair?

Finally, the night was over and I could escape to the confines of my bedroom, away from the two crazy people downstairs. Things were starting to feel unreal. I wanted to pinch myself and wake up.

Please, God, tell me my Mother isn't having an affair.

Even though I had lost a lot of respect for my dad through the whole Kythera mess, I still couldn't bear the thought of Mother cheating on him. My mind was racing as I stepped into my bathroom and turned on the Jacuzzi tub. Maybe there was a perfectly good explanation for why she was wearing that dress and sneaking out through the back. Maybe it really was a Women's Club thing, and they were all required to dress up like a movie star or celebrity. She did have a Jackie Kennedy-meets-Marilyn Monroe thing going on. It could have been a themed meeting or party, right?

Who was I kidding? Those women were stiff and their idea of fun was leaving the crusts on their tea sandwiches. But before I jumped to all sorts of conclusions, I needed to give her a chance to explain.

The next morning I got up late and missed breakfast. I expected to be scolded by Mother the minute I walked into the dining room, but she was too busy with her morning list to even notice me. I sat down at the table and took a piece of fruit from the bowl in the middle of the table. Dad must have already left. His chair was empty, but his coffee mug was still there, along with a crumpled stack of newspapers.

Christina sat a plate down in front of me with a spinach and egg white omelet, watermelon chunks on the side. The pink liquid from the watermelon had seeped over toward the omelet. I picked up my fork and tried to save the eggs from the sweet juice. What I wouldn't give for a Krispy Kreme donut.

"Will you go out and check the mail, Casper?" Mother asked, still scribbling on her notepad. There was so much blue ink on the yellow sheet of paper, it was turning green. I was terrified of what she had me doing on that list today.

"Sure, after I eat," I said quietly, spearing a piece of watermelon and popping it in my mouth.

Mother looked up at me, her clenched jaw relaxing. "Oh, I thought you had already eaten."

I shook my head and she went back to scribbling. I decided to take a couple of bites of the omelet. It had a sweet aftertaste that wasn't appetizing at all. I put my fork on the plate and took it into the kitchen for Christina.

I scooted out of the kitchen and down the long hallway to the front door. As I opened the front door, I was once again hit by the stifling heat. Instantly, my skin was covered in the humid, salty air, and I felt like I hadn't taken a shower in days. I still wasn't used to the smell of the sea clinging to me all the time or the moisture.

I looked toward White Point Gardens, just across the street, and over to the bay. I stared at the gold-flecked waters of the harbor. I pulled open the heavy cast iron mailbox door and pulled out the mail. Down the street, there was a loud *thwack*, and I instantly looked toward the noise.

A man in a tan suit was hammering a sign into the front yard of Mrs. Hamilton's house. I walked down the street a little bit to see that it was a sign for Goldman Realty. Wow, they didn't waste time. Mrs. Hamilton hadn't been dead that long, along with her daughter Kelly Winters. The newspaper listed it as a tragic burglary gone wrong, but I knew that wasn't true. Mrs. Hamilton had been pretty nosy, and she was the one who warned me about Kythera when we first moved in. She got me asking questions about them, and I opened my mouth to Alex, who had said she should mind her own business and stop talking about Kythera. Days later, I came home to see blaring blue lights in front of her home, and body bags being wheeled out.

That's when I realized that Kelly Winters, the news reporter who had written an article about

Kythera, was Mrs. Hamilton's daughter. When I snooped around the newspaper office, I found out Kelly had written critical articles about what Kythera was really up to—then she had suddenly left town and hadn't returned until a few days before her death.

As I started to turn back toward my own house, I noticed a black car blur by me and pull up in front of Mrs. Hamilton's house. I turned to see the familiar red "K" staring back at me on the trunk of the car. Figured. Alex's dad, Mr. Alamilla, stepped out and shook the realtor's hand. They both walked up the steps and into the house. Kythera was probably looking to add another home to the collection.

They owned ours and my dad had used our horse farm to secure the lease and our membership into the group. Who knew what the next family would be forced to do to move in to that house and become a part of the elite Kythera, which seemed to be above the law. I wondered if I should caution them about the *other group* that's after Kythera?

I finally whirled around and headed up the steps into the house. I walked back into the dining room and handed the mail to Mother.

"They just put up a for sale sign on Mrs. Hamilton's house," I said.

She looked up again from her list, her eyes wide with surprise. "Really?"

I nodded my head, and she started scribbling

again. She usually was never *this* preoccupied with her list. Something had to be wrong with her.

"Hey, where did you go yesterday? I saw you leaving through the back yard wearing a red dress." I put my hands on the back of the mahogany dining chair, wringing them around the smooth surface.

She stopped writing. Her knuckles turned white, she was gripping the pen so hard. "I had a Women's Club meeting. Didn't you hear me last night?" she asked, an icy edge in her voice.

"Yeah, but I just didn't think you would wear something like that to one of those meetings. That was more like something you wear out on a date or to some special party."

Her eyes darted back and forth across the paper she was scribbling, then she sat the pen down on the pad. "It was a costume party. I had to dress up," she said impatiently, rubbing her temples.

"I thought you said it was a meeting?"

"Meeting . . . party, whatever. I had to dress up." She got up from the table, her mouth pursed. She picked up her list and walked out of the room without another word. I stood there awkwardly for a moment staring at the closed door. I didn't know what to think.

Sure, we always had a rocky relationship, mainly because I wasn't the daughter she wanted. I had no desire to be a socialite, busy with parties and charity events that were meaningless. I wanted to spend my life free to be who I wanted to be, not some trophy wife only capable of directing fancy parties. But our relationship had taken a turn for the worse lately. I didn't even feel like her daughter anymore.

I had always felt like an outsider in this family. I had even thought for a while that I was adopted and my biological parents would show up at the front door any day. But then my parents would always do something that made me feel like I was really their daughter and the thoughts would go away. Now, I was wishing it was true and that I could open the door to find my real family waiting on the doorstep to take me away from all this.

Anger started to flood my thoughts and I stormed into the kitchen. Christina was busy wiping off the counters, and the chef was pulling vegetables out of the refrigerator, several peppers and onions in his hands. He pulled out another pepper and then a candy bar, staring at it as if he had just found a radioactive spider. *Great*, guess I had to find a new place to hide my candy and Coke stash. Why did I have to hide chocolate and soda like they were drugs? It was another thing I didn't understand about my mother.

I stormed out the back door and into the garage. I stared at the little black Audi coupe that had gotten me into so much trouble and wished I had the keys. Okay, maybe I had gotten it into trouble, but I was still going to blame it on the car.

I looked at the vehicles, and an idea popped into my head. I'm sure one of them held clues to where Mother had really gone yesterday. She usually drove the Land Rover or the Mercedes coupe. I opened the door to the Mercedes and started searching in between the seats and the center console. It was empty except a twenty-dollar bill in the console. *Dad must have been using this car recently*, I thought.

I closed the door and walked over to the Land Rover and opened the driver's-side door. I jumped up into the seat and pulled open the center console. There was a pair of sparkly diamond earrings and a piece of folded-up paper. I opened it and there was an address on it that I didn't recognize. There was also a time on it. It said six-thirty—and that was about the time I had seen her slipping out the back door.

I held the paper in my hand and just sat in the driver's seat, my legs hanging out to the side. I wished I had a car so I could find out what this was about, but if I attempted to leave, I knew I would never be allowed to leave the house again . . . *ever*.

Then a thought hit me, and I knew exactly how I was going to find out where Mother had gone and who she was meeting. I would just have to wait for the perfect time for my plan to work.

Chapter

6

I STARED AT THE BOARD IN my first class of the day, barely registering what was going on. I had nervous butterflies in my stomach as I thought about my plans after school and how I was going to accomplish them.

Last night, I had stayed up for several hours, listening to Adele on my iPod, lying on my bed, and working out the details of how I was going to find out some information about my mother's mysterious meeting. I did a Google Maps search of the address and tried to memorize where the house was, so I would be able to convince to whoever I could get to take me there that I had been there before.

There was only one person that I would be allowed to go anywhere with . . . Dev. Sure, I had only had a couple of casual conversations with him in the hall, but he had offered to take me to his house to go horseback riding. Why couldn't I use that? I could pretend I lived at the address and ask him to drop me off there, and not only accomplish my goal in finding out about Mother, but I would also be performing my "job" for Kythera. It was a win-win situation.

But what if he didn't say anything about going riding today? I was a terrible flirt and I hated to ask people to help me out. I had always been an independent person, hell-bent on doing things on my own. Then I thought about the horses and Cal. I wanted to save them both, and that required me to act out of character.

The bell rang and I rushed to the door, but Alex caught my arm as I hurried out. "Casper, are you all right?" he said in his smooth, deep voice.

I turned to look at him. His black eyebrows knit together. I plastered a goofy grin on my face. "Sure. Everything's *great*," I said—with a little too much sarcasm.

He immediately let go of my arm and frowned. I didn't care.

I opened the door to my locker and threw my books in, a loud metal thud sounding as they hit the back wall. I waited a couple of seconds, then looked around for Dev. He wasn't anywhere in the crowded hallway. I picked up a notebook in my locker and slowly put it in my backpack. Still no Dev. I pulled out a pencil sharpener and sharpened a pencil. The noise in the hallway died down, but there was still no sign of Dev. I finally closed my locker and started down the hallway toward my next class.

Finally, I saw Dev's tall figure walking toward me. He walked past a group of girls, who immediately started giggling. They all stared him up and down as he passed. He spotted me, oblivious to the girls practically drooling over him, and a big smile formed on his face.

I felt myself smiling, too.

"Hey, Dev," I said as he stopped in front of me.

"Hey, Casper, how was your weekend?" He shifted his backpack from one shoulder to the other.

"It was okay . . . lots of homework. How about yours?" I said quietly.

I was so nervous, because I knew I had to make a good impression. There was so much riding on my friendship with Dev.

"I spent some time horseback riding, and at the beach."

"Fun," I said, unsure of what to say next.

"Listen, we should hang out sometime—when you're no longer grounded,"

I felt a sense of relief wash over me. "Yeah that sounds great. I'm sure my parents will make an exception if I tell them I have a school project or something."

"You are bad, aren't you?" He chuckled.

I shrugged my shoulders. "Hey, gotta live a little, right?"

"Yeah, I guess so. What about you come over and we can go riding this afternoon?"

"Oh, I would love to, but the driver is busy this afternoon and I'll be lucky if I don't get left at school all night." I pulled on a loose purple thread on my backpack strap, hoping he would take the bait.

"Why don't you come home with me after school, and then I'll take you home after we go riding?"

He was making this *so* easy. "You would do that? You're so sweet," I said, batting my eyelashes at him. Is this what girls were supposed to do? *Ha, who needs Veronica's sexy hips?*

"Yeah, no problem. It'll be fun actually having someone to go riding with me."

The bell rang and I realized we were the only two people in the hall.

"Oh, I've got to get to class, but I'll see you after school. Just wait for me on the bench out front?" he called as he ran down the hall.

"Sure!" I said, and scurried to my own class. I pulled the strap of my backpack closer as I walked into my calculus class.

"Someone's in a good mood," said Charlotte as I sat down at my desk.

I looked up at her face, her eyes bright with curiosity and her lips curled into a mischievous grin.

"Huh?" I said, her words not registering.

"You look *sooo* happy? Something happen this weekend I don't know about? Did Cal call?"

I had finally decided to start speaking to Charlotte again after she cornered me at the Kythera meeting last weekend. She had apologized for not telling me about Cal, and she said she desperately wanted to be friends again. I was happy to have her to talk to again, even if it meant playing twenty questions.

"Oh, um, no, it's just been a pretty good day, I guess." I pulled out my notebook and scribbled my name and the date at the top.

"Uh-huh. I'll take that answer for now, but I know there has to be something else going on. I know that look . . ."

"All right class, let's get started," called Mr. Perry.

"I expect all the details at lunch," she said, then swirled around in her chair to face the board.

Great, something to look forward to, I thought. Not.

The bell rang and I started getting my stuff together.

"Miss Whitley, I need to speak with you for a minute," called Mr. Perry. *Uh-oh.*

I walked up to his desk, not sure what to expect. It wasn't like me to be called to the teacher's desk. I was normally a straight-A student, but I knew things weren't going as well as usual.

"Your work hasn't been up to par lately. I saw your records from your old school and you were an excellent math student. I had been expecting more. Is everything okay? Something distracting you from your school work?" He adjusted his tortoise shell glasses on his slender nose.

"I'm just having a hard time adjusting to a new school, that's all," I said.

"You've seemed to have made a lot of new friends. Maybe they are taking up too much of your time after school instead of your homework?"

I felt my cheeks burning, which always happened when I was embarrassed. I hope he didn't notice. "No, but maybe I should cut back time at the Hunt Club," I lied. There was no way I could tell him what was really going on.

"You're a hunter?" he asked, his eyes widening.

"No, I like to go horseback riding and we board one of our horses there. I've been spending all my time out there because I miss home and all our horses." That was the truth, even though it wasn't the reason for my sloppy school work.

He nodded. "I understand. But you need to make at least a ninety on the next test to keep you're A and your GPA. You'll need it if you are going to Harvard."

"What?"

He looked confused. "It said in your file you were planning on going to Harvard."

I rolled my eyes. "That's my parents' plans. I'm going to the University of Kentucky and managing our family's thoroughbred farm. Harvard is my dad's idea."

"Oh, well, either way. You still need a good GPA, just in case you change your mind."

I nodded, not willing to argue with my teacher about the fact that I wouldn't be changing my mind. I turned and headed for the door, relieved to be out of there. I was completely embarrassed—and disappointed in myself. I had always paid attention to my school work. School and the horses had been my life—until I moved to Charleston. Then Kythera came along and ruined everything. Now, it had taken away the one thing that made this place bearable . . . Cal.

———◆———

Finally, school was over. I waited patiently for Dev on the bench, watching as everyone left. I pulled out my latest reading assignment for Renaissance literature, and began reading it so I wouldn't have to spend too much time tonight on my homework. After the speech from Mr. Perry, I didn't want another one. I planned to try to balance getting out of Kythera, tracking my mom, figuring out who was trying to kill us and completing all my school work. *Ha.*

"You don't waste any time do you?" said the sickeningly sweet voice of Veronica. I hadn't even heard her walk up to me.

I looked up at her and rolled my eyes. "What are you talking about?"

She put her hand on her hip. "With Dev . . . that's who you are waiting for isn't it?"

"You were at the meeting this weekend right? You heard you know who." I looked down at the page and hoped she would just keep walking.

"Yeah, but you look like you're enjoying it. At least, you did in the hallway when you were drooling over him."

"Do you have nothing better to do than watch my every move? Are you really that jealous?" I closed the book and put it in my backpack.

"Don't flatter yourself. I'm just still trying to figure out how they let someone like you in, that's all."

I took a deep breath and pinched the bridge of my nose. "Listen, can we just call a truce? I'm in *the club* and, believe me, I would do anything to get out. But since I'm stuck, can we at least be nice to each other in the hall?"

Veronica swept her long dark hair back, and raised a perfectly manicured eyebrow. "I'd rather die," she said, and abruptly turned and started walking to the parking lot. I shook my head as she swung her hips with every step, the guys going to football practice stopping in mid-stride to watch.

"Hey, sorry. I had to talk to my chemistry teacher after class." I looked behind to see Dev rushing toward me.

I got up from the bench. "Not a problem."

"So, do we need to let the driver know that I'm taking you home later?" He reached out his hand for my backpack. I slung it off my shoulders and handed it to him, our hands touching momentarily, and I felt something between us.

Don't fall for him, you're doing this for Cal, I reminded myself.

"No, I borrowed my friend Charlotte's phone and told him what I was doing after school."

I'd hated to ask Charlotte to use her phone, but I'd had no choice if my plan was going to work. Of course, she gave me the third degree and I had to tell her my plan . . . or, at least, most of it. I was able to keep the part about my mother's possible affair under wraps.

"Great, then let's get going." Dev started walking to the parking lot and I followed behind.

The passenger-side door groaned as he opened it and threw in my backpack. I jumped up into the seat and buckled my seat belt as he closed the door. He ran around the other side and hopped in.

"So, how's Charleston been since you've moved here? You ready to run away yet?" Dev asked as we pulled out of the parking lot.

I laughed nervously, wondering if he knew I had tried to run away or if his wording was just a coincidence. "Not yet, but it's crossed my mind."

I figured he'd been in India and wouldn't have known anything about it. Plus, he didn't really hang out with any of the Kythera members, so it was unlikely anyone had told him about my stunt. Although, it had been the gossip around school for a few days, so he had to know. *Whatever*—he didn't *act* like he had a clue.

"I'd love to get away for a long time," he said as he turned onto a two-lane road, heading away from Charleston.

"Where would you go?"

He was silent for a moment as he turned onto a single-lane road lined with oak trees. "I really like the time we spend in India with my family. I think I would go there," he said, slowing the vehicle down.

"I've never been to India." I stared out my window. There were tons of beautiful old oaks with Spanish moss not only lining the drive, but all over the yard. There was shaded cover over most of the landscape, which gave off the air that it was protected and sheltered from the rest of the world.

"It's a beautiful place, with lots of bright colors and sounds. Families are close-knit, and it's just a happy place to be."

Finally, the oak trees gave way to a big white house with columns and a pebbled circular drive. The house was huge and felt like something out of *Gone with the Wind,* but there was something about it that didn't feel so imposing or fancy. Maybe it was the pretty pink and yellow rose bushes lining the large porch, or the lavender wreath on the front door.

Dev stopped the truck in front of the steps and I jumped out and waited for him to walk up the steps. He opened the front door and we stepped into a very open room. The staircase to the second floor was completely visible, and the wooden steps were lined with a red runner. I followed Dev through a door near the staircase, and we were in the kitchen. Several pots were boiling on the stove and a small woman was bent over, placing something in the oven.

"Mom, I want you to meet somebody."

The woman stood up, and her face was beaming. Her ebony hair was up in a bun, and she was wearing a pair of worn jeans and a three-quarter sleeve black T. She stuck her hand out for me to shake it.

"This is Casper Whitley. She's new at school and she loves horses so I thought we could go for a ride together," said Dev.

"Hello, Casper, welcome to our home."

"Thank you," I said, mesmerized by what I was seeing. Dev actually had a mother who could cook *and* who wore faded jeans like me.

"You are welcome to stay for dinner. We're having one of Dev's favorites . . . chicken Tandoori," she said, as she took the lid off a pot and stirred.

"That sounds wonderful, but my parents are expecting me for dinner with another family."

"Maybe next time," she said with a big smile.

Dev walked down a hallway off the kitchen, which led to the back patio. We stepped into the large back yard, and I couldn't help but stare in envy. The yard was an open space, with a large swimming pool and a split-rail fence that separated the pool area from a field that seemed to go on for miles. I could see in the distance a couple of black horses grazing, and beyond them

I saw the ocean. As I looked out over the beautiful scenery, I had to hold back a couple of tears.

"Wow," I said, barely able to breathe.

"It's pretty, isn't it?" he said, motioning for me to follow him once again. I could barely keep my eyes off the horses as we walked into a white barn with a green tin roof.

There were several rows of stalls on both sides of the barn. A gray horse head appeared from behind one of the stall doors.

"Oh, you have Arabian horses!" I exclaimed, as I went over to rub the broad forehead of the horse.

"You really do know your horses, don't you?" said Dev as he pulled out a saddle.

I nodded my head. "So who's this?" I kept rubbing the horse's forehead all the way down to its short black muzzle.

"That's Alister Stella Gray, but we just call her Stella. You'll be riding her."

I stepped back as he opened the stall door and put the saddle on her.

"What a pretty name. Where did you get it?"

"My mother loves roses, if you couldn't tell from the yard. And she loves horses, so most of them are named after roses." He led Stella out of her stall and motioned for me to jump on.

I gave Stella a pat on the back and did a quick check of the saddle to make sure it was on properly. Everything looked okay and I put my foot in the stirrup and swung up onto the saddle.

"Go ahead and ride out into the field and I'll catch up with you in a minute," said Dev.

I walked Stella out to the pasture and took a deep breath. I felt so alive and free, like I always did on a horse. Sure, I got to spend plenty of time with Wendy at the Hunt Club, but here it was different. I was still on someone else's property. Sure, this was Dev's house—but it just felt like *home.*

I gave Stella a nudge and she went flying. Before I knew it, we had flown by the two black Arabian horses in the pasture to where the grass ended at the sandy beach. We stopped there, and I just stared out at the deep blue ocean. This was one thing that was different from our farm in Kentucky. Our borders didn't end at an ocean, but at a thick forest where birds were always chirping. There weren't any birds chirping, but the pounding of the ocean waves a few feet away was equally breathtaking.

"You're pretty fast!" yelled Dev from behind. He was galloping toward me on a roan-colored horse. I stopped Stella and waited for him. Dev came up beside me, and we stood near the edge of the beach, the waves roaring onto the sand.

I smirked. "It's not me. Stella's just fast. Are they race horses?"

"They definitely could be. Their bloodline is full of race horses, but my parents aren't into all that. A couple of them are in dressage competitions, but mainly they are just for us."

"Guess that explains why you don't know who I am." I leaned forward and patted Stella on the neck.

"Oh, I know who you are—I just didn't think it mattered." Dev started moving forward and we walked the horses onto the sand.

"Oh," I said. We started following the surf down the beach.

"If you have horses, you know who the Whitleys are. You're a horse legacy."

"Do you know why I am in Charleston, then?" I asked, hoping I wasn't being too forward in letting out the Kythera secret.

"Not really—I assumed it had something to do with the Romans."

"Yes, it does. Our dads worked out some kind of business deal."

"He's always bringing new people to town and they drag along their kids. It's kind of weird how many people at school are here because of the Romans, but I guess it's just business. I hope it hasn't been too bad on you," he said, shrugging his shoulders.

"No, it's not been that bad," I said, also shrugging. I thought about Cal, and his unbelievable blue eyes. I wanted more than anything to see him, to know he was okay and that he still loved me.

"Made any friends this summer?" he asked, and I was brought back into the here and now.

"Yeah, Charlotte, Sarah, and Alex . . . well,

he's sort of a friend. Also, Marcus . . . have you met him? And Cal." I said Cal's name quickly, hoping he wouldn't detect the sadness in my voice. I was sure I wasn't supposed to let on that he was my boyfriend if I wanted to get Dev interested in Kythera.

"Yeah, Marcus and I have chemistry class together. He seems pretty cool. Oh, and I know Cal," he added, but I didn't ask him if they were friends or anything.

I looked out at the darkening water. "Hey, we better head back. I need to meet my parents at their friends' house for another boring dinner," I lied. I was shocked at how easy it had become to lie.

"Sure," said Dev, and we headed back to the barn.

After a quick goodbye to his mother, we left in a flurry. I hated to say goodbye to the horses, and I stared out the back window of the truck as his beautiful house and roses disappeared.

I gave Dev the address I had found in my mother's car and he seemed to be familiar with the area. Thirty minutes later, we pulled up to a dark house near downtown Charleston. There were no lights on or any signs of life.

"Are you sure this is the right address?" Dev hunched down to look past the Spanish moss to glimpse the silent front porch.

I started to panic. "Yeah, this is it. I think they may be out back. It was supposed to be some garden party or something." I gathered my backpack and jumped out of the truck.

"I don't think I should leave you here. I can wait with you till your parents get here."

"No, their car is across the street," I said, pointing to a random black sedan.

"Okay, but give me a call when you get inside?" he asked, his voice still worried.

"Yeah, no problem. Thanks again for this afternoon. I had a lot of fun," I said, leaning against the truck door.

"Me, too. We should hang out again. See ya at school," he said with a smile.

"Sure thing, see you tomorrow."

Dev shifted the truck into drive and disappeared down the dark street. Once his tail lights disappeared, I looked up at the house.

It was a pink stucco house, with big sago palms on either side of the walkway. I didn't know what I should do next. What would I say if I rang the doorbell? *Hey, are you having an affair with my mother?* What if he had a wife, and she answered? Could I really destroy her world?

Finally, I decided to walk up to the front door and see if there was any mail in the box located next to the door. Maybe I could find out his name or something without having to ring the doorbell and talk to someone.

I tiptoed up the steps onto the porch and carefully pulled the mail out of the box. It was mostly generic junk mail that came to every house, but there was the electric bill hidden in the clutter.

The owner of the house was a Mr. Franklin Gray. It was Marcus's dad.

Chapter

7

STARED AT THE ENVELOPE, UNABLE to move. Could it really be? It just didn't make sense. This wasn't Marcus's house. They lived only a couple of blocks from me, which was on the other side of the Charleston peninsula. This had to be a mistake, or maybe there was another Franklin Gray. It was a common last name and Franklin wasn't exactly original either. But, deep down, I knew it was the Franklin Gray who was my best friend's father.

I threw the mail back into the box, ran down the steps, and started walking down the sidewalk, unsure of where I was going. A cool wind blew across my face and then thunder sounded from above. I looked up at the dark clouds that had rolled in from the harbor. I crossed my arms over my chest and started walking faster. I knew there was no way I could walk home, but I didn't have a way to call a cab either. I really hadn't thought through what I was going to do after I got here. Maybe this hadn't been such a great plan after all.

After a couple of blocks, it started to sprinkle. I pulled my blazer off and put it over my head, but it did little to help as the rain drops fell harder. A few more blocks and I was drenched. I saw a neon sign for a restaurant and hurried across the street to step in. I took my soaked blazer off my head and held it in my hands. I looked around the half-empty booths. Everyone was staring at me, including the guys playing pool in the far corner. This wasn't as much of a restaurant as a bar. I had an uneasy feeling, but I walked up to the bar and motioned for the bartender.

"Honey, hope you aren't asking for alcohol, because we don't sale to underage prep school girls," he said, chuckling.

"I don't drink, but I would like to borrow a phone. I need to call a cab," I said.

The man raised his red eyebrows, and laughed. "Doesn't a girl like you have a fancy iPhone or something?"

I looked around and a couple of the guys from the pool table had moved closer. "Not when they're grounded."

"Oh, so you're a *bad* girl?" asked the guy who had slipped up to the stool next to me.

He was close enough I could smell the alcohol

on his breath. I started to shiver. How did I get myself into this mess?

Then something came over me and I turned to face him.

"No, not unless you count going against one of the most powerful people in this town," I said, raising an eyebrow and pointing to my ankle.

The man looked down, squinting to see the tattoo. I tilted my leg to help him out. Once what it my ankle tattoo said finally sunk in his brain, his eyes widened and he coughed. "Oh, didn't know. Benny, get this girl a phone!" he shouted to the bartender, and I took a deep breath.

Sometimes that tattoo paid off in a big way.

Without another word, the bartender handed me a wireless phone. "Thanks, Benny."

I dialed the number of the cab company I had written down earlier. I dialed the number and was assured that a cab would arrive in ten minutes. I handed the phone back to Benny and sat down on the stool to wait. I stared at the shiny bar, rubbing my fingers across the surface.

"Could I have a Coke?" I asked Benny, and he nodded, filling a glass with ice and pouring a can of Coke over it. He slid it toward me and I took a sip, the bubbles tickling my nose.

"So, do you know about the others?" said the guy. He was still sitting by me, holding onto a bottle of Budweiser.

"What do you mean?" I asked, rubbing my fingers against the cold glass in front of me.

"The others who want to take the place of that tattoo on your pretty ankle."

I was suddenly very interested in what he had to say.

"Do you know anything about them? Like a name or something?" I asked, turning my head toward him. Benny put another beer in front of the guy.

"I don't know a name, but I know these people are hardcore. They've been asking everyone for information about the K, and they are willing to pay a lot of money for it."

"Have they asked you to get info?"

He laughed, his whole body shaking. "Hell no, when would I ever come in contact with people like you?"

"Then how do you know about it?" I turned my attention back to the bar, annoyed. I prayed the taxi would hurry up.

"Because my cousin is a lawyer downtown. His office is next to that fancy French restaurant where the K meets."

I swung back around. "What's his name?"

The guy took another drink of his beer, and then set it down on the counter. "Edward Whitaker."

I felt like the room was swirling around me. Kythera's attorney, Martin Charles, had an office that was next to the French restaurant—and, if I remembered correctly, the name of his firm was Charles & Whitaker.

The guy picked up his bottle of beer and took

a long gulp. I swiveled around on the stool and saw the taxi out the window.

"Thanks for the Coke," I called to Benny, laying down a five-dollar bill.

Once the cab pulled up to my house, I paid and got out and just stared at the house. I had expected to get some answers tonight, but I had ended up with more questions—as usual.

Life had been so much simpler in Kentucky, where studying for my next test and training for the next jumping competition were the biggest issues that I faced. Somehow, all this felt so unfair, because I shouldn't have to worry about things like this. How could my mother have an affair—and with a friend's dad!? Should I ask Marcus about it? It was hard for me to think about keeping it a secret from him, but I also didn't want to be the one to cause him so much pain. Despite how I had treated him recently, Marcus had been a great and reliable friend. Come to think of it, he still *was*, even though I had been awful to him these past few days.

And then there was the whole issue with the attorney. Had Edward Whitaker been paid off by the other group? Is that how they were getting information on us now?

I shook my head and walked up the steps, tired of all the questions swirling in my head. I took the key out of my pocket and unlocked the door. The house was dark, as I had expected, since my parents were at some dinner party. They sucked when it came to punishments, because they were never around to make sure I was at home and behaving.

I actually wished—for the first time—that they had been home earlier and had stopped me from my plan, because all it had done was make me feel more miserable than I already did.

I sat at my usual table in the cafeteria the next day, staring at the barely-touched salad in front of me.

"You okay?" I looked up to see Marcus staring at me, his eyes full or concern.

I picked up my fork and stabbed a couple of carrots. "Yeah, nothing's wrong. I just miss Cal," I said, feeling like I wasn't totally lying.

It was true I missed Cal more and more every day, but I also didn't like carrying around such a big secret that involved not only my family, but my friends. I had avoided Marcus when I saw him in class and when we had passed in the hallway this morning. I'd pretended like I didn't see him, or that I was busy taking notes.

"You're just acting really weird today. I wanted to make sure there wasn't something that I could do." He sat down beside me, opening a can of Mountain Dew.

I took a deep breath. "Listen, there is something bothering me and I don't know how to tell you this, because I'm afraid you'll be upset."

"What is it?" he said.

"Promise you won't like blow up or anything?" I pushed my tray away and turned to look at him.

"Yeah, have I ever blown up on you before? You're my closest friend here, you can tell me anything," he said with a cautious laugh. Marcus was the calmest person I knew, but I'd never had to tell him anything like this before.

"You know I went riding with Dev yesterday?"

Marcus nodded his head, and I looked around the cafeteria to make sure no one else was heading to our table.

"I had him drop me off afterward at an address I found in my mother's car. I saw her sneaking out the back of the house this weekend in a fancy red dress. The kind of dress she only wears on a date with Dad, but he wasn't with her. Anyway, I had Dev drop me off at the address after we went riding. When I got to the house last night, I looked in the mailbox for the owner's name or something . . ." I paused, unsure if I was able to tell him everything.

Marcus looked at me, raising his eyebrows waiting for me to finish.

"And the name on the electric bill was to your Dad," I finally stuttered out.

I waited for some kind of response, but Marcus just stared past me. I turned around to see if there was something that had caught his attention, but it was just an empty table with a couple of milk cartons left on it.

I turned back around. "Marcus? Are you all right?"

"Yeah, sure. I mean that doesn't mean anything, right? Maybe they had some kind of Kythera business, you know?"

"Yeah, but why would your dad need another house you didn't know about to talk about Kythera with my mother? Did you know about the house?"

"No. I mean, maybe it's a piece of property he's trying to sell. He does some real estate deals every now and then. " Marcus looked down at his open can of soda and started bending the tab back and forth until it broke off.

I knew there was no reason to keep pushing him about it. He wasn't going to believe what this all meant. I didn't want to make him mad at me. "Maybe you're right. Sorry I brought it up."

"Nah, don't be sorry. You probably needed an explanation, too. Glad we could work it out," he said, swirling the broken soda tab around on the table with his finger.

Before I could say anything else, Alex sat his tray on the table. Charlotte showed up a couple of seconds later, along with Sarah, chatting about some cute guy they had seen at the mall this weekend. Sarah had had a crush on Jacob, but she had no idea that he was only interested in her because she was a part of Kythera. After Jacob's death, it was easy to tell that Sarah had been shaken by the whole thing, but it hadn't taken her too long to rebound as if nothing out of the ordinary had happened. It scared me how easily they all took the death in stride, as if it was normal.

A sickening knot formed in my stomach.

I tried to refocus my attention on Marcus and making sure he didn't hate me now. He would only smile and nod occasionally, but he didn't contribute much to the conversations at the lunch table. He was usually laughing and cutting jokes the entire time. Finally, the bell rang and we all got up to leave for class.

I put my tray up and went to say goodbye to Marcus, but he was nowhere to be found. I guess he was pretty upset and I felt even worse for bringing it up. I hoped I could find out some information that would make him feel better, but until then, there wasn't much I could do. I picked up my backpack and headed for the hall. I walked to my locker and pulled out my books for the next class. As I slammed the door shut, Dev appeared.

"Whoa, someone having a bad day?" he asked.

"You could say that." I dropped my books in my bag and zipped it up.

"Maybe another ride would make you feel better? I've got nothing planned this afternoon." He opened his own locker, and pulled out some books.

"I would, but I really need to see Wendy. Stella is great, but she's not Wendy. You understand, right?"

"Yeah, completely. Maybe later this week?"

"Sure," I said with a smile.

Dev turned slowly and headed down the hall. He turned his head to look back at me before walking into his class. I hated how he could make me feel better even when I was in a bad mood. And he had the best timing ever. He always showed up when I felt the worst and always left me feeling better.

Cal usually was the one who did that. I was desperate to hear Cal's voice and to tell him what had been going on. He would understand, and make me feel better about it all. Well, better about everything except the Dev thing. He would understand why I had to spend time with him, but I was sure he wouldn't like it.

The rest of the school day went by in a blur and, before I knew it, the bell rang and we were all clamoring to leave. I went to sit at my customary bench and hoped that Veronica would just walk on by. She did, because she was on her cell phone, but she did look back at me with a sneer on her pouty lips.

Marcus walked by slowly, staring at the ground.

"Hey, Marcus!" I shouted, waving my hand at him. He looked over at me, but his face was emotionless.

"What's up?" he said softly. I felt like I had crushed all the happy spirit he had.

"Are you okay? I mean, ever since our conversation at lunch, you've been acting different. I'm sorry I said anything."

He nodded, and then sat down heavily next to me. "I'm sorry—it's not your fault. I just can't believe he would do something like this. My parents always seemed so happy." He linked his hands together as he slumped down the bench.

"I was surprised, but not completely. My parents have their fair share of fights—and, lately, they don't seem to be on the same wavelength."

"Maybe there's more to the story?" he asked.

"I dunno," I said doubtfully, not wanting to stoke the hope in his words.

"There's gotta be another reason they were meeting there."

I looked over at Marcus, who was staring out at the nearly empty parking lot. I scooted next to him and leaned my head on this shoulder. "Maybe, and if not, it would be pretty cool to have a brother."

I felt his head turn toward me, his chin grazing the top of my head as he fake laughed. I tilted my eyes up.

"Hey, I'm trying to find the positives in the situation."

He turned his head back, quiet for a minute. "You would be a pretty cool sister."

I sighed heavily, letting my head completely rest on his shoulder and closed my eyes. Although I hated what was going on with our parents, the thought of having not only a friend, but a brother like Marcus was phenomenal. Most of the time, being an only child was great, but there were times I wish I had someone to lean on. Marcus had easily fallen into that role when we had met. There was just something about him that was comforting and protective. I think we were what each other needed when our lives were uprooted and brought here for the all-mighty Kythera.

"Mother, can you drop me off at the Hunt Club?" I asked, as I walked into the family room off the kitchen. "It's the driver's day off and I really need some time with Wendy."Mother was sitting, perfectly posed on the edge of the couch in a slinky gold dress with a short skirt that grazed the top of her bony thighs. "I've got a party to go to in a few minutes, so, no, I can't take you. Maybe Kristin . . . Christina can drop you off on her way home?" she suggested, still barely able to remember our maid's name or the fact that the Hunt Club would be way out of the way for her.

"I think she's already left, and what party are you going to at four o'clock?" I said, looking at the large clock on the wall.

"It's another women's club thing," she said absently, pretending she was more interested in the news.

"They sure do like to dress up a lot more than the club at home. I've never seen you wear such sparkly and short dresses before," I said with some sarcasm.

She pulled at her skirt so it covered a little more of her thigh.

"Is Dad going with you?" I asked.

"No, he's got a meeting with Tyson all afternoon. Do you have any homework?" she asked, probably to get me to stop asking questions.

"I have a reading assignment," I said, leaning against the back of the couch.

Mother didn't say anything. I think she thought if she didn't acknowledge me, I would just go away and leave her to her secret meeting with Mr. Gray. She was going to get her wish . . . for now.

I turned and went back through the kitchen and up the servant stairs, pretending that I was going to my room to read or work on homework. I heard the back door slam shut and I knew Mother had left to meet her mystery man. I ran back down the stairs, hoping I could get some answers about what she was doing, which would make me feel better—and Marcus . . . maybe. If I found out she really was having an affair, neither of us would be really happy

But how could I find out without a car? I looked around the empty kitchen. There was no one else home, and it wasn't like the keys were locked up. I could just take them and hope to beat Dad home. *No*, I thought, *there's no point.* I already knew the truth, and I should just leave it alone. I had bigger issues to deal with than Mother's affair. There was the whole thing with Dev and Kythera, and then there was Cal.

I turned back down the steps and into the

butler's pantry. I dialed Cal's number and it started ringing. My heart started to thud in my chest.

Please pick up.

After several rings, I thought about hanging up, but then I heard someone pick up the phone. My heart stopped.

"Hello?" I asked anxiously, but no response. Then the phone was hung up. My mind went blank. What just happened? Had he dropped the phone? Or maybe he was with somebody and he couldn't talk, but he wanted me to know he was there. Or . . . he heard my voice and he did not want to talk to me. *Oh, no,* that couldn't be it . . . could it? I felt sick, as if I had eaten something bad. I tried to convince myself that it wasn't that he didn't want to talk to me, but the thought was hard to ignore.

Was it really over? Tears started to form in the corners of my eyes at the thought of no longer being with Cal. Then I started to sob uncontrollably. My heart literally ached in my chest, and I slid down onto the marble floor. Cal didn't want to be with me anymore, that's all it could be. I was devastated. I let the tears pour down my face and blur my vision. I was so upset, my face grew hot and my tears felt cool against my skin. After a few minutes, the tears slowed and I wiped them away with a dish towel from the towel bar.

I looked around the small room as I sat on the

floor. This was not me. I was not this weak—or was I? Had Kythera sucked everything out of me? Anger started to rise up in my throat and I jumped up to my feet. I was being ridiculous. I had no proof that Cal even had his phone and that Tyson hadn't been the one who answered. And why would I fall apart, just because he *might* have hung up on me? I always thought that was something other girls did . . . not me. Plus, I didn't feel like it was over, so no use spending time worrying about it.

I wiped the remaining tears from my face and went straight to where the keys were kept. No one would know I had even left—but, as I reached for the keys to the Audi, the home phone rang. I raced to answer it. Maybe Cal was trying to call me back.

"Hello?" I said anxiously.

"Hey, is this Casper?" It was Dev.

"Yeah," I said, trying not to sound too disappointed.

"It's Dev. I know you said you were going riding at the Hunt Club, but I thought you might like to go eat dinner or something after?" his voice was low and sheepish.

"Actually, I'm not going to the Hunt Club. The driver is busy and my mother is out." I wrapped the long telephone cord around my wrist.

"I could take you out to the Hunt Club, and hang out with Wendy."

"No, that's okay. Thanks for the offer, though.

I've got homework tonight, so it's probably better if I don't go out there anyway," I lied.

I didn't want to share that part of me with Dev, since our relationship wasn't genuine. Wendy was like my kid and I didn't just let anyone meet her.

"So, no to the Hunt Club, but yes to dinner?"

He sounded so hopeful that I giggled to myself. He wasn't supposed to be that hopeful.

"Sorry again, but I'm going to have to pass. Remember, I'm still grounded." For once, my punishment was going to be useful.

"I understand—maybe they can make an exception again?"

"I doubt it. They have a family dinner planned." The lies were becoming so easy, I didn't even have to think about them anymore.

"Okay, well, maybe later this week. See you at school."

"Yeah, sure. See ya," I said hastily and hung up the phone.

I knew I shouldn't have been so rude, especially considering my task, but I had too many other things on my mind. Like how to pull it all together and quit being a pouty drama queen.

I needed to stop letting Tyson defeat me. What had happened to my defiant attitude? Was I really going to roll over that easy? No—I wasn't a quitter. When I took a bad fall on one of my horses, I always got back on without even thinking twice. I had to do the same thing here.

Tyson might have been the king, but I was one

subject who couldn't remain loyal. I wasn't above a kingdom takeover. Besides, I would make a pretty damn good queen.

Chapter

8

I WALKED INTO THE LIBRARY, SAT down at the desk, and turned on my laptop. I did a couple of spins in the rolling desk chair as the computer booted up. Then I stopped and stared out the large windows that looked out into the backyard, aggravated it was so small and that my view was a large stucco fence covered in vines instead of rolling hills and pretty horses.

I started thinking about what I needed to do to get myself out of this mess. First, I needed to find Cal somehow. I was going to do an internet search for boarding schools in North Carolina and call all of them to find out which one Cal was at. Second, I needed to find out more about the attorney the guy in the bar had mentioned. Was his cousin bought off and giving the other group information or had he turned them down? Either way, he would have some kind of information about the group who had it in for Kythera. Third, I needed to find out for sure if my mother was having an affair with Mr. Gray.

I chuckled to myself. If this wasn't so serious, it *would* be funny. It sounded like I was talking about the book *Fifty Shades of Grey*. I had never read it, but I knew the main guy was named Christian Grey, and I really hoped Mother wasn't living out some fantasy from the book. I *had* seen it on her nightstand not too long ago.

Finally, the computer home screen appeared and I clicked on the internet icon. I typed "boarding schools, North Carolina" into Google. Fortunately, the list wasn't too long. I grabbed a piece of stationary from the desk with "Whitley" in pretty cursive at the top, and wrote down the schools' names and the numbers for the administrative offices. I looked at the large clock on the wall. It was five o'clock. I doubted anyone would be in, so I would have to wait till tomorrow to get some answers. I folded the paper in half and tucked it into my blazer pocket.

Task two would have to wait till tomorrow, too, since the law office was more than likely closed, too. Plus, I needed time to think about my strategy for getting information from them anyway. It wasn't like a seventeen-year-old could walk in and demand information. That wouldn't believable, especially since not many teenagers need a lawyer's help.

ALL THE KING'S MEN

That left task three, and I was almost positive that Mother was with Mr. Gray right now. I closed the laptop, got up, and went to the pantry to grab the keys. But what would I do when I got there? I couldn't knock on the door. I wasn't supposed to be driving, and I didn't want her to have any excuse to turn the situation around on me. I could spy in the windows, but I might see something I didn't *want* to see. It was just a chance I was going to have to take.

Twenty minutes later, I pulled up near the house I'd been at the night before. Tonight, the lights were on, and my heart started to beat wildly. I looked around for a place to park, but the street was jammed with cars. I drove another block and finally found a small space between a Volkswagen Beetle and a MINI. I walked down the street slowly, looking around in every direction. I didn't need them to come out of the house and see me.

Finally, I reached the front steps and almost walked up before realizing the door was halfway open. I made a quick decision and tried to hide behind the overgrown boxwood next to the walkway.

"I think we've made a lot of progress, tonight. Meet you here in a couple of days?" said Mr. Gray in his deep, resounding voice. He was a tall man, something Marcus had inherited, and he had the booming voice to match.

"Yes, that sounds great," said my mother with a demure smile.

He walked her to her car, which was parked directly in front of the house, opened the door for her, and gave her a quick peck on the cheek.

My feet started to burn and tingle as if I were standing in hot coals. Great, I must have stepped in a fire ant bed! I moved my feet around, but tried to keep the rest of my body still. I bit my lip to keep from letting out a cry. Mr. Gray turned back to the house, walked up the steps, and closed the door behind him. Fortunately, Mother didn't linger and drove off quickly. I jumped from the bush and did a little dance in the street, trying to wipe the ants off the tops of my exposed feet. After a couple of seconds, I was pretty sure that I had gotten rid of them. The tops of my feet were already red and pulsing. As I stared at them, I began to panic, as I realized Mother was probably on her way home. I started to sprint toward my car, sped out of the spot and barely missed the MINI.

As I drove, I thought about Mr. Gray's words. "Made a lot of progress." What did that mean? That didn't sound like something you would say to your mistress. Sounded more like something you would say to a therapy patient—and, besides that, what was with the puny kiss on the cheek? Don't get me wrong, I didn't want to see a make-out section, but this was the worst affair I'd ever seen. And I had seen my fair share, considering the circle my parents floated in, which included a lot of horny old men and young, bored housewives.

I could still remember, when I was in seventh grade, walking in on my best friend Maggie's mother and the gardener, making out on top of the kitchen island. How cliché—but, by high school, that had been the norm. Who needed soap operas? But the other thing I remember about that incident is that when I had told my mother what I had seen, she called Maggie's mom and chewed her out, and then told her she was a whore. I had also heard her talking to Dad later, and saying how she couldn't believe someone would cheat and do it in front of the children.

She had been so upset about what had happened, she had banned Maggie's mother from all her parties for the rest of the year. My mother was the queen of Lexington's finest society. Her banishment was social suicide for Maggie's family.

So how could she turn around and do exactly what she had hated so much? Had she become that fed up with Dad? He was gone now more than ever, busy trying to keep Tyson happy and our family's fortune. Truly, we had already lost it when we joined Kythera. It was now property of the K, and the moment we left, it would be all but lost. Unless I could figure out some way to save it—or, at least, the horses. That was all we needed anyway, because that was what my dad's fortune had been built on. I knew our family could do it again.

I scooted under a yellow light and coasted onto our street. The house was only a block away, and I prayed Mother hadn't gone straight home after her little meeting. The house was in view and I sped up before swerving into the driveway. I parked the car in the garage, breathing a sigh of relief that her car was still missing.

I wiped away the beads of sweat that had formed on my forehead as I got out of the car and locked it. I walked into the house, my feet now not only burning, but itching like crazy. I walked faster. The smell of sweet and spicy Asian food filled my nose as I stepped in the back door. The chef was busy over a wok, tossing in some red pepper strips and soy sauce, steam rising from the bowl.

I hung up the keys in the pantry, grabbed a bag of peas for my feet from the freezer, and walked up the servant stairs, waving at the chef as I walked by. I laid down on the chaise lounge in the corner of my room, balancing the bag of peas on my feet. They were going numb from the cold, but that was better than the burning and itching. That was one thing I hated about Charleston. In Kentucky, I could have walked barefoot in a field of soft grass without thinking twice about it. Besides the horses, I missed soft grass in general the most. Here, at any point in time, you could be attacked by vicious ants.

At least I had made it home safely and undetected. I knew the staff wouldn't tell on me, so I had nothing to worry about . . . except what to say to Marcus tomorrow. I had caught our parents together, but what had I really seen? I wasn't completely convinced it was an affair, but I had no other explanation as to why they would be meeting in secret.

School tomorrow was going to suck. Not only would I have to limp around in pain, but I would have to tell Marcus what I had seen.

———◄◆►———

I hobbled out of the girls' locker room and into the gym. The top of my feet itched so badly, especially since I had on socks and tennis shoes. It took everything I had not to strip the shoes and socks off in the middle of class and just start scratching away while everyone stared at me in disgust.

The P.E. teacher had pulled out a wire cart filled with basketballs and put them next to the court. A couple of the guys had already grabbed a few and were trying to dunk them into the net at the far end of the court. I spotted Marcus as he easily dunked the ball, and hung onto the rim like a pro. Marcus had been always been great at sports. Apparently at his high school in New York, he'd been scouted by some of the biggest colleges to play for their teams, and he was the MVP of the high school varsity basketball team. He had a future in the NFL—which he'd had to give up when his parents wanted him to join Kythera.

I walked across the floor, barely dodging a basketball that was flying toward me.

"Hey," I said softly, as Marcus dribbled the ball.

"Hey," he said, but kept his attention on the net.

"Listen, can we talk? I've got something to tell you."

He dribbled a couple more times, then nodded and threw the ball into the basket with ease. It thudded against the gym floor before rolling to the wall. We walked over to the bleachers and sat down on the front row.

"What's up?" he asked as he leaned against the second row of bleachers.

"I saw our parents together last night in front of that house I told you about," I said in one breath. I had thought about some small talk before letting it loose, but realized it would be better just to go ahead and get it over with.

He nodded. "Huh, I guess that answers that." He looked down at the floor.

I waited a minute, hoping he had something else to say, but he just stared at the guys on the court.

"But I'm not one hundred percent sure they are having an affair," I added after a few long seconds.

He instantly perked up. His big dark eyes turned on me and they were filled with hope. Part of me wished I hadn't mentioned it, but I was desperate to see some glimmer of the old Marcus I had come to know.

"What makes you think that?"

"I went back to the house yesterday to see if I could catch them there and I got there as they were walking out. Your dad said something like, 'I think we are making progress,' which didn't sound very flirty to me. Plus, when she left, he only gave her a quick peck on the cheek. I'm not an expert on affairs, but I think it would have been a lot more passionate if they were involved." I pulled up one foot on the bleacher and stuck my finger underneath the tongue of my shoe and scratched. *Ahh.*

"Yeah, that doesn't sound like an affair—or, at least, not a good one. But there is only one problem with your theory. What he said doesn't make sense, sounds like something a shrink would say."

I nodded, smiling that he had thought the same thing.

"But they were on the street, so that could explain the quick kiss. He couldn't let her leave without something, so he just gave her a quick one on the cheek."

I frowned. I hadn't thought about that. "Still, I think there is more to the story."

"You might be right," he said, a ball rolling to his feet. He picked it up and threw it back to the group of guys who were still goofing around.

"You could help me figure it out, and then we'll know for sure," I suggested.

He paused for a minute before turning to me. "Okay, I'll help."

I smiled as I continued to scratch the top of my foot. "Great!"

"What's up with your foot?" he said, laughing for the first time since I told him about the affair.

The teacher blew his whistle for the class to begin. Marcus got up and held his hand out for me. I took it after getting one last good scratch in. "Fire ants in a bush."

He pulled me off the bench, a knowing look on his face. We had both come from places where fire ants were like Big Foot. We knew they might exist, but we had never seen them firsthand, so we weren't sure if they did. Myth solved . . . they definitely existed.

"I'll come over and we can work on our homework this afternoon," he said, emphasizing *homework* as if it were a secret code.

I nodded as he jogged over to the court with the rest of the guys. He had some spring in his step again, which made me happy. What was even better was knowing that I had some help.

Next step was to get him on board to help me with the rest of my tasks.

━━━━◁◇▷━━━━

Marcus had said when I saw him in the parking lot after school that he would come straight over to my house to work on our "homework," but I didn't know how long it would take him to really get here. He'd been talking to Charlotte in the parking lot when I'd seen him, and they were now boyfriend and girlfriend—as of last week. Charlotte had been trying to get with Marcus since he moved to Charleston. Marcus had made comments about how pretty she was, and I'd finally spilled the secret that Charlotte liked him, too. I knew I'd broken some sort of girl code, but she didn't seem to mind that I did. I was happy for them and I hoped it worked out, but I couldn't stand to be around them too long. They were so lovey-dovey, always hugging and kissing. Plus, it made me miss Cal, and I couldn't think about that right now.

I stepped into the front foyer and immediately stopped, because the butler was up on a chair, hammering a nail in the wall. That could only mean one thing . . . my mother was decorating. When we had moved into this house, it had been completely furnished with beautiful antiques that matched the 1700s architecture, but had not met my mother's decorating taste. She had quickly set out to get rid of the antiques and replace them with some of our things from Kentucky and new things she had bought recently. I knew if she saw me, she would want me to give my opinion on her latest purchase. I wasn't in the mood to give her my opinion.

I shook my head, feeling sorry for our poor butler as I turned toward the steps. I had so much respect for him, but I also pitied him because he had to work for someone like my mother. Mother was never kind to the help, and she always ordered them around as if they were incapable of doing anything right without her direction. I chalked up her attitude to being a born and bred blue blood, who had been raised to be the perfect wife and hostess in her rich circle. She didn't know how else to respond.

I threw my backpack on the uncomfortable excuse for a desk chair and flung open the burnt-orange curtains. The dark room was flooded with light and a pretty view of the tops of the trees in the park and the harbor. I flipped on the desktop computer, pulled out my notebook and the folded piece of paper I had with the phone numbers for the boarding schools on it. I was *so* ready to find Cal. I looked around the room for a telephone, but didn't find one, which was weird—I figured most offices would have one. Maybe it was because most people had cell phones now? It was probably better if the call came from Marcus's cell phone number anyway, just in case they had caller id.

As I sat down in front of the computer, the door flung open and Marcus walked in, his face beaming. "You ready to do some snooping?" he asked, as he threw his huge duffel bag he called a "backpack" on the floor and then flung himself into one of the wing chairs opposite the desk. The chair screeched against the wood floor.

"Yes, definitely. But I have to tell you that I've

got a couple other things that I want your help with . . ." I said, putting my head in my hands, hoping I could persuade him with my smiling face.

"Like?"

"I need to find Cal. I can't take it anymore, and he can help me with my other task." I clicked on the internet icon and typed in the address for Google.

"How many you got?" he asked with a raised eyebrow.

"Three." I typed, "Martin & Whitaker, Charleston, SC," into the search field.

"You've been busy. So, what's the other one?"

"When I went to see the house where our parents were meeting the first time, I had to wait for a cab in some bar," I said absently, clicking through the search page results.

"By yourself? On that side of town? Have you lost your mind? Why didn't you call me?" he said, in a stern tone like a parent.

"Sorry, but you were so upset that I didn't think you would want to go with me." I shrugged my shoulders.

Martin & Whitaker's page was third in the search results. I clicked on it, and classical music started playing out of the ancient computer's speakers.

"I'm sorry about that. I just didn't know what to think. My parents have always been happy. They've actually been who I've looked up to when it comes to relationships and to think it's been a lie was hard to hear."

"I get it, plus maybe it's not a lie. Maybe they are still madly in love and he's meeting my mother for some other reason."

He looked at me doubtfully. "I like your optimism."

"Anyway, while I was waiting at the creepy bar, this guy kept talking to me. I got scared and I flashed him my tattoo. Of course, everyone left me alone after that, but the guy started asking me if I knew about the other group after us. He didn't have the name of the group, but he said they had been asking people around town for information on us and they were willing to pay money for it. They said they had approached his cousin, Edward Whitaker, who's an attorney with Martin Charles."

Marcus raised an eyebrow. "For real? I mean, how do you know that guy wasn't part of the other group and sending you on some wild chase?"

I shrugged my shoulders. "I don't. That's why I need to find out if it's the truth or not. If it is the truth, it might be valuable information for later."

"What do you mean?"

"Maybe I can use the information to help me get out of Kythera."

"You're smart and you never give up do you?" he said as he pulled out his cell phone. He got a goofy grin on his face as he typed a text. It had to be Charlotte.

"Nope," I said and turned my attention back to the screen, which now had a cheesy photo of the attorneys standing together in a hallway plastered on the top scroll bar.

It was a large firm, with about ten attorneys listed. I searched for Edward Whitaker and he was second to last on the list. I clicked on his name and landed on his personal page, a smiling photo of him in a suit next to his bio. It said he practiced in the area of business litigation and real estate transactions. It sounded kind of boring to me.

"So, what do you need me to do?" asked Marcus.

I handed him the crumpled piece of paper with the boarding school numbers on it. "Can you call these schools and find out which one Cal is at?"

He studied the list. "Sure. I'll go down the hall and make the calls," he said as he got up.

"Great, just make sure my parents aren't up here, so they can't hear what you're doing. They shouldn't be, but I told them you were coming over to do homework, so my mother might get nosy."

He nodded as he walked out of the room, the cell phone already pressed to his ear as he closed the door.

I stared again at the picture of Edward Whitaker. He was a far cry from his cousin who I had met in the bar. He had red hair that was cropped short, and he was well-groomed in his navy suit. His big green eyes were creased at the corners as he mugged for the camera.

I didn't know much about the law or how much an attorney made, but I was pretty sure they weren't hurting. So why would he take money from another group, knowing that his partner worked for us? Either it was a lie, or these people were offering more money than he could make at the firm.

I needed to find a way to get into the office and nose around. But what kind of excuse could I come up with? He wouldn't believe I had any real estate transaction or business issue to discuss with him, plus he would wonder why I hadn't gone to Charles Martin. I put my hand under my chin and stared at the screen and his freckly face again. I scanned his suit and noticed something strange. What kind of pin did he have on his lapel? I leaned forward to try to make it out, my face an inch from the screen. It was a capital "M" with an arrow through it. It didn't look like a fraternity pin, but I couldn't be sure. I went back to the main page and started looking at the other attorneys. Only one other attorney had a pin and it was obvious it was an American flag.

Marcus walked into the room. "I found him!" he shouted, raising his arms in the air like he had just won the state championship.

He brought me the piece of paper, the boarding school in Asheville circled. I felt my heart jump a mile.

"I can't believe it, thank you!" I got up from the chair and ran to hug him. "One task down, now only two to go. Come take a look at this. What does that look like to you?" I asked him, pointing at the small gold pin.

He squinted at the screen. "It looks like an M with an arrow through it."

"Does it look like a fraternity pin to you?"

He studied it a little longer, "No . . ." He paused. "But it does look familiar. Like I've seen it around New York, on somebody's suit on Wall Street or at my dad's accounting firm."

"Huh." I sat back down at the computer, pulled up another tab, and typed in a description of the pin and clicked enter.

To my surprise, there were a lot of hits and they were all asking the same question. There were photos of people walking down the street, people passing by and taking photos of the pin. And then there was a group standing in some banquet hall, all wearing the same pin, but it didn't have a caption.

I scrolled down the page to find some more information and found a page entitled, "Marrow, the secret society." I quickly cleared my search field and typed in the title of the page, and it was like looking for Kythera all over.

"Oh, no, this has to be the other group . . . Marrow," I said aloud.

Marcus looked at me, his eyes wide. "So he's been bought off?"

I nodded. "I think it's time to go to Tyson."

Chapter

9

AS I WALKED DOWN THE hallway at school, I stared at the piece of paper with the boarding school numbers on it. Marcus had put a big red circle around the phone number and name of the school Cal was at in Asheville. I felt a little bubble of happiness every time I looked at it. Phase two would begin this afternoon, with another call to the boarding school and a dreaded conversation with Tyson about the pin. I had made a little sketch of the pin on the bottom of the sheet with the boarding school numbers.

Suddenly, I bumped into someone, my head making contact with their shoulder, and I dropped the paper on the floor. "Oh, I'm sorry," I said breathlessly, startled from my thoughts.

"No problem," said Dev. He bent over to pick up the paper I had dropped.

He looked at it, trying to read my scrawled writing. Unfortunately, I had the same terrible writing skills as my mother.

"Are you transferring to a boy's boarding school? I think you might need a pretty good costume to pull that one off."

"No, and not all those schools are just for boys." I laughed, gently pulling the paper from him.

"Yeah, but the one you have circled is."

"Oh, I know—it's just some research for my mother's cousin. She's looking for a boarding school to send her son to." *Where the heck did that come from?*

He looked at me, puzzled. "Why couldn't she just look it up herself?"

His question was legitimate, but it irritated me. What was it his business, anyway? I was about to snap at him, then remembered I needed to play nice, according to Tyson.

"She isn't computer-savvy," was all I said, as I started down the hall.

Dev chased after me. "Hey, you want to come over for dinner? My mom really liked you and wanted me to invite you over again."

"That's sweet," I said, pausing to think of my answer. "Sure, what time?"

"Six o'clock? I can come pick you up and bring you home," he offered.

"No, that's okay. I'll have the driver bring me," I said, because I didn't want him to know that I was stopping by the Romans' house later.

"Great, see you then," he said, touching my shoulder. The warmth from his hand lingered, but I tried to forget about it as I walked into class.

I sat down at my seat and was about to stuff the paper back into my pocket—but then I saw Alex sit down across the room from me. I got up and walked over to his seat.

"Hey, can I ask you a question?"

He finished a text and looked up at me. "Sure." He looked excited that I was actually speaking to him.

I showed him the symbol I had drawn on the bottom of the page. "Have you ever seen this as a pin on somebody's suit or anything?"

He studied it for a minute, and I watched as his eyes drifted to the boarding schools up top. His jaw tightened. "No, I haven't."

"Okay, thanks."

He handed the paper back to me, and I walked quietly back over to my desk.

Things had been so tense with Alex ever since he had admitted to me that he had feelings for me. He had thought that once I knew the truth about Cal and how he had used Kythera to bring me here that I would give him a chance. Things hadn't worked out as he had planned. We were on speaking terms, but things were touch and go.

"Casper," Alex called from across the room.

I turned and looked at him, as he got up from his chair.

"Actually, I think I have seen that pin before."

He stuck his hand out and I gave the paper back to him. He looked at it closely. "Yeah, at Club Ultra a couple of weeks ago. I remember it because it kind of shined when the strobe lights hit it."

"You're sure it was the same pin?" I said, hope filling my chest.

"I'm pretty positive."

"How old was he? Had you ever seen him before? Was he from here?"

"Whoa, what's with all the interest in this pin? Or is it the guy?"

"The pin—and I can't tell you why just yet."

He smirked. "What if I told you that he's probably going to be there next Saturday, and I'll take you there, then will you tell me what this is all about?"

He handed the paper back to me again, his hand brushing against mine. He let it linger for a minute. Alex would never give up.

"I'll tell you after you take me and we get the information that I'm looking for." I raised an eyebrow.

He stared at me for a minute, clearly thinking about whether or not he was going to settle. "Fine," he said.

"Do you have a fake id or something to get into this place?" I looked up to see the teacher walk into the room. I stuffed the paper in my blazer pocket.

"Yeah, it's on your ankle, remember?" he said with a laugh.

"I didn't think about that. Just come by the house around ten o'clock Saturday."

He nodded in response and went to sit back down in his seat. I went to my seat and pulled out my political science notebook. I hoped that this guy would show up at the club. One, because I needed to figure this Marrow thing out and, two, I would hate to waste a Saturday night at a club. I wasn't really into the club scene.

Ms. Epling started talking and writing on the board about the fall of Napoleon. I looked up to take notes, and I could see Alex grinning from ear to ear at me. *This better pay off.*

———◆———

I closed the door of the Lincoln and stared up at the Romans' massive house hidden behind the oak trees. I stomped across the gravel, my throat going dry. I hadn't talked to Tyson since the Kythera meeting, and I had *never* had a conversation with him alone. We weren't exactly friends, but right now I had to get past that, especially if I wanted Cal back and to get out of stupid Kythera for good.

I pushed the doorbell nervously, rocking back and forth as I waited for the butler to answer. The door opened slowly, and I walked in. "I need to speak to Mr. Roman, please," I said, staring up at the tall, frescoed ceilings of the foyer. I always felt like I was walking into a Roman cathedral, which had always been ironic to me since their last name was Roman. I wondered if it was a coincidence or on purpose?

It was hard to be back in this house after what had happened the last time I was here. My nerves were on edge and I had to concentrate really hard to keep from barreling out the door. The butler motioned me down the hall, and I prayed that he wasn't leading me to the library. But, of course, he turned to the left to the set of double doors leading me straight to the library. As he opened the door, I held my breath.

I stepped in, but stayed close to the door. Tyson was sitting at his desk at the far end of the room, rows of books surrounding him in the built-in cases. He looked up from his desk.

"Ah, Casper, to what do I owe this pleasure? Good news about the Chavan kid, I hope?"

He didn't get up from his desk and I knew he expected me to come over to him, but he had another think coming. I looked down at the rug where Jacob's blood had smeared the light pink pattern, turning it a deep, violent red. Of course, that rug was gone and a similarly patterned rug had replaced it.

"Nothing about Dev, but I am having dinner at his house later this afternoon. I came here to tell you I have some information about the other group who's after Kythera." I clutched my hands behind my back, twisting my fingers together.

"Oh," he said, and immediately got up from his desk. He walked toward me and stopped in the middle of the rug that I refused to step on. He waited for me to continue.

"I've found some information about who they are, but before I share anything with you, I want to make a deal," I blurted out.

He sneered and almost laughed. "What kind of deal? I hope you've given up on trying to get out. You saw how that turned out last time." He put a hand in his pants' pocket.

"No. I want you to sign over Wendy if I get you the name and information about this group—and I want Cal brought back from his boarding school in North Carolina." I bit my bottom lip.

"Wendy? Who's Wendy?" He moved from the middle of the room, and over to a cart with a decanter of liquor. He poured himself a glass of dark liquid into a cut-crystal cup.

"My horse. The one that's in Charleston."

He laughed. "I should have known it would have something to do with those damn horses." He took a sip of the drink and stared at me. He was waiting for me to back down, but I wasn't going to.

Finally, he sighed. "Sure, if you find out who they are, I'll sign the horse over to you."

"Good, but I want this deal in writing, so you can't go back on it. And what about Cal?" I crossed my arms over my chest.

He laughed. "Fine, but I can't make any promises about Cal. You've had too much influence on him, so don't expect to see him anytime soon. He won't be leaving the boarding school until he starts school at Tulane next fall. I might even send him to Europe next summer," he said with a smirk.

He was enjoying this, and I wanted to cry. I really wouldn't see Cal for a long time. Tyson was going to make sure we were never together again, and it felt like my heart was being crushed. I swept away a tear that escaped my eye before he could see it. I had to focus on Wendy right now. At least he was giving her to me.

Tyson went over to his desk and scribbled something on a piece of paper. He walked over and handed it to me. I looked at it, and it read that Mr. Roman would relinquish the title of Wendy the horse to Casper Whitley, if she was able to provide a name and evidence as to who the other group was that were after them. He had signed it with his undecipherable signature.

"Is that good enough?"

"Yes, thank you," I said, and turned to leave the room. I could hear Tyson laughing, and I wanted to turn back around and tell him to go to hell, but I knew that wouldn't help. I wasn't going to forget about Cal that quickly—but I tried to get my heart to believe that it was truly over, because otherwise the pain would be too excruciating. Cal was gone, and there was nothing I could do about it.

But getting Wendy back was the first step to getting my freedom back, and then maybe someday I could see Cal again. I pulled out the slip of paper with the boarding school numbers on it, and tore it up. There was no point in calling right now. There was nothing I could do to bring him back. Another tear slid down my cheek as I threw the pieces of paper out of the car window.

The driver dropped me off at the front doorstep of Dev's home, where he was standing on the porch, waiting for me. He looked happy to see me and I fought back the feelings that were bubbling up inside of me.

"Hey, glad you could make it!" he shouted, as I walked up the steps and through the front door he held open for me.

"Yeah, me, too," I said, feeling a little nervous at how excited he was to see me.

We walked through the hall and straight into the kitchen, which had so many smells, it was hard to decipher what all was floating in the air.

"Hey, Casper, glad you could join us," said his mother, who was busy putting some rice into a large bowl.

"Thanks for inviting me."

She nodded and motioned for us to take a seat at the table in the kitchen.

It felt weird to actually use a breakfast nook. Mother never used it, not even to sit down with coffee in the morning. She said it was where the help should sit and that it wasn't proper for us to eat there.

Dev's mother brought over the bowl of rice,

which was so hot, steam curled up to the ceiling. There were footsteps coming down the hall, and a young girl popped through the kitchen door, texting away on an iPhone.

She looked at me and scowled.

"This is my sister, Preema; she's in middle school," said Dev. She had the same shiny black hair as her mother, which was shorter and cut at her shoulders. She wore pair of pretty pink glasses and a matching headband in her hair.

"Hey," she said in a sarcastic tone, as she slumped down into one of the chairs. She continued to text on her phone until her mother came over and whispered into her ear. She immediately dropped her phone on the table, but began staring at the wall, annoyed.

"Have you ever had Indian food?" Dev asked.

"Not really," I said, trying to think back if I really had. I loved Chinese and Thai, but I don't think Indian was something I had ever tried—at least not the authentic food that his mother was probably able to whip up.

"Then you are in for something special," his mother chimed in, as she sat another bowl on the table. "This is naan."

It looked a lot like pita bread that had bubbled up from being put in the oven. I picked up a piece and tore off a bite. It was light, buttery, and delicious.

The back door slammed and a man in dark jeans, a plaid shirt, and cowboy boots walked in.

He wiped at the sweat on his forehead with his forearm and went to the sink to wash his hands. He looked over at the table and spotted me. He quickly wiped his hands off with the towel, and walked to the table.

"You must be Casper—it's nice to meet you. I'm Dev's father," he said, extending his hand for me to shake it.

His hands were rough and calloused, like my dad's used to be when he spent most of his time on the farm. Now, he wore suits, Rolex watches, and shiny shoes. I preferred him in his jeans and T-shirts.

"Nice to meet you," I said. He sat down to the table and his wife joined us, bringing another bowl filled with meat and a red sauce.

It was one of the most fun dinners I had ever had with a family. There were no fake laughs, waiters buzzing about, or talk about the latest Louis Vuitton purse. We talked, laughed—even his sister joined in. *This must be what a normal family dinner is supposed to look like,* I thought at one point—and I liked it . . . *a lot.*

After dinner, his dad helped his mother clean up the kitchen, and Dev and I went to sit on the swing of their massive back porch. I looked in the window at his parents as they grazed elbows at the sink and smiled at each other. They looked like young lovers who were just starting out. It looked like a scene out of a romantic movie.

"How are your classes going?" Dev asked, and I looked over at him.

"Fine, not too exciting or anything," I answered looking at my feet, which barely touched the ground as we swung back and forth.

"You've seemed pretty distracted the past couple of days. Something going on?"

"No, just the usual . . . tons of homework and, of course, the whole being grounded thing sucks," I said. Something in me wanted desperately to tell him what was really going on, but a part of me thought it wasn't such a good idea.

"It can't be that bad. You got to come over here. When I'm grounded, my parents won't let me leave the house but to go to school."

"They still let you drive?" I looked out over the vast landscape of his backyard. The sun was low, and the faint glimpse of the shore looked like a dark line of ink across the horizon.

"Yeah, they don't have time to take me to school. But they do make me take my sister and pick her up as punishment and to make sure I don't go anywhere else. My sister would rat me out in a heartbeat."

"Your family seems really nice," I said quietly, a little jealous of the perfect setting of his life.

"They are, but I'm sure your family is, too. Do you have any siblings?"

I smiled to myself. "Yeah, about thirty."

"Okay . . ." he said with a confused pause.

I looked up at him, putting my hand on the edge of the swing. "I don't have any human siblings, but I count every one of our horses as one. They mean that much to me. Besides, I can't think of any better siblings to have . . . they don't talk back or tell on you."

He smiled back at me, and I felt my cheeks turning red. What was happening here?

"True, I think they make a great family," he said, scooting a little closer. I didn't budge from where I was sitting, enjoying the slight breeze and cooling air.

"They do," I said quietly.

Dev went silent and I looked up to get a glimpse of his face. He was smiling at me, and our eyes locked on each other. I wanted to look away, but I couldn't. I held my breath.

Dev leaned in close to me, but paused for a moment, as if asking permission to kiss my lips. I moved forward so our lips would meet, and I felt a spark ignite in my chest. He kissed me slowly and tenderly. But, as he brought his hand up to my hair, I suddenly broke away, the spell of the moment disappearing.

I got up from the swing, the chains rattling from the sudden movement. "I'm sorry, I can't do this," I said, my voice shaky.

Guilt overtook my entire body, and I felt like I was on the verge of tears. An image of a crushed Cal entered my mind and I had to get out of there—fast. I opened the back door and rushed through the now-empty kitchen and to the front door. As I walked onto the front porch, I started to run, but stopped when I realized I had nowhere to run to.

"Wait, Casper!" called Dev, as he rushed out the front door and down the steps to where I stood in the gravel driveway.

He stopped in front of me. "Sorry. I mean, I shouldn't have done that. I thought it was okay, and you just looked so beautiful. I felt such a connection to you . . ." he said, his words trailing off.

I stood there motionless, unable to speak. I had felt a spark, but my heart belonged to someone else. I felt tears forming against my eyelids; I looked up to try to keep them from falling, but one escaped down my cheek.

I opened my mouth to speak. "I . . . I feel something, too . . . but," I stuttered, wiping at the tears.

Before I could finish the thought, Dev swept in and hugged me. The warmth returned again to my body. I didn't want him to let go, but I felt so confused. My face was crushed into his chest, but I forced myself to look up at him again. His eyes were sad, but there was some spark of fire in them. I was not able to wait a second longer, so I pushed myself up on my tiptoes and kissed him again. I pushed past the feelings of guilt, and focused on the softness of his lips and our mouths meeting each other so perfectly.

Finally, I had to step back unable to take the intensity any longer. I took a couple of deep breaths, and tried to refocus my thoughts that were pinging back and forth in my head like a Ping-Pong ball.

My mind finally cleared, and the tears dried up. "I have a boyfriend," I blurted out.

Dev's eyes went wide. "Then why have you been hanging out with me?"

"He's been sent to boarding school, and I haven't talked to him since." I crossed my arms over my chest and looked at the ground.

"Who is it?"

"Cal Roman," I said, his name lingering on my lips and making me feel like a really crappy person.

"Oh," Dev said, and then there was a moment of silence. A *long* moment of silence. "How do you know you are even still together if you haven't talked to him since he left?"

I instantly looked up to see a serious look on Dev's face.

"I don't know."

"Maybe it's time to let that go? I mean, wouldn't he have tried to contact you by now? What happened the last time you two were together?"

I kicked the gravel with my right foot, the top of my black ballet flat turning gray. I didn't like thinking about that moment in the jail. Cal had been pretty distant, but, considering what we had just done, it had made sense. But so did the idea that he blamed me for everything. I had decided to run away; I had tried so hard to get away. Maybe Dev was right—and although I couldn't forget Cal so easily, Dev was making it easier.

"We got grounded."

"Oh, now this all makes sense. Cal's always getting into trouble."

"Yeah, but it was my fault, so he probably hates me."

"Don't worry about it. I'm here, and I don't care what you did." He reached out for my hand, and my first instinct was to grab it away, but I didn't. His grip was strong, reassuring—and we had way more in common. He loved horses as much as I did, and his family was amazing and it was just peaceful here with Dev.

I gripped his hand. "Thank you."

He leaned in again and kissed me softly on the lips. The guilt was fading, and I felt Cal's image fading into the background. Tyson's word also echoed in my mind—he had guaranteed that Cal wouldn't be back in my life anytime soon. By next year, when he would be surrounded by cute girls at Tulane University, I would be just a memory for him. I would miss Cal, but it was time to move on with my life . . . wasn't it?

Dev took me home, and we didn't talk much in the car, but he did give me a quick kiss as I got out. I was too stunned to know what to say to him, so I smiled and waved like an idiot.

I did have feelings for Dev, but I was so confused. I needed time to think. Normally, I would go hang out with Wendy and that would help me solve whatever problems I was having, but I didn't think Wendy could help me with a boy problem. This was too complicated and I was wading into deep girl-drama territory. I could only think of one person who could help me . . . Charlotte.

I dialed her number on the home phone in the butler's pantry and waited patiently as her cell phone played Demi Lovato's song "Give Your Heart a Break" as the ring tone.

"Hello?" asked Charlotte.

"Hey, it's Casper."

"Oh, hey! I didn't recognize the number, where are you calling from? Why didn't you call me on your cell phone?"

"My parents took it, so I'm using the home phone." I picked up a box of gluten-free crackers that had been left on the counter in the pantry.

"Why do they have a home phone? Isn't that old-fashioned or something?" she said, laughing.

"I dunno, it came with the house. Listen, I need some help," I said, popping a cracker into my mouth. I chewed it quickly and swallowed.

"Uh-oh, boy trouble?"

"Yeah, how did you know that?" Charlotte was a gossiping, shopping-obsessed, stereotypical girl, but she was also very smart. Smarter than any seventeen-year-old should be about love.

"Because I've seen Dev. He could cause a problem for almost any girl. He's totally hot."

"Hey, you have a boyfriend."

"Doesn't mean I'm blind, hon."

I closed the box of crackers, and shoved them to the back of the counter. "True," I said.

"Dev's a really nice guy, and he's gorgeous. You all have a lot in common. And now you have to be friends with him for Kythera. You feel guilty because you think you're cheating on Cal, right?"

"Yes, but how . . ." I said, stunned how easily she had it all figured out.

"You're too easy to read, Casper. I can see how you look at Dev. You pretend you don't feel anything, but you do."

"Is it that obvious? I still love Cal, though," I said, the sadness obvious in my voice. My heart was aching for Cal, but it also wanted Dev.

"If Cal weren't in the picture, would you go out with Dev?" she asked not missing a beat.

"Yes," I answered, a little too quickly.

"Then go for it. You know I'm Cal's number-one fan. I love him like a brother. But Tyson isn't playing. He'll do whatever it takes to make sure that Cal stays in Kythera. He's not going to let Cal come back. And, sure, when he's in college, Tyson won't be able to control him as much, but that's like a year away. He would want you to move on," she said, her tone serious.

I knew she was right. It was time to face the fact that Cal was gone, no matter how much it hurt.

"We won't judge you for going out with Dev . . . I promise. First loves are tough. But it gets easier after a while," she added, breaking my thoughts.

"How many boyfriends have you had?" I asked, surprised by how experienced she sounded.

"Enough. See you tomorrow. Call me if you need anything else, 'kay?" she said.

"Thanks, bye," I said, and the phone line went dead. I put the phone back in its cradle.

It hadn't even crossed my mind, but she was probably in a hurry because she was hanging out with Marcus. I had seen them leaving school together. *Crap*, did that mean he'd heard everything we were talking about? I started to panic, but then I realized I didn't care if he knew. Charlotte had said "We won't judge you." She had to be referring to Marcus—or was she talking about the whole group?

Ugh, why couldn't everything be like horseback riding? You told the horse what to do and that was that. This was way too complicated for me, but Charlotte was right. If Cal was really gone, I needed to move on—and I could see myself with Dev if there wasn't going to be Cal.

Chapter

10

THE SCHOOL WEEK WENT BY slowly—even more so because Marcus and I had made little progress in finding out what our parents were up doing at that mysterious house on the other side of Charleston. Marcus had even gotten brave enough to go out there with me one night, but the house was dark and no one ever showed up. Our parents didn't meet each other the rest of the week, and it was as if the whole problem had disappeared.

We spent our afternoons playing Scrabble, analyzing his relationship with Charlotte and my new relationship with Dev. Yes, Marcus had been there that afternoon when I was talking to Charlotte and, yes, she had blabbed all the details to him. But he was okay with it all and he didn't blame me for moving on.

I abandoned my search for Cal, and Marcus and I focused on finding out more information about Marrow.

Saturday night finally came around and I had to do some serious begging to get to go to the club. Dad told me no, but for some reason Mother took my side. She said it was time for them to loosen the restrictions on me. I couldn't figure out why, but I was grateful for whatever her reasoning was.

Alex asked to pick me up at ten, but I said that Dev was coming along, because I was supposed to be recruiting him. Most everyone at school had figured out that Dev and I had something going on, but I still didn't want to throw it in his face. Alex was completely bummed, but he relented because he couldn't argue with my logic. Being the recruiter sucked in most ways, but it did have its perks.

Dev was at my door at ten, dressed casually, as usual, looking like he was ready to go for a ride across the fields. I smiled at him as I opened the door. He stepped to me and gave me a kiss on the lips, took my hand, and led me to his truck.

He knew where Club Ultra was, saying that he had been there a couple of times. When I had asked him to come with me, he'd thought it was strange, because he knew I wasn't the clubbing type—but I'd said that a bunch of my friends were going and they wanted me to come along. I still didn't feel comfortable telling him why I *really* wanted to go. I *was* supposed to be making Kythera look good, and telling him I was looking for some people who were trying to get rid of us all was probably not the best way to recruit him.

We pulled into the parking lot of the club, where tons of people were walking up to the front steps to wait in line to get in. After we parked, I spotted Alex at the front door and he waved us over.

"Hey, Casper, come this way," he said, not acknowledging Dev. We swept past the line and up the concrete steps, a bouncer opening the shiny gold door for us.

The thumping music hit my body the minute we stepped into the dark room. Strobe lights danced above us, illuminating the dance floor. There were not that many people out on the dance floor yet—it was still early—but Alex wanted to get here so we wouldn't miss the guy we were looking for. Alex led us to a round booth, which was far away from all the other tables and overlooked the dance floor.

We approached the table, where Charlotte and Marcus were already sitting, cuddled up in the corner of the booth. To my surprise, Veronica was sitting with them as well, her legs thrown over Matt, another Kythera member. She looked at me and Dev, her plump lips curling up into a sinister sneer. She leaned over and started making out with Matt. As if I cared.

Sarah was quietly sipping a drink on the other

end of the booth, obviously feeling out of place next to Veronica and Matt. She waved at me, a look of relief on her face as she motioned for us to sit next to her. I sat down, and scooted close to Sarah to give Dev room.

"Hey, I didn't know you liked clubs!" shouted Sarah over the heavy bass music.

"I don't," was all that I said, aggravated that I would have to shout to be heard.

We sat around for a little while, watching as more and more people flooded in. I watched for the suspicious guy wearing the pin, but nothing. Charlotte tapped my shoulder and motioned to the dance floor. I looked at Dev and he nodded. I shrugged my shoulders and followed her to the dance floor. What did I have to lose? I wasn't the best dancer, but the floor was so packed, it wasn't like anyone would notice me.

The dance floor was so crowded, there was barely room to breathe. Charlotte took me by the hand and guided me into the middle of the crowd and we started moving to the music. I felt the temperature rise in the room, and I could feel sweat on my forehead. After several minutes, we really got into it and we were dancing like crazy with the rest of the crowd. Soon, I lost Charlotte in the crowd, but I was actually having too much fun to leave. I kept bumping into other people and dancing with them, the light so dim I could barely tell who I was dancing with half the time.

I felt someone put their hand on my shoulder

and I was about to turn around and tell them to back off, but there was a familiar spark. I could feel his body behind mine as he danced really close. The electric between us was off the charts and I thought Dev must have joined in the crowd. I turned around to look at him, but it wasn't Dev and my mouth dropped open.

Dev wasn't behind me—it was Cal.

At first, I thought I was dreaming, but Cal pulled me to him and kissed me hard. I knew then it wasn't a dream, and I eagerly kissed him back. So many emotions flooded my body . . . relief and excitement.

After a minute I pulled away, and leaned into his ear. "How did you get here?"

He leaned into my ear, chills going up and down my spine. "I have my ways . . . I just had to see you."

Cal grabbed my hand and pulled me through the crowd and toward the exit. The minute we were outside in the alley, he grabbed me and started kissing me. We ended up against the wall of the building, my back against the cold concrete. It felt like I was coming alive again, and Dev was no longer any part of my thoughts. Cal was just so overwhelming in my mind and heart that nothing and no one else could compete.

Finally, we stopped, and I looked into those incredible blue eyes that I had been missing. "I'm so happy you're back," I said breathlessly.

"Me, too—I just couldn't stand to be away from

you." He put his hand on my neck and pulled me to him again and hugged me. My face fell into the comfortable crook of his neck.

"Are you here for good?" I asked, my lips inches from his neck.

He didn't respond, because a scream echoed through the alley. The kind of scream I'd only heard before in scary movies. It made the hair stand up on my arms. I immediately raised my head and looked at Cal. The screaming continued. We ran toward the sound. It was coming from the parking lot across the street from the club.

Crowds of people were starting to run in the same direction we were, and a sense of panic started to rush into my chest. Finally, I saw the distraught face of Sarah, her screams now quieter. Cal and I pushed through the crowd to see what was going on, and when I finally caught sight I felt my knees buckle under.

Veronica's lifeless body was draped over the hood of her Mercedes, her face staring up blankly at the dark sky. A single line of dark blood dripped down her arm and wrist, covering the "K" in her Kythera tattoo. Her upside-down tattoo mirrored the blood-red writing on the wheel well of the car.

I was unable to move, but also unable to look away. Cal was shouting something, but my ears felt numb and fuzzy. There was a blur of activity in front of me, like a movie; the actions were sped up all around me, but I was standing completely still, watching.

I looked over at Alex, and he was frozen, his eyes on his sister. I wanted to run to him, but I literally was unable to move.

"Marcus, get Casper out of here!" shouted Cal, and within seconds, I was being pushed along by Marcus, away from the chaotic scene. I heard the shrill sound of the ambulance as it pulled onto the street.

Marcus was pulling me along like a rag doll, as I struggled to watch the chaos unfolding behind me. People were covering their mouths, frantic voices on cell phones, the paramedics rushing through the wall of bystanders.

Once I was no longer able to watch, I turned to Marcus, noticing for the first time Charlotte being dragged along the other side of Marcus. We reached Marcus's Land Rover, and he opened the back door for me. I jumped in without a word, and Charlotte got in the front seat.

We zoomed away from downtown at a fast pace. I looked out the window, unable to focus on anything.

"Wait, where's Dev?" I said out of the blue, panic dripping in my words. Since seeing Cal and then the chaos in the parking lot, I had forgotten all about him. I felt terrible that I had left without another thought about him until now.

"We didn't see him in the crowd in the parking lot before . . ." Marcus said not finishing the thought.

"Before what?" I asked.

"Before we saw Veronica," chimed in Charlotte.

"Oh," I said, quietly deciding it was best not to talk the rest of the way home—or wherever we were going.

Marcus pulled up to the Romans' house, and my heart fluttered. I should have known we would have to gather together as a group and focus on "cleanup" for Kythera instead of focusing on the death of a teenage girl. It finally sunk in—Veronica was *dead*. I had no doubt in my mind. Her body had been completely still, and her beautiful caramel-colored skin had been ashen and gray. Who would do such a thing?

I shuddered, realizing what a dumb question that was. Plenty of people would kill us, simply because of the tattoo we had been branded with. I would bet it was the mysterious group after us who were trying to send us a strong message. That was what I hated most about this stupid club—killing had no more meaning than sending a message to the other party. Our lives were worthless pawns in a giant game of chess.

The Romans' house was all lit up, the glow of the lights illuminating the otherwise dark yard. I jumped out of Marcus's SUV as he pulled up to the steps, not waiting for him to come to a complete stop.

I ran up the steps and into the house. The people milling in the foyer looked at me, and I could tell they already knew what had happened. I walked slowly into the living room, where my parents were sitting on the sofa. My mother had her head in her hands, her shoulders heaving as she wept softly. My dad had a reassuring hand on her back.

Mr. Gray was standing near the fireplace, a glass of liquor in one hand as he stared down at the wood floor. He would glance up occasionally at my mother. I felt the need to run over and punch him in the face, but I didn't.

"Listen, everyone, I've gotten word from the police and it's not good," said Tyson as he breezed into the room, his booming voice echoing in the cavernous room.

I stood with my arms crossed against a column.

"Veronica didn't make it," he said slowly.

The whimpers began immediately from the women in the group, and the men had their jaws tight in an effort to not show their emotions. I couldn't look at anyone, my own tears threatening to cascade down my face.

"The police have no leads on who did it, but they did find this at the crime scene." I looked up to see Tyson holding the small gold pin I had spotted earlier in the attorney's photo—the one Alex had described seeing at the club before.

The door slammed and I jumped. Everyone looked toward the door and Cal strode in, blood on his crisp white shirt. He looked around and when he found me came straight over to me.

He put his hands in my hair. "Are you okay?" he asked, ignoring the rest of the people in the room. They had all gone silent, including Tyson.

I nodded, searching his eyes. They were dark and determined. I had seen that look before. He turned around to face his father near the mantel, but he put a protective hand around my shoulders.

"Ah, Cal, so glad to see you," Tyson said mockingly. "As I was saying, the police found this pinned on Veronica's dress."

"It's the other group's pin," I blurted out.

"And how do you know that?" Tyson asked, skeptical of what I was saying.

"They're called Marrow, and I think they have a spy in your attorney's office."

"What? Who?" piped in Charlotte's father, Mr. Watson. He normally reminded me of Santa Claus, with his jolly face and white beard, but right now he looked like an angry gnome.

"Edward Whitaker."

Tyson looked at me, a sneer on his face. "And what makes you think that?"

"Have you ever seen the pin on his suit? The one in his picture on their webpage?" I said, raising an eyebrow.

He hesitated, holding his jaw tight. "No, I haven't." The room was quiet, all eyes on Tyson.

"You mean someone in our attorney's office is one of them?" interjected Mr. Watson. He turned an angry glare toward Tyson. "How could you have not known this?"

"It must be relatively new . . . I promise I'll have it looked into."

"You better," Mr. Watson said as he sat down on one of the wing chairs.

"That's actually what I was doing at the club tonight. Alex has seen someone there a few weeks ago with the same pin," I said, my confidence growing. I liked making Tyson look like an idiot.

"No need to do that, Casper—you should have just told me and I would have taken care of it," said Tyson, his face now a deep shade of purple.

"I think Casper should continue to look into it. She seems to be getting further that any of us— especially you, Tyson," chastised Mr. Watson.

The temperature in the room instantly went up a couple of degrees; the tension was thick and palpable.

"But that may be dangerous," piped in my mother, who was still sitting on the couch. She held a tissue in her hand to dab her now-puffy eyes. I had never seen Mother look so unhinged in public.

"What choice do we have? Obviously, she's been able to find things out we can't. They are targeting the kids, and the kids are the only ones who can get any information," said Dad, a hand patting my mother's exposed knee.

"But that's our daughter you're talking about. She's not a detective. She could get hurt!" Mother yelled angrily.

"I'll make sure she's okay, I promise," said Cal.

Mother looked at me and at Cal, worry creasing her forehead, but she didn't say anything. She knew she was outnumbered and there was no way she could go against everyone else, even though she was my mother.

I'm not going back to boarding school—am I, Dad?" he asked, knowing Tyson couldn't disappoint the Kythera members now.

"Of course not," he responded.

My heart leapt with joy. He was back and I wouldn't be alone anymore. But what about Dev? I hadn't thought about him except for a second in the car. That's when it became clear to me that when I was given the choice, Dev didn't hold a candle to Cal.

Then it hit me—I had way bigger problems right now. Like a murdered girl, who, sure, I hadn't liked, but I never wanted to see her dead.

The group started to slowly separate and make their way to the front door. My mother came up to me and hugged me. "You will be careful, won't you?" she asked, her voice low and soft.

"Yes, always."

She looked over at Cal and grabbed his shoulders. "Please take care of her. I love her so much and I wouldn't know what I would do if I lost her."

He nodded. "I don't know what I would do without her either."

I felt my heart ache. My mother wasn't one to tell me that she loved me. I knew deep down she did, even in those moments we were almost to the point of scratching each other's eyes out. But she never said it and neither did I.

The house quickly emptied, and we were left alone. Tyson scurried down the hall without a word to Cal or me. We sat down on the couch, and I looked at him, still amazed he was finally back here with me.

"Are you okay?" I asked.

Not only was Veronica a friend—or a frenemy, if I was being honest—she had, at one time, dated Cal. I knew his feelings for her were gone, but he had to be shaken up by all of this.

"Yeah, I'm fine. I can't believe she's gone. I feel so bad for Alex and his parents. Unfortunately, death's become too big a part of our lives around here. I'm starting to become numb to it."

It was true; I had been horrified to see Veronica like that, but it was starting to feel normal and that scared me. Were we all becoming numb? It shouldn't be like that. Every person's heartbeat was important and held meaning beyond whether they were a member of Kythera or Marrow.

I didn't want to become like these monsters who could kill without thinking twice about it. That included becoming like Tyson. I wanted to be free before I became completely numb, too.

———◆———

St. Luke's was packed to the brim with people, all in the customary black clothes. Cal and I sat on the third row from the front, surrounded by members of Kythera. The priest asked Alex to come up and say a few words about his sister.

Alex's face was gray, and his eyes were glazed over. He cleared his throat before beginning.

"My sister was my best friend. We had our sibling rivalries, but she was always there for me, and I'm just sorry I wasn't there for her . . ." he said, his words breaking up. He took a moment to try to collect himself before going on.

"She was so vibrant and alive, and there will forever be a hole in my heart. You will never be forgotten, I promise," he said, turning to look at the giant portrait of Veronica.

No matter how much we didn't get along, there was no denying her obvious beauty. Her perfect caramel skin and wide brown eyes were sparkling. She looked so happy and perfect in the photo. I realized I had never seen her smile like that. She didn't look so intimidating in the portrait. Maybe we could've have been friends eventually.

I still couldn't believe this had happened. No, that was a lie. I knew eventually they would succeed in picking us off one by one. I had to figure out who they were before more people were killed.

The priest said the final prayers. The casket, dripping in red roses, was hoisted above the pallbearers' heads and brought slowly down the aisle. We all stood to our feet, Cal grabbing my hand. The crowd was silent, except for the muffled sniffling that echoed in the large cathedral.

The doors were flung open and bright white light penetrated the darkness surrounding us.

People began shuffling toward the aisle. As I waited for Charlotte and Marcus to move in front of me, I looked up to the large cross on the wall. Thoughts of the night I had been chased into the church infiltrated my thoughts. How did things get this messed up? Did God dislike Kythera as much as I did?

As we walked out the front door, I caught a glimpse of Dev standing on the sidewalk. He looked like he was waiting for someone—maybe even me. Cal noticed him and his eyes narrowed. Dev motioned for me to come over to him.

"Go ahead, I need to speak to someone anyway," Cal whispered in my ear.

I walked down the steps and stopped in front of Dev. He had a frown on his face and he looked like he wasn't completely awake. He was dazed, like everyone else.

"Hey, sorry I couldn't find you the other night. When I went to go look for you, I saw a couple people I knew and got stuck talking, and when I turned back around, everyone was rushing outside. I saw you get in the car with Marcus, so I knew you were safe. Sorry I haven't called. My parents had me on lockdown. This has really scared them. I don't even know what to say Alex or his parents," he said at maximum speed.

I was silent, not sure what I needed to say.

"I see Cal's back," he said, nodding toward Cal who was talking to Charlotte's parents.

"Yes, he is. And it's okay—I understand why

you didn't call. I haven't been thinking about much except what happened at the club."

"So . . . are you back together with him?" he asked quietly.

"I'm sorry how things worked out. I really like you, but Cal's always had my heart," I said, looking down at the dirty concrete sidewalk, a pink spot of gum plastered to it.

"You don't have to explain. I get it. We can still be friends, right?" he said, a small smile on his face.

"Of course," I said, some of the tension disappearing. He took that better than I thought he would. Then again, we were at a funeral—how mad could he get?

"Great. Well, I've got to get going. My parents are waiting on me. I just wanted to pay my respects. I knew Veronica, but not real well. It's so sad." He pointed at an older model Lexus, his parents inside.

I watched Dev walk over to his parents and I waved at them. They looked the other way. They weren't as friendly as before, probably because I had broken their son's heart. Maybe not—I mean, we had just started really talking when everything happened. I felt awful. I knew I had been using Dev to get over Cal . . . at least, that was what I was telling myself. I knew I had felt something between us that day at his house, but it wasn't a strong as what I felt for Cal.

I turned and walked back toward Cal, who was now talking to Alex.

"I'm so sorry, Alex. I just don't know what to say," I said, as I approached him.

His deep brown eyes were puffy, and he looked like he hadn't slept in days. His normally put-together appearance was anything but. His black suit was wrinkled, and his hair was going everywhere.

"Thanks," he said quietly. His phone buzzed in his pocket. He pulled it out and silenced it. "I got to get going, they're waiting on me," Alex said hastily and walked down the steps without another word.

I grabbed Cal's hand and squeezed. "We've got to figure out who these people are."

"Yes, before they kill us one at a time," he added, and I felt a chill race up and down my spine.

"I was thinking the same thing."

This was no longer a game. The other group had decided if they couldn't scare us away, they would take us *all* out of the picture for good. I didn't want to go to another funeral for a classmate and Kythera member, nor did I want to be the one in the casket.

Chapter 11

SCHOOL WAS SOMBER THE NEXT day. There wasn't a lot of chatter in the hallway, and everyone looked too scared to talk. St. Mary's had brought in grief counselors for anyone who needed to speak with one. I would have taken the time to speak to one if I thought they could get the image of Veronica's lifeless body out of my head. Every time I closed my eyes, all I could see was her wrist, thick blood dripping over her tattoo.

I opened my locker to get my political science book and slammed it shut as I raced off to class. The seat directly across from me was empty. Alex was out of school and would probably be out for several days—that was what Ms. Epling said when she told us that we could get an excuse from her to speak with one of the counselors. Alex had looked terrible at the funeral, but nothing compared to the way his parents had looked. His mother hadn't stopped crying through the entire funeral. Even when everyone was quiet for prayers, we could still hear her muffled sobs. It was heartbreaking.

Ms. Epling was writing notes about World War II on the board, but I wasn't really paying attention. I scribbled the symbol from the attorney's lapel over and over again in the margins of my notebook. He was the only solid lead I had in cracking the mystery of the other group. I had to come up with an excuse to see him, but what kind of business could a seventeen-year-old have with an attorney?

"Ms. Whitley, what's the date of Japan's bombing of Pearl Harbor?" asked Ms. Epling.

I dropped my pencil as my mind went blank. "Uh . . ."

"Just as I thought. Please pay attention or leave," she said in a harsh tone.

I felt my cheeks burn red and I wanted to hide under my desk. Until we'd moved here, I had always been a good student who never got into trouble, but apparently trouble was determined to follow me around.

I was glad that the bell rang and I could hurry away from class and forget what had happened. As I ran down the hall, I saw several of Veronica's friends. They looked at me with their usual sneers, but quickly put their faces downcast, as if they suddenly remembered that one of their friends had been murdered. I didn't pay any attention to them, but I did miss seeing Veronica—even if it was only to see her give me the evil eye.

I opened my locker, and Dev appeared, opening his own squeaky locker. I closed mine and was about to act like I was in a rush and say a quick bye before escaping the awkward situation, but a photo of me on Stella in his locker caught my eye.

"Hey," Dev said and I realized I had been staring at the photo.

"Oh, hey, sorry. Is that a photo of me riding Stella?" *Way to sound a like an idiot—of course it was, genius.*

He looked at the photo and his cheeks turned deep red. "Yeah, it is. I had my cell phone when we went riding last week and I snapped the photo. You looked so happy and I wanted a photo of you smiling," he said sheepishly.

"Oh."

I felt even more like a terrible person. Dev was such a nice guy and I had dumped him like he was nothing. Heck, I didn't even tell him straight out what had happened. I had waited till I saw him at the funeral, where he saw me with Cal. He deserved better than that.

"I'm sorry about everything. I should have told you as soon as I had the chance that Cal was back. You're a great guy, but . . ."

Dev waved his hands at me. "It's okay. I get it. I knew that day at my house you still had feelings for Cal, but I kept pressing you. Let's be friends and forget about it? I still need someone to go horseback riding with me, so let's leave it at that."

"Okay, thanks," I said with some relief.

Dev closed his locker, leaving the picture of me up in the door. "See you later?" he said.

I nodded and he turned and walked down the hall. I leaned against my locker, feeling like he was letting me off the hook and being the nice guy that he was, which made me feel even more like a complete witch.

"Why are you frowning?" asked Cal, who had walked up beside me.

I turned to look at him. "Because I'm a terrible person."

He smirked. "Why would you think that?"

I hadn't told Cal the whole story of what had happened while he was in North Carolina. "While you were at boarding school, I was hanging out with Dev a lot," I began, pausing to read his reaction.

He shrugged. "Yeah, because Dad wanted you to recruit him and he likes to ride horses. Don't feel bad—I understand." He grabbed my hand and squeezed.

I looked up at the clock in the hall, knowing the bell was going to ring any second and I was going to be late for calculus again. "That's not everything, though. I thought I was never going to see you again and your dad told me there was no way you were coming back, and I kind of liked Dev," I said, staring at the floor.

Cal let go of my hand, and I immediately looked up and searched his face. His blue eyes were wide. Was he shocked? My stomach started churning and I felt nauseated.

He started laughing, and I didn't know what to do. "Casper, Charlotte already told me everything. It's okay, trust me."

"She can't keep anything secret, can she?" I asked angrily, vowing to never tell her anything again.

The bell rang and the hall emptied, but I didn't care.

"Don't be upset with her. She told me how you called and were so torn about everything, and that she told you to move on. If I wasn't able to make it back, I would have wanted you to find someone else because I want you to be happy. Don't beat yourself up about it," he said. He put his arms around my shoulders and hugged me.

How did I end up liking two totally awesome and nice guys? And why did they like me?

Cal let go of me. "Why are you still frowning?"

"Because I don't deserve you."

"Oh, hell, Casper, if anything, I don't deserve you. You're the one that's too good. I got you in this whole mess to begin with," he said, running his hand through his hair.

I lifted an eyebrow. "You're right. I'd forgotten about that. It is your fault."

We looked at each other and both smiled. "Come on, let's get to class," he said, and gave me a kiss on the top of the head.

My forehead tingled; as bad as I had felt about dumping Dev, I knew I had made the right decision.

Cal left me at the door of my next class and I tried my best to walk in quietly. I sat down behind Charlotte painfully slowly, hoping I wouldn't make any noise. She didn't even bother to look back at me. I sighed with relief when Mr. Perry didn't either, as he wrote out a calculus problem on the board. I was safe this time.

I was feeling happier, at least, about my guy problems, but that didn't solve my other problems—including Marrow. I had to find a way to meet with that attorney. As I opened up my notebook it finally hit me. I could get him to write up a formal contract for ownership of Wendy. That idea made me smile to myself, because not only would I get more information about him, but also make sure I got ownership of Wendy when I got Tyson the information he needed.

I walked to my car as soon as the bell rang. All my privileges had been restored so I could effectively help Kythera. I tried not to stop and talk to anyone, because I knew I only had a couple hours to make it to the law office and catch Mr. Whitaker.

Traffic was slow and I thumped my fingers against the steering wheel impatiently. It was almost four o'clock when I pulled up in front of the law office downtown. I parked in the garage across the street and practically ran into the chilly office.

I looked around the glitzy lobby, which contained several large leather couches and oil paintings in gold frames. The floor was a shiny white marble, and a giant Chinese vase stood in the corner.

"Can I help you?" asked the petite secretary behind the enormous Victorian-style desk. She looked like she was a four-year-old sitting behind her mother's large office desk.

"Um, yes. I'm looking for Mr. Whitaker, is he in?"

She looked me up and down with her large doe eyes. "Are you sure you aren't looking for Mr. Charles? He usually helps all Mr. Roman's friends," she asked sweetly.

"That's right, I forgot. Is he busy?" I hadn't thought this little plan all the way through. I had no excuse for not asking for Mr. Charles. I just hoped he wasn't available.

"Yes, he's in a mediation this afternoon. I can get your name and number and have him give you a call when he's available." She pulled out a sticky note and a pen, ready to jot my name down.

"No—I mean, it's kind of urgent," I said nervously, playing with the hem of my school blazer.

"What's your name?"

"Casper Whitley."

She picked up the phone and talked quietly with someone. Once she hung the phone up, she got up from her desk and motioned for me to follow her. Her towering heels clacked on the floor as we walked up a wide staircase. She had on a black pencil skirt, crisp white dress shirt, and the red soles of her Louboutin heels flashed as she walked up the steps. She looked more like she belonged at an office for a fashion magazine like in *The Devil Wears Prada* than a law office.

We walked down a long hallway and opened another door without knocking. The room opened into another lobby-like room, with a secretary sitting behind another ornate desk.

"Kari, this young lady is here to see Mr. Whitaker."

Kari nodded her head and motioned for me to take a seat. The woman in the Louboutins walked out of the room as if she was walking on a runway in Milan.

I picked up the *South Carolina Bar Journal* to flip through while I waited, but it was not very interesting. I looked around for another magazine, but nothing was appealing unless you were into tech gadgets, law, or the stock market.

"Kari!" yelled a man from behind the closed office door, which startled me.

The tall brunette got up quickly and walked into the office. Had this guy never heard of an intercom? She came back out with a folder and a handful of papers.

"You can go in now," she said to me with a friendly smile on her face.

I got up from the couch and walked confidently into his office, and stood in front of one of the wing chairs opposite his desk.

"Hey, I'm Edward Whitaker. Nice to meet you," he said, standing up to shake my hand. He was a lot shorter than I was expecting, as I was about an inch taller than him in my ballet flats. He had a full head of black hair cropped short and small, round brown eyes.

"Nice to meet you. I'm Casper Whitley," I said as I sat down in the wing chair. I looked at his impeccably tailored navy pinstripe suit and the gold pin on his lapel.

"So, what can I do for you, Ms. Whitley? Don't you all usually see Mr. Charles?" he asked as he relaxed back into his desk chair.

"Yes, but he wasn't available and I needed to speak to an attorney today. It's pretty important."

"Okay, so what do you need?" he said with a laugh, clasping his hands together.

"I need to have some papers drawn up for horse ownership. Mr. Roman is signing a horse over to me, and I want a legal document showing that it was a legal transaction," I said, trying to use legal mumbo jumbo that I had picked up from episodes of *Law & Order*.

"I don't know much about equine law, but I'm

sure I can come up with something." He pulled out a yellow notepad and looked around his desk. He pushed the intercom button and called for Kari. She appeared at the door within seconds.

"Can you bring me a pen?" he asked her. "Mine have all disappeared." She wordlessly turned back into the lobby.

"So, you go to St. Mary's right?" he asked, as he waited for her to bring him a pen.

"Yes, it's my first year there. Do you have any kids?"

"Yeah, but none in high school. My little boy is in third grade, but he'll eventually go to St. Mary's, too. Best school in the city."

Kari came in with a handful of blue pens.

"Thank you," he said. "Oh, and can you staple this for me?"

I looked at the black stapler two inches from his hand.

She had a defeated look on her face as she took the papers from his hands and stapled them and handed them back. And I thought my mother was an elitist, but this guy made her look like Mother Theresa. Kari was about to walk out of the office when he summoned her again.

"Can you refill my coffee?" he asked, smiling. She took the mug and left. "Now, where were we? So, Tyson is giving you a horse? That seems a little odd," he said, clasping his hands together.

"It was my horse, but . . ."

I heard the sound of a phone buzzing in a drawer.

"I'm sorry, I need to get this," he said. He picked up the phone, walked out of the room, and shut the door behind him. I hadn't planned on getting alone time in his office, but this was perfect. I jumped up and started pulling out drawers in his desk. I tried to scan the papers as quickly as I could for anything that might help me. I went through his middle drawer, sifting through the blue pens he had in his desk despite requesting his assistant to get him more. As I landed on my hands on a piece of paper with the pin emblem on it, his assistant walked in. I froze as she let out a little gasp.

"I'm sorry," I stammered, as I wracked my brain for an excuse as to why I was looking through her boss's desk. I couldn't think of anything. She stood still, the steaming cup of coffee in her hand.

"Listen, I think your boss is helping someone attack me and my friends. One person's already been killed and I'm trying to stop anyone else from turning up dead," I spit out, hoping she would understand.

She looked at me for a moment, chewing on the corner of her thin lips. She looked out into the lobby, then closed the door quietly behind her as she walked toward me.

"You're part of Kythera, right?" she asked, as she set the coffee cup on his desk.

"Yes," I said, my hand still on the paper.

"He's been asking for information about Kythera and Mr. Charles," she said.

"Because he's part of another group? People who wear this pin?" I asked as I pulled out the sealed piece of paper, pointing at the "M" with the arrow through it.

She nodded. "Yes, there are a lot of people that come in here with that pin."

"Do you have any information—like their names, addresses?" I pleaded.

She hesitated again. I could almost literally see the mental fight in her mind.

"Did you read about Veronica Alamilla's death in the paper?" I asked, breaking her thoughts.

"Yes."

"The police didn't release this information, but this pin was found near her body. She was only seventeen."

She looked at me, her soft green eyes searching mine, as if trying to decipher if I was telling the truth. She took the paper from my hand and placed it back in the drawer. My heart sunk. She wasn't going to help me.

"Please sit down," she said, as she walked out of the room. Beads of sweat started forming on my forehead. Maybe I hadn't picked the best time to stop perfecting my lies and tell the truth. I had no way of knowing whether Kari would rat me out to her boss. I looked to the window, but there was no way I could escape as the windows didn't open.

I jumped as Mr. Whitaker stepped back into the office.

"I'm sorry about that. Where were we?" he asked, as he sat down heavily in his chair. He took a sip of the coffee and yelled for Kari. "This coffee is cool and there can't be any sugar in it," he said, handing her the cup.

She looked at me, blushing.

I took a deep breath and slumped down in my chair a little bit, thankful she hadn't said anything to him. That was a good sign, right?

The rest of the meeting was pretty boring and didn't give me any information beyond what I knew before I walked in, other than that he was a narcissist and thought he was cool because he had stayed at every Ritz-Carlton in the country.

I shook his hand as he stood up to show me the way out of his office. We walked out into the lobby, where he asked Kari to get a business card for me from his desk in his office.

A few seconds later, she put the card in my hand, and gave me a knowing look. I walked into the hallway and out to the large stairwell. I looked at his card and flipped it over. Kari had written her phone number and "Call Me" on the back.

I rushed to my car and raced home, excited that I might have gotten a break in finding out who was after Kythera and who was responsible for killing Veronica. I knew I should probably wait a couple of hours until Kari left the office before calling—in the meantime, I could fill Cal in on what I had found.

I walked into the house and the smell of steak

and butter wafted from the kitchen. I dropped my backpack into the hall and walked through the door into the kitchen. The chef was busy tending to flames at the stove, and mother was standing at the bar, looking over something.

"Where have you been?" she asked, as she put down the yellow piece of paper and put her red-manicured hand on her bony hip.

"Doing research at the law firm," I said. I walked to the bar and picked a couple of grapes from the fruit bowl.

"Really? Did you find out anything?" she asked, her blue-gray eyes turning wide.

"Not a whole lot," I said.

For some reason, I didn't want to tell her about the secretary. It wasn't that I didn't trust her, but a gut feeling told me I needed to keep as many people out of what I was doing as possible.

"Oh," she said, and turned back to her paper. The conversation was over. I headed to the family room to watch some TV before dinner. I looked up at the clock anxiously, counting down the seconds until I could call Kari and get some more information.

My cell phone buzzed in my blazer pocket, Cal's name scrolling across the screen. "Hey," I said happily.

"Hey, it's so nice to get to talk to you and hear your voice every day," he said.

I felt my face grow hot. "I'm so glad to hear your voice, too."

"Did you find out anything at the law office?" he asked.

"Yes and no. He didn't give me any information, but his secretary slipped me a note to call her later. I'm going to after dinner. You want to come over?" I picked up the remote and started flipping through channels.

"Sure, sounds great. See you in a few," he said, and hung up the phone.

Dinner went by awkwardly, and not because Cal was over. My parents barely spoke a word to each other or to us. Dad asked Cal about school, and Mom asked me to help her with a charity dinner she'd volunteered to organize. I could barely wait to escape the room. I glanced over at Cal ever so often, a puzzled look on his face. All I could do was shrug my shoulders.

When the worst dinner of my life finally came to a close, I jumped up, grabbed Cal's hand, and pulled him into the front living room.

"What was that all about?" he asked as we entered the room.

I hesitated, dreading what I was about to say. "I think my mom is having an affair."

Cal's mouth dropped open. "What!?" he said, his features stretching out in surprise.

"I saw her sneaking out the back one day wearing a really tight, fancy dress, and then I followed her one day to a house owned by Marcus's dad." I looked down at the rug, moving the end tassels with my shoe.

"You mean Mr. Gray?"

I nodded.

"Wow," he said as he sat down heavily on the couch. "Are you sure?"

"I saw them come out of the house Mr. Gray owns on the other side of town together. I mean they didn't seem all that into each other or anything, but what else could they be doing? Why else would he have bought a house on the other side of town that Marcus doesn't know about?"

Cal looked up at the mantel. "There could be other reasons. Just don't think about it too hard until we figure this out. I'm not sure your mother is having an affair."

"What makes you think she isn't?" I walked over and sat down next to him.

He put his arm around my shoulders. "Do you know how I ended up back here?"

"No, there's been so much going on, I haven't even bothered to ask. I was just so happy to see you. I didn't care how you got here."

"Well, your mother was the one who called the boarding school and arranged for me to come back. No one knows this, not even my dad. He thinks I just figured out how to get myself out, like I always do," he said with a smirk.

"Huh, why did my mother get you out?" I asked, puzzled she would do such a weird thing.

"She knew how much you missed me," he said with a wink.

"Maybe," I said with a shrug, still totally

stunned my mother had taken an interest in helping out my boyfriend.

My mother very rarely did things that weren't a direct benefit to her. There had to be some other reason that she made the effort to bring Cal back, especially since she could feel the full wrath of Cal's father and Kythera for doing it. But as I sat there, my head leaning against Cal's shoulder, I couldn't think of any other reason than that she wanted to help me. The thought of my mother being loving and caring made me question if she really was having an affair at all . . .

I looked up at the clock on the mantel, realizing it was almost seven. I jumped up from the couch and headed toward the stairs.

"What are you doing?" Cal called, still sitting comfortably on the couch.

"I have to go get my phone to call Kari," I said, as I disappeared up the steps.

My phone was somewhere on my bed, and I flung all the covers back until I heard the familiar thud of the phone on the rug. Cal appeared at the doorway as I picked up the phone, and pulled out the attorney's business card with Kari's number on the back.

Cal plopped down on the bed, his hands under his head. I dialed her number and it began to ring. I looked over at Cal anxiously.

"Hello?" said the familiar voice.

"Hi, this is Casper," I said, almost whispering.

"Oh, yes. Meet me here at my house in thirty

minutes. The address is 1142 Vine Lane," said Kari, and the line went dead. I scrunched my eyebrows together.

"What?" Cal asked, sitting up.

"She gave me her address and then hung up." I stuffed the phone in my blazer pocket.

"Are you going over there?" he asked.

"Yes, why wouldn't I?"

"Because it's not safe. You aren't thinking this through. How do you know she isn't helping him and this is just a trap? She knows who you are."

"If you had seen the way Mr. Whitaker treated her, you would know that she isn't helping him." I walked back into the bedroom and picked up my purse off the wing chair in the corner.

"Stop," Cal said in a forceful voice as he grabbed my forearm. "You aren't going."

I jerked my arm away. "And who do you think you are to tell me what to do?"

"I'm your boyfriend and I love you, but I've also been a Kythera member my whole life. You don't know what lengths people will go to get to us. This isn't a good idea." His eyes were dark and pleading.

"But I have to, Cal. If I find out who these people are, your father agreed to give Wendy back to me," I said.

Even though Cal and I understood each other most of the time, I still don't think he truly knew how much I needed Wendy and my freedom.

"I need this, Cal," I pleaded.

He searched my eyes. "Fine, but I'm going with you and we're taking my car."

"Okay, but we need to hurry." I turned around and headed for the stairs. I had my purse, keys, and now Cal in tow.

Chapter

12

ABOUT THIRTY MINUTES LATER, WE pulled up in front of the address Kari had given me. The street was neat, filled with tiny well-kept yards with equally tiny, but cute clapboard homes. Cal decided to go a block down and park in an alley, the bright red "K" on the back invisible from the street.

I had changed into a pair of jeans and a light blue T-shirt and Cal had removed his St. Mary's blazer. We didn't want anyone to be able to identify us. We strolled down the street, hand in hand, as if we were just taking a late afternoon walk. An elderly couple was talking as they walked a large German shepherd. They smiled and nodded as they passed. They seemed so happy and carefree. I couldn't help but imagine that one day that would be Cal and me. I knew it sounded crazy to imagine that, since that felt like a million years away, but it was still nice, all the same.

I walked up to the bright red door of Kari's house and knocked, taking a step back to wait for her to answer. The door cracked open and she stuck her head out. Once she recognized me, she opened the door and ushered us in quickly.

"Come in," she said quietly, showing us into her small but tidy living room. She motioned for us to sit down on the red plaid love seat.

"Would you like anything to drink?" she asked, sitting down in the brown chair across from us. We both shook our heads.

"You're Mr. Roman's son aren't you?" She asked looking at Cal.

"Yes, I think we've met before."

"Maybe in the hall or something at the law firm. Your dad was always in there speaking to Mr. Charles. He's a really nice guy,. He's great to his assistance." She looked around nervously, crossing her arms over her chest.

"So, what can you tell me about Mr. Whitaker and Marrow?" I said, wanting to go ahead and get the information we were here for. She looked frightened and I wanted to get out of here as soon as possible. I didn't want anyone to know that we had spoken to her.

"A group of men came in a few months ago, demanding to speak with Mr. Whitaker. They were all wearing really nice suits, and the gold pin on their lapels. I didn't get to hear much of their conversation except when I was called in to get them coffee. They were asking questions about Mr. Roman and Kythera came up. They said Kythera was getting out of hand, and they needed someone on the inside to get them information on them."

"Getting out of hand?" Cal asked, propping his arms on his knees.

Kari shrugged her shoulders. "I'm not sure what it was supposed to mean. Something about needing to show Kythera who's in control."

Cal looked at me, a puzzled look on his face. I didn't know what to make of it.

"Did you happen to get the guys' names?"

She nodded, but as she opened her mouth to speak, the sound of shattering glass echoed into the room. I screamed as Kari slumped down into the chair. Cal grabbed my arms and pulled me onto the floor. Several more shots rang out, breaking the other window and pummeling the walls and the furniture. I couldn't see much, as Cal laid his body on top of mine.

I was barely able to breathe, my heart thumping in my chest. I looked between Cal's forearms to see Kari's legs, a gush of bright red blood running down her calf.

Oh, no, this can't be happening. How did they know we were here? How are we going to get out?

The gunshots finally stopped. The only noise I could hear was Cal's heavy breathing and my own pulse thudding in my ears.

Cal leaned his head to my ear. "Stay here."

I didn't respond, but I felt for my cell phone in my pocket. I pulled it out and dialed 911, slowly lifting it to my ear.

I watched him as he crawled on all fours across the room, his hands and feet crunching across the broken glass. The 911 operator answered and as I started to tell her our situation another shot rang out. I dropped the phone and it slid under the couch. Cal dropped to the ground, landing hard on his stomach.

"Cal!" I screamed as he started crawling back toward me.

"Don't move," he whispered.

I turned my attention back to finding the phone. I put my hand under the couch searching for it. I could hear the operator asking if anyone was there, but I couldn't put my hands on it.

Loud banging came from the front door and I instinctively looked up, my heart beating hard against the floor. Someone was trying to get in, and it wasn't going to take them long to break down the flimsy door.

"What do we do now?" I said, Cal now lying beside me.

He looked around, his jaw tight. "We start crawling for the kitchen."

He pointed to the doorway about ten feet away. He motioned for me to go first. I tried one more time to reach the phone, but couldn't. I just hoped the operator could hear what was going on and trace my phone to here.

I started crawling, my hands and knees rubbing the glass into the carpet. I didn't dare take the time to look at my palms, but I could feel the tiny stinging cuts from the glass.

The noise from the front door was deafening, but I tried to block it out as tears started to stream down my face. I didn't want to die, not like this. I refused to let it all end like this, but I wasn't sure what we could do. The house had to be surrounded. We had no idea where the shots were coming from.

God, I prayed, *I need you now*.

We finally reached the kitchen's linoleum floor. I breathed a small sigh of relief as I leaned up against the cabinets. I finally looked down at my palms, which were shaking uncontrollably. They were streaked with tiny red cuts.

I looked over at Cal, and prayed he knew what we had to do next. He was looking straight ahead, his breathing ragged and uneven. The front door finally busted open and I jumped up, panicked. Cal pushed me into another room, which must've been Kari's bedroom, and closed the door and locked it. He looked around the room for what felt like minutes, but couldn't have been more than a few seconds before he went over to the window and tried to pull it open. It wouldn't budge.

My pulse was racing so fast, I was about to fall over. We were trapped, and I had no clue how we were going to get out of this one. Cal ran to the closet and looked up.

"Come here!" he yelled. I did as I was told, as he pulled open the trap door to the attic. He unfolded the ladder, the springs groaning loudly.

The knob on the bedroom door jiggled. I was paralyzed, but Cal forced me up the stairs. I scampered into the hot, dark space, my hands and knees resting on wobbly wood planks. Cal headed up behind me. I watched as he strained to pull the ladder back up so he could shut the attic door. Finally, he got it to shut with a loud bang, the springs vibrating against the wood.

"Now what?" My voice was shaky as I spoke, and I struggled to catch my breath in the unbearably hot room.

"I don't know," Cal said as he flipped on the light, a single naked bulb. He ran his hand through his hair. "I didn't bring a gun, and I'm pretty sure I'm outnumbered anyway."

There was a loud crash, the floor shaking underneath us.

"Oh, no," I said, my eyes filling with tears. It would only be a few minutes before they found the attic door.

A faint glimmer of light reflected on the pink insulation across the room.

"Cal, look it's a window," I said pointing.

He put a foot on one of the beams, and reached his hand out for mine. He pulled me close behind; we walked across the attic like two acrobats until we were right under the decorative window. Cal pushed against it, but it wouldn't budge. It wasn't a window meant to be opened. He looked around again as we balanced on the beam, trying not to fall into the cotton candy insulation.

There was a short piece of wood behind me that looked like a remnant from when the house was built. I picked it up and handed it to Cal. He shoved it through the window, and it broke with ease, pieces shattering across the insulation like drops of rain.

I heard the loud squeak of the springs of the ladder. I couldn't help but look back to see two men emerge at the top of the ladder, looking directly at us. One of them pulled a gun out and pointed it at us. I covered my head with my hands and waited to be struck, but nothing happened. I heard him pull the trigger—but instead of a loud bang, there was only a click. He cursed a couple of times and looked at the gun. I guess it had jammed on him.

I sighed in relief—but my relief was quickly replaced with sheer panic as they started walking across the beams toward us.

Cal ripped his white button-down off, wrapped it around his hand, and smashed the rest of the window out. He quickly wiped away the fragments with the shirt and motioned for me to come to him. I jumped to the beam in front of the window and he helped me squeeze out of it.

I scrambled onto the hot roof, not caring that my skin felt like it was being melted off by the scalding hot shingles. I tried get to my feet, but I quickly fell back to the roof. I need to crawl using my hands, knees, and feet to hold myself on the sloped roof. Cal climbed through the window and joined me. We looked around, the sky a deep purple and orange. We could see for miles across Charleston. Under any other circumstances, I could have stared at the beautiful scenery.

Another shot fired, hitting the roof, bits of shingles flying up and hitting my arms. We ducked and Cal started crawling toward the chimney that was above the window. I followed behind. This was more terrifying than anything I had experienced, including the night the man in the mask had a knife to my throat. At least then, I knew right where my attacker was and how many there were. Cal had a gun then. Today, we didn't have anything.

Once Cal made it to the chimney, he extended his hand out to me to help me get to him. Cal's breathing was heavy and I could feel his pulse in his wrist when I grabbed his arm. That didn't make me feel any better about the situation. We both leaned up against the chimney. I braced myself against the rough stone, digging my heels into the shingles and laying my palms on the hot, gritty roof. I bit my lip to keep from screaming, the pain radiating from my already cut and blistered hands.

"What do we do now?" I asked, afraid to move at this point.

Cal breathed out heavily. "I don't know."

The men grunted as they tried to work through the tiny window, their heavy steps grinding the shattered bits of glass into the roof. The memories of being carried in Cal's arms across the broken glass of my parents' home flashed through my head. My parents . . . what would happen to them? Although my mother and I had rarely gotten along, something in the air had changed recently, and I was sorry that I wasn't going to see how things turned out between us. I just hoped she knew how much I loved her. And Dad . . . I couldn't think about him without tears welling up in my eyes.

I looked into Cal's eyes, his own a little glossy. He mouthed the words, "I love you," before he pushed himself off the chimney and started sliding down toward the window.

I screamed in horror as I watched him crash into and tackle one of the men. "Cal! No!"

They both slid to the edge of the roof and I held my breath. Cal shoved the man off the roof, a loud thud echoing across the street as his body fell on top of a parked car below. He slowly started working his way back up the roof. The second guy hadn't budged from his perch near the window. I could tell he was afraid of heights as he stared at the nearby ground. Cal started crawling back up to the opening, but someone started shooting again.

A shot rang out, burrowing into the roof only a few feet from Cal.

"Cal, please!" I yelled, my voice hoarse from screaming and the tears that had me choked up.

Cal grabbed the second guy, but he lost his footing and they both started tumbling down the sloped roof, dropping out of view and onto the street below.

"Cal!" I edged myself down to the ledge, sliding on my butt, trying to stay in control of my descent. I had to see if Cal was okay. Another shot snapped by inches from my head, jolting me, and I started sliding down the sloped roof. I lost control and ended up sliding head first down the steep roof. Lying flat on my stomach, I tried to spread my arms and legs out like an X to keep from tumbling onto the street. The smell of hot tar burned my nose and I stopped, unable to move. I wanted to see if Cal was all right, but I could only lie there, motionless and afraid. I didn't know if I was out of sight from the shooter or if I was in his crosshairs. I closed my eyes and prayed.

The sounds of sirens ripped through the stifling air. I tried to catch my breath, feeling like I was about to faint. I could see several cop cars zooming down the street, but lost sight as they pulled up in front of the house. I heard the noise of slamming doors and people shouting. I started to slide again, trying to get off my stomach, but there was no way I could without falling, nor did I know if the shooter would try to take a second shot at me. My palms burned against the rough shingles, and I couldn't keep the hot tears from streaking down my face, not knowing what had happened to Cal.

"There's somebody on the roof!" shouted a cop, and I heard the sound of guns cocking.

"It's Casper! Don't shoot!" I shouted.

"Okay, we'll be up to get you!" a male officer shouted back.

My neck was hurting from holding it up from the roof, but I craned it as far as I could, hoping I would be able to see Cal. He had to be okay.

"Cal!" I shouted. No response.

Now there was the sound of an ambulance coming down the street. I felt completely helpless, and all I wanted to do was see if Cal was okay. It was terrible not knowing, and the fact that if I could only slide down a couple more feet I could see him was excruciating. I tried one more time to pull myself up a little, but the minute I started lifting my chest off the roof I slid a few more inches down.

"Hold on, don't move!" said a female voice from above me. I looked up to see an officer dressed in blue crawling backward toward me.

When she reached the area just above me, she threw a rope down, the end touching my hands. I grabbed it and started climbing up toward her. Once we finally reached the broken window, she instructed me to climb through and head back downstairs.

The officer helped me through the kitchen, and

into the living room. Kari's body had already been removed, but dark splotches of blood covered the chair she had been sitting in. I looked away as I rushed out of the house, leaving the cop behind. I ran past the broken front door and onto the street, searching for Cal, but he wasn't lying on the ground. I sighed in relief, until I realized neither of the other men were on the ground either. Had the ambulance already taken them?

The officer finally caught up to me and grabbed my arm. I looked at her.

"Where's Cal?" I asked her.

"He's been taken to the hospital." Her brown eyes were flat and emotionless. I looked at her shiny gold name plate, which identified her as Alvarez.

"How bad was he hurt? Can you tell me what hospital they took him to?"

"No, I don't have any information. You need to let a paramedic take a look at you and then you need to come to the station with us and give us a statement," Alvarez said, her face still blank.

I didn't know what to make of it. Was she emotionless because he already knew Cal was dead and this was something she had to deal with on a daily basis?

"I'm going to the hospital first to see Cal. You can take my statement there," I said as I turned to head down the street to Cal's car.

"I'm sorry, but I can't let you leave. You have to come with us right now," she said, pulling gently on my arm.

I pushed her away. "No, I have to know whether he's alive or not. You can't tell me *anything*?" I begged, the tears starting to blur my vision.

I couldn't stand not knowing whether he was alive or dead. I loved him, and my heart would be broken if he died. Just the thought started to make the tears flow down my face and I had to take short breaths in order to breathe.

Another cop came up to us as I tried to wipe away the tears on my face. "What seems to be the problem?" he asked in a gruff tone.

"Sir, she wants to go to the hospital to check on her friend, but I told her she needs to be checked out by a paramedic and then we need her to come to the station and give a statement."

"Nonsense, let her go. A doctor in the ER can check her out and we can get her statement at the hospital. Go ahead and take her there," he instructed Alvarez.

My eyes were too blurry to really see the man, but I whispered a thank-you to him as I was led to a police car. The ride was silent and terrifying. I didn't know what to expect when I got to the hospital. Would I walk into lobby filled with people already mourning his death?

The tears started flowing again at that thought. I tried desperately to convince myself he wasn't dead, but I couldn't help this sickening feeling in my stomach that Cal was gone forever.

Chapter

13

LVAREZ PULLED UP NEAR THE front door of the hospital and I jumped out before the she had even come to a complete stop. I ran into the building and straight for the information desk. The volunteer behind the desk told me he was in the ICU on the third floor.

"Casper," said someone, and looked behind me to see Dev standing in the lobby.

"What are you doing here?" I asked, not caring that I hadn't bothered to say hello.

"I was with Marcus, working on a school project, when he got the call about Cal. I came with him because he said you were with Cal and I wanted to make sure you were okay," he said as he stared at the floor.

"Is he okay?" I asked, ignoring what he had just said.

He shrugged his shoulders. "They wouldn't come tell me anything, even when I asked about you. They just told me to come and sit down here until someone in the family could give me more information. They let Marcus go up though, which is weird, since he's not family," he said, shoving his hands into his jeans pockets.

"Thanks for stopping by, but I have to go make sure Cal's okay."

He nodded. "I'll be waiting here if you need anything."

"Thank you," I said sincerely, before turning and heading toward the staircase. I was too anxious to wait for the elevator.

On the third floor, I almost took out an orderly carrying a tray of food, and barely missed a patient in a wheelchair. I frantically followed the blue line that was supposed to lead me to the ICU, but I felt more like I was running in circles.

Finally, I reached the double doors, *ICU* in big red letters above them. I opened the doors, and walked in. Heart machines were pulsing, and other hospital sounds filled my ears. I looked into the windows of rooms, searching for any sign of Cal.

"Can I help you?" asked a petite nurse with bright red hair.

"Yes, I'm looking for Cal Roman."

"Are you family?"

I shook my head. "Can you at least tell me if he's okay?"

"I'm sorry, but I can't give any information unless you're family. Go through that door to the ICU waiting room. I'm sure some of his family is there and they can fill you in on his condition," she said pointing to the door.

"Thanks," I said as I walked into the waiting room.

Mrs. Roman was sitting on the couch, her face in her hands. Mr. Roman was standing, looking out the window, his square jaw tight. As the door closed, Mrs. Roman looked up at me, her eyes red and ringed with black smears like a raccoon. She didn't say a word, but quickly turned her head to the window. Tyson didn't even look at me.

"How are you?" asked Marcus, as he stood up from a chair to come give me a hug.

"I'm fine, but how's Cal? You think I could see him?" I asked.

Marcus looked over at the Romans, who had still not acknowledged my presence. "You'll have to ask them, but I can tell you Cal's not doing very well."

I felt my heart drop and my legs almost gave way, as if gravity was going to pull me to the floor. I was speechless.

"You can go see him," Tyson said quietly. I looked over at him as he still stared out the window.

"Third room on the left," Marcus added.

Without another word, I walked back out to the ICU.

I walked up to Cal's room and slid open the glass door. Cal looked barely recognizable. He lay perfectly still on the bed. Tubes were running all over him, including a tube going into his mouth.

The tears came without warning and I covered my mouth in an effort to keep from sobbing out loud. If he could hear me, I didn't want him to know I was bawling my eyes out. I wanted to be optimistic.

I walked over to his bed and carefully picked up his hand. It was warm, which sent tingles of hope through my body. I kept waiting for him to squeeze my hand, but nothing happened.

The door slid open and I looked behind me, brushing away the tears with my free hand. Tyson walked in, his hands at his sides, and stood near the door.

"He's in a coma. He got a pretty hard knock on the head when he hit the sidewalk. The only reason he's even alive right now is that one of the men broke his fall." Tysons eyes floated to mine for a second before looking back down at the ground.

"Do they know when he'll wake up?" I asked in a shaky voice.

"They don't know. It depends on how long it takes for the swelling in his brain to go down. Could be a few days, a couple of months, or he might not wake up at all," he said, his voice halting at the end.

"Oh," I said, fresh tears rolling down my cheeks.

"Did you find out anything about the attorney?" he asked.

I looked back at him, disgust on my face. "How can you ask that right now? Your son may never wake up."

"Because I'm angry and these people are responsible for what happened to him. I want to know who they are so I can get rid of them for good."

"So you want to kill them, like Jacob? Is that the only way you know how to deal with things?" I held tightly to Cal's hand, being careful not to press too hard on his I.V.

"You have no idea what the real world is like and how it operates. Do I enjoy killing people? No, but sometimes it's necessary when that's the only way to stop them from coming after us and killing us all." He took a couple of steps toward me, but still kept a few feet between us.

"Couldn't you just expose them in the media? Or get the police involved? I know they're on your side."

He shook his head, a slight smirk on his face. "It is not that simple, Casper."

I looked back at Cal's calm face. He looked like he was peacefully sleeping and would wake up any second, his bright blue eyes staring back at me. "I think it can be that simple," I whispered.

"You are welcome to try. God knows Kythera could use the help right now," Tyson responded.

I felt my jaw go tight as I gritted my teeth. I

let go of Cal's hand gently, and turned around my arms crossed against my chest. "I'm not doing this for Kythera. I'm doing this for Cal and for Wendy."

"Wendy? Who the hell is Wendy?"

"My horse that you promised to give me if I get you information on this stupid group."

"Oh, yes, right. I forgot about that."

I walked up to Tyson, all fears of him disappearing into the air. "I won't let you forget when I bring you the information you need."

I walked out of the room, my adrenaline pumping fast and hard through my veins. I was angry. I was upset that I had somehow ended up in this nightmare. I loved *The Godfather* movies, but I never wanted to be a part of them, and that's what I felt like every day now. I was going to find out who these people were, get Wendy back, save my family and Cal. It wasn't the normal to-do list for a high school senior, but I never had ever really been normal.

I stepped into the house through the back door and looked up in surprise to see my mother sitting on the couch, a solemn look on her face. I was about to ignore her and go upstairs to my room to plot my next move, but she stopped me with her hand.

"Casper, I need to talk to you," she said, her voice weak and quiet.

I took a seat on the love seat near her.

"How's Cal doing?" she asked, her eyebrows furrowing.

"He's in a coma. They don't know yet how long it will be or if he will wake up." I felt sadness creeping up in my throat as I looked at my mother. I bit my lip so I wouldn't cry again.

"Oh, no, I'm so sorry. Hopefully he will be awake in a couple of days. He's a strong boy," she said, a small smile on her red lips.

"Yes, he is." I thought about the moment on the roof when he had looked at me. His eyes had had a blue fire in them and he had been so determined. I wouldn't have been able to stop him from going after the men. He had saved my life . . . *again*, but this time he may not live to hear my thank-you.

"Were you able to find out anything while you were there?" she asked softly.

I shook my head. "No, they killed her before she could say anything." My lips started quivering as I thought about the chaotic scene.

"They did? I'm so sorry, honey, this isn't anything a child should have to see or endure. I can't believe we are in this position in the first place. If your father wasn't so stubborn . . ." she said, trailing off. Mother reached her hand out and put it on my knee.

Her touch made it impossible for me to hold the tears back any longer. I began to cry uncontrollably. I wanted to hug my mother, but I was too afraid to reach out and grab her. Fortunately, she got up and put her arms around me. I rested my head on her shoulder as I just let it all out. She stroked my hair and held onto me tightly. It felt so good, but weird at the same time. Normally, this was something my dad would be doing—or I would be hugging tightly to Wendy if he wasn't around. The thought of my dad made me cry even harder. He hated me right now, and I didn't know how to fix it. I wished he would wake up and realize we needed to be running as far as we could from Charleston.

I finally felt the tears slowing and I could breathe evenly again. I took a couple seconds longer before picking up my head and staring at my mother with my red, puffy eyes. She was looking at me, her own eyes glazed over with tears. Why was she so nice all of a sudden?

"Are you having an affair?" I blurted out.

"What? Why would you think that?" she asked, her voice screeching and her cheeks turning bright red.

"I saw you leaving the other day wearing a dress that you wouldn't be wearing except on a date . . ."

"I already explained that to you," she said, interrupting me.

"I found an address in your car. I followed you there one day and saw you with Marcus's dad."

She was silent her lips in a thin line. So it was true.

"It's not what you think," she finally said.

"Then what is it?" I sat back on the love seat and wiped my eyes with the sleeve of my T-shirt.

"I can't explain right now; you just have to trust me on this one."

I stood up and balled up my fists at my sides. "I'm tired of hearing that line. That's what I kept hearing about Kythera and what has it gotten me? I've become target practice for some group who wants to kill me so they can take over Kythera's territory. Is this what you pictured our lives to be like?"

"No, it isn't, but we have to deal with it for now. There isn't anything that I can do but make the best of it," said Mother as she stood. Her face was stony, void of any emotion.

"You may not have any intentions of getting us out of this mess, but I do," I said, narrowing my eyes at her. I turned to walk through the kitchen and up the servant stairs.

I walked into my bedroom and over to the mantel. I picked up the framed photo of Cal and me at the Hunt Club with Wendy. We were both smiling, Cal's fear not evident as he put his arm around Wendy's neck. *I'm doing this for you*, I said to myself.

I had no idea if I could figure out who was behind this. In fact, what made me think I could when Kythera couldn't? But I had to try—even if it was the last thing I did. I couldn't live my whole life like this. I didn't want to be a caged bird. I was meant to be free, to ride across the fields on a thoroughbred, breathing the crisp air into my lungs—not worrying if someone was following behind with a gun. This wasn't going to be my life.

I looked out the window at our small backyard and envisioned the rolling fields of our farm. I would do anything to get that life back.

Chapter

14

I WALKED INTO THE LUNCHROOM THE next day and everyone stared at me, whispering to each other. It didn't bother me. I was getting used to being the gossip in the cafeteria for one reason or another.

I walked over to our usual table and set down my tray. I slung my backpack over the chair and sat down and opened a bottle of water, the scratches on my palms burning as I twisted the cap. I put my fork into the salad I'd picked up in the line, but it didn't even look appetizing. I just didn't feel hungry.

Seconds later, Charlotte appeared, setting her own tray down at the seat across from me. "Hey, how are you feeling?" she asked quietly.

I shrugged my shoulders. "Okay, I guess."

"I went by and saw Cal last night. He looks good. I think he'll snap out of this," she said.

I looked up at her smiling face as she opened a fruit cup and placed a spoonful of mandarin oranges into her mouth.

"I hope so, but I plan on getting us out of this so it doesn't happen again." I pushed the giant pieces of lettuce around with my fork.

Charlotte choked down an orange slice. "What is that supposed to mean? Haven't you already tried to get out? Why can't you just be happy?"

I felt anger rising up in my chest. "Just be happy? How many times have you had someone shoot a bullet at your head? This isn't the life I want. Maybe you are willing to live looking over your shoulder, but I'm not."

"Why are you so dramatic? Things aren't that bad, and once they get everything under control, things will go back to being normal." Charlotte rolled her eyes and looked around the cafeteria.

Marcus sat down beside Charlotte. "Who are you rolling your eyes at?" he asked her.

"Nothing, just some drama queen," she said, lowering her eyes to her tray.

I felt my pulse speed up and heat rise to my cheeks. What was wrong with her? Couldn't she recognize when something was falling down around her? She was living in a glass house with a mob outside ready to throw stones.

I didn't want to be the girl staring out at the mob and doing nothing to protect myself from the shards of glass when they started flying. There was too much to live for, including Cal, who may have given his life to save mine. I wasn't going to dishonor him by idly sitting by and waiting for the end to come.

I got up from the table with my half-eaten food.

"Where you going?" asked Marcus, a puzzled look on his face.

I shrugged my shoulders. "I'm not hungry anymore." I walked to the counter and dropped off my tray, then exited the busy cafeteria and walked into the quiet hallway.

I leaned up against the lockers and took a deep breath. It was taking everything I had not to slide to the floor and put my head against my knees. My heart was aching again, more than it had before, when Cal was at boarding school. At least there, I knew he was alive and I would get to speak to him at some point. Now, I could only pray he would wake up.

I looked up at the clock on the wall. Three more hours until school was over. I made the quick decision to walk through the front doors and out to the parking lot. I pulled my keys out of my backpack and got in my car. I had never skipped school before, but this year seemed to be all about firsts.

I drove the familiar drive out to the Hunt Club. As I neared the gate that seemed to be guarding nowhere, I thought about the first time Cal had brought me out here. I pulled my white entrance card out and swiped it in front of the sensor. The gates opened slowly and I drove down the familiar gravel path.

I remembered getting so annoyed with Cal because he wouldn't tell me where we were going and the random gate had told me nothing. He had been smiling from ear to ear, which had irritated me even more. But what had happened next would forever change the way I felt about him.

I pulled into the gravel parking lot and headed straight for the barn. My nose filled with the sweet smell of fresh hay and horses. Wendy poked her head up over her stall door, as if she knew I was coming to see her. I couldn't help but smile. I opened her stall and stepped in, putting my arms around her neck and hugging her. Her steady breathing was loud in my ear. I focused on her strong heartbeat, letting it block out all the thoughts in my head, concentrating only on her. Touching Wendy was like getting a jolt of life. The horses had always been that for me . . . the gateway to freedom. I never felt like I fit into my parents' world, but I'd always known that I was born to be with the horses.

I let go of her neck, the smell of her now on my face, and looked into her big brown eyes. "I've got to fix this, Wendy," I said quietly.

Wendy slowly blinked, showcasing her long, dark lashes. I went to the corner and sat down in the straw, pulling out the apple I had stuffed in my backpack from the cafeteria. I held it out to her. Wendy quickly moved toward me, taking the apple in her mouth. The loud crunch as Wendy gobbled it up filled my ears.

I started thinking of what I could do to make things better, hoping being near Wendy would help me focus. It always had before. If things were crazy at school or with my parents, being near her always made me think clearer.

Marrow was trying really hard to get rid Cal and me, but why? And they had succeeded in killing Veronica. Why not go after the adults? Why would getting rid of us make sense instead of going after Tyson? That was something that I didn't understand. Tyson was the one in control, so wouldn't it make more sense to get rid of him? Then Kythera would fall apart on its own.

What would Marrow gain if only the kids were all gone? If Cal were gone, then Tyson wouldn't have an heir to pass his Kythera membership to—especially since Kythera was all about family bloodlines. If Tyson couldn't pass on leadership to Cal, then who was next in line? Alex and his sister Veronica would have been next, because their father was basically second-in-command. Explains why they went after Veronica, but doesn't explain me.

I picked up a couple of pieces of straw and twisted them in my fingers. I looked over at Wendy, who had walked over to her trough and was munching on some hay. My mind was blank. This wasn't helping me any. I stood up and rubbed Wendy across her back.

I pulled her face toward mine and kissed her lightly on the muzzle. "See you later."

I had to get some real answers and fast. But where could I get any information? The parking lot was crowded as I walked toward my car. I glanced up at the group of men getting into a white SUV. Normally, I wouldn't have looked for more than a second, but they stood out in their black suits and shiny shoes. Most of the people here were more casual in their riding and hunting gear. The sun glinted against something on one of the men's suits. It shone bright gold, and I held my breath. As he opened the door, the glare disappeared and I could make out the pin that had now become so familiar to me.

As he looked back at me, I ducked behind my car. I didn't move an inch until I saw them drive by—then I got into my car and followed them. I tried to keep a pretty good distance between me and the white Suburban SUV as we exited the long drive out of the Hunt Club. I stared at their license plate. It wasn't anything special— except, wait . . . did it have the Marrow symbol in the corner of the plate? I leaned forward over the steering wheel as I tried to get a look at it. Suddenly, they put on the brakes, and I hit my chin hard on the steering wheel as I stomped on my brakes to keep from rear-ending them. I was afraid they had noticed how closely I was following them, but when I looked around, I realized we were back at the gate in the middle of the forest.

As they waited for the gate to open, I looked in the middle console for a pen and some paper,

knowing I should write down their license plate
number. I found a receipt, but no pen—and my
backpack was in the trunk. I tried to think fast
before we started moving again. I looked over
at my cell phone which I had thrown into the
passenger seat. I picked it up and tried my best
to secretly take a photo of the plate. Hopefully,
they would think I was just another teenager
texting and driving.

I snapped the photo and quickly threw the
phone back on the seat. Finally, we were moving
again, and we crept along the gravel road. They
were moving pretty slow—too slow. Did they know
I was taking a photo? My heart started thumping
in my chest. I hoped they couldn't recognize me
or my car. Stupid Kythera—all their obvious
markings on their vehicles made it hard to be
incognito. Fortunately, there wasn't a big "K"
symbol on the front, so I felt sort of safe.

The SUV stopped again at the highway,
turning their left blinker on. I debated in my
head whether or not to follow them. I made a
split-second decision and turned my own left
blinker on.

I was nervous because I didn't have a plan.
I guessed I would follow them to wherever they
were going and keep on driving past them. The
sun was still bright in the sky, so there was
no way for them not to see me behind them. I
hoped they would just think I happened to be
going in the same direction. But if they started

making a lot of turns I would have to abandon my plan, because they would know exactly what I was doing.

The SUV was heading away from Charleston. The road sign I passed said it was five miles to Canaan. We came to a crossroads, where the SUV paused for a stop sign. I looked around at the deserted intersection. As my eyes came back to the road, I noticed that one of the doors of the SUV was opening. A man got out and looked squarely at me. I froze, staring at his sunglasses as I recognized his face. It was my calculus teacher. I could feel the blood draining from my face. Mr. Perry started walking toward my car.

I had a sickening feeling in my stomach and I did the only thing I could think of—I threw the car into reverse. I took my eyes off the SUV as I reversed down the road, afraid to turn around because they would see the "K" on the back. It was a good thing I had always been good at reversing. My driver's ed teacher, Ms. Echols, had said my reversing was better than going forward. She hadn't meant it as a compliment, but if she could see me now, she would have.

I could feel the adrenaline pumping through my arms and legs and I wondered if they were following me. As I came up on a curve, I reversed into a driveway. I looked at the road, but the SUV was nowhere to be seen. I breathed out in relief, but it dawned on me. If I had recognized Mr. Perry, he had to have recognized me—didn't he?

I put the car in drive and sped back to Charleston as fast as I could. I had to get the photo of the license to Tyson and tell him who I had seen. I couldn't believe my teacher was basically a spy for Marrow. Really? Did this kind of stuff happen outside of the movies? I'd been attacked countless times in the past few months, joined a secret group, my boyfriend was in a coma, and now my calculus teacher was a spy. When was the rollercoaster ever going to end?

The streetlamps flickered on as I neared the Romans' house. I pulled into the driveway. The house was dark except for the gas lamps on the front porch. I walked up to the front door and rang the doorbell. I could hear the church bell-like sound echo in the hall and the heavy steps of the butler as he came to the door.

"Yes?" he said, as he looked me up and down in the darkness.

"Is Tyson home?" I asked.

"Yes." Without saying another word, he motioned for me to come in.

I looked around the dark house. Normally, it would be full of light and sounds from dinner and cocktail parties, but now it was still and mausoleum-like. There was a sadness in the air that was so cold, it penetrated my skin. It was the same sadness I was carrying in my heart.

I followed the butler into the library, where Tyson was sitting on the leather couch, drink in hand. He looked rough; his normally perfectlycoifed hair was messy and his tie was loose around his neck.

He looked up at me and started to smile, but quickly erased it when he realized I wasn't someone else. He took a sip of his liquor and set it on the coffee table.

"Why are *you* here?" he asked, his words slurring together.

I could smell the bourbon on his breath from across the room. It smelled like our box at the Kentucky Derby after everyone had had several mint juleps.

"I have a photo to show you, and I know someone else that's involved with the other group." I pulled my phone out of my back pocket and handed it to Tyson.

He took it from me, and stared at the screen. "It's a license plate? What do I need this for?" He laughed, the sound eerie and hollow.

"It's a vehicle for Marrow. I saw them at the Hunt Club. I followed them from there, and I saw my calculus teacher, Mr. Perry, get out of the vehicle. He saw me."

Tyson's face went pale as he picked his glass back up. "You sure it was Mr. Perry?" he asked as he took another sip.

"I'm positive."

He smirked. "I wouldn't be too worried that he saw you. He already knows who all the members are, not to mention he has access to school records and all of your schedules. He should be more concerned that you saw him."

I felt my stomach twist into knots. "I'm not telling you this so you can go out and kill him."

"That's none of your business, little girl, but thanks for the info." He waved me away like I was a servant.

My blood boiled. "I may be a little girl, but at least I can solve problems without killing. And I've figured out way more than you and your almighty Kythera, so who's the little one now?"

He looked at me, his knuckles turning white around his glass just before he threw it at the wall near the fireplace. "How dare you talk to me like that!? Who do you think you are? Cal may see something in you, but you're just a spoiled brat."

"Do you think it makes you big to talk to a little girl like that?" I moved toward the door, afraid he would have better aim next time.

He was quiet for a moment, as he stared at the shattered pieces of glass near the fireplace. "I'm sorry. I'm just upset about Cal."

I turned back around and leaned on the door, "So am I. That's why I'm trying to figure out who's responsible."

He nodded. "Thank you for the information. But I can't promise what will happen to Mr. Perry."

I sighed. "Can you at least promise he won't end up in a dumpster or on the bottom of the harbor?"

He smirked. "I think I can manage that."

Without another word, I walked out of the library and out of the Romans' home. I felt tears forming in my eyes—not because of what Tyson had said to me, but knowing that those words were out of sadness for his son, who I loved, too.

I wiped away a tear as I sped away, trying my best not to dwell on the situation too much. I was going to go home, but I had the urge to go see Cal. He might not be able to speak to me, look at me, or smile, but I knew just being near him would help.

I walked into the lobby of the hospital and headed straight for the bank of elevators. I stepped into the elevator as the doors opened and an elderly man stepped in as the doors were about to close.

He grinned at me and punched the button for the third floor. "Where are ya headed?"

"Same floor," I said quietly, leaning against the hand rail.

"My wife is in the ICU. Second time this month, but we're hopeful," he said, trying to start a conversation. It wasn't going to work. "Who you here to see?" He obviously wasn't going to give up.

"My boyfriend." I started tapping my shoe on the faux-wooden floor.

"Is he going to be all right?" he asked, concern in his voice.

I nodded, because I didn't know what else to do. I hoped he would be okay, but I had no way of knowing if he would be or not. He could wake up tomorrow and be perfectly fine, or he could not remember who I am. Or, worse yet, he could never wake up and just lay there in a hospital bed, machines breathing for him and keeping him alive.

"Oh, I'm sorry, honey. My wife's always said I have a big mouth and one day I need to listen to her. I'm sure he will be okay. God will take care of him, you'll see."

The doors of the elevator opened and I wanted to rush out of there.

"Everything will be fine honey, you'll see. Just have faith," he repeated reassuringly.

I stepped out of the elevator, but stopped and turned to look at the man. His small, round eyes were scrunched up as if he was in physical pain. I could tell he didn't mean any harm.

I whispered a quick, "Thank you," before continuing down the hall.

As I walked into the ICU, I was overcome by the strong smell of antiseptic. I looked into the open curtains of several rooms, patients asleep and unmoving in their beds. As I approached Cal's room, I noticed that the curtains were drawn. A nurse quietly exited the room, closing the door carefully behind her, which was funny to me, because it wasn't like she could wake him up shutting a door.

As she walked down the hallway, she bumped hard into my shoulder. She said a quick sorry as she scurried down the hall and into the elevator.

That was odd, I thought. I opened the door to Cal's room. His eyes were still closed and my shoulders drooped. Every time I walked in, I hoped to see him sitting up and smiling at me.

I sat down in the chair that had been pulled over to the side of his bed. I was surprised his mother wasn't sitting in it—she barely ever left his side. I rubbed the top his forearm and grabbed his hand, squeezing it, intertwining my fingers with his, and instantly felt a sense of warmth in the otherwise frigid room.

I moved his hand a little closer to the edge of the bed and felt something sharp rubbed against my hand. I held my breath as I picked up the gold pin, an "M" with an arrow running through it. There was a note attached that read,

Humpty Dumpty sat on a wall,
Humpty Dumpty had a great fall.
All the king's horses AND ALL THE KING'S MEN
Couldn't put Humpty together again.

I looked up at Cal's blank face and then to his monitors. Seconds later, the heart monitor started beeping wildly as I watched his heart rate drop. I stood up and several nurses ran in, nearly knocking me over.

"Code blue! Get the doctor in here!" one shouted as another grabbed my arm and dragged me out.

I wanted to fight her, but all I felt was numb

and unable to think; I let her lead me out without a word. In the hallway, everything was playing out in front of me as if I were a ghost, watching in horror, unable to do anything.

The doctor ran into Cal's room, along with a flurry of more nurses. They were shouting, but I couldn't hear what they were saying. It felt like they were a thousand miles away. I wanted to cry, scream, or move, but I couldn't. All their movements were slow and blurry, as if I were not awake at all, but in some awful nightmare.

Cal's mother started running down the hallway toward his room, but she was stopped at the door by a nurse. He had to physically hold her back as she screamed and beat her arms against him before she finally slumped down onto the floor. She shook violently as she cried, but her wailing barely penetrated my thoughts.

Then, as if I had physically been struck by something, the pain rushed into my chest. I couldn't breathe and it was a deep emptiness I had never felt before, so wrenching I could no longer stand on my feet. I fell to my knees and I let out the air I felt like I had been holding for several minutes. The tears finally started flowing down my face, so fast my vision was like I was underwater, the hospital staff blurry blobs swimming in the distance.

Someone picked me up easily from the floor and started walking with me in their arms down the hall. I immediately recognized his strong cologne and knew it was my dad, who was carrying me as if I were a rag doll. I buried my head into his shoulder without looking up at his face and wrapped my arms around him, crying uncontrollably.

"I'm so sorry," he whispered, but that only made me cry harder.

It felt good to be in his arms. It reminded me of all the times as a kid he had comforted me when I had gotten hurt, and how he was always there with his arms open wide for me to run into them. When I was little, I had thought my dad was a superhero who could take away any pain with one hug.

But as good as it felt, this time he couldn't take the pain away. I heard the hospital doors slide open and felt the cool air on my skin, and the smell of Charleston's salty air.

I lifted my head and tried to open my swollen eyes. "Wait, we can't leave," I begged, my voice crackly and uneven.

"You don't need to stay here. There's nothing you can do. You need to be home," he said with Dad-like authority.

"But what if he's still alive? I want to know. I can't stand not knowing," I said, the tears threatening to flow again.

"Honey, I know how much you love and believe in Cal, but I doubt he can survive this," he said, still walking toward the parking lot.

"You said that about Trio, and he survived," I said, feeling like a little girl again.

When Ghostly Trio, our newest foal, contracted colic, it had looked like he wasn't going to make it, but I'd begged Dad to do whatever he could to save him. I was only nine at the time, and Dad had tried to explain that sometimes these things happened, but I hadn't wanted to hear it.

I stayed in the stall with Trio night and day for several days, sleeping in his stall with my blanket and teddy bear, afraid to leave his side. Finally, Dad couldn't take it anymore and he had Trio flown to one of the top equine veterinarians in the world. He was saved with surgery and became one of our Triple Crown winners. Today he was happily prancing across the fields of Ghost Hill Farms.

"Cal's not a horse. He's strong, but he's been through a lot," he said, as he put me back on the ground.

I stood next to our car, wiping the tears from my eyes. "But he could survive. Please, I need to know. I don't want to get a phone call later. Please," I begged.

Dad looked at me for a long moment, the sadness evident in his moss-green eyes. "Fine, but—"

Before he could finish his sentence, I was sprinting back to the hospital.

I weaved my way through people as they walked in the lobby, none of them registering in my mind. They were merely obstacles in my way. I was too impatient to wait for the elevator, so I raced up the stairs, out of breath as I stepped out into the hallway of the third floor. I didn't stop until I reached the ICU nurse's desk. I looked over to Cal's room, which was empty. But I wasn't giving up hope yet.

"Where's Cal Roman?" I asked the nurse behind the desk.

"Are you family?"

I was so tired of that question. "Yes, I'm his cousin," I lied.

She looked at me skeptically.

"Please, give me some information," I pleaded, hoping my puffy red face would persuade her. My heart was beating wildly in my chest.

"He's in surgery now."

"So he's not dead?" I asked, barely able to breathe.

"No, but I can't give you any more information, even if you are his cousin," she said and returned to her computer.

I ran down the hallway to the ICU waiting room and burst through the door to see Cal's mother and Tyson sitting in the far corner. They looked up at me, their faces puffy as mine.

"He's alive?" I asked.

Tyson nodded. "Yes, for now. He had a heart attack and they're trying to repair the damage."

I sat down heavily in one of the chairs, feeling light headed. So there was still hope. *Thank you, God.* I put my head in my hands, trying to keep the tears at bay as I said a little prayer.

After a few minutes, I was able to think a little more clearly, and I looked back up at Tyson. "Why would he have a heart attack?"

Tyson shrugged his shoulders. "They don't know why he would have one at his age. There were no indicators of it beforehand."

That's when I finally remembered what I had seen moments before Cal had the heart attack. "I found a pin and a note on Cal's bed right before his machines went crazy."

Tyson's eyes got wide, and his face turned blood red. "*What!?*"

I almost didn't want to continue, because it felt like he was mad at me. "I found a note and a Marrow pin on his bed."

"Why didn't you tell anyone!?" he shouted, standing. His wife tried to comfort him, placing her hand on his forearm, but he just shrugged her off.

"I saw the note and then the machines went crazy and I was dragged out of the room. I was terrified I was going to lose him. I couldn't think!" I shouted back, irritated he was treating me like I was a criminal.

"Tyson, calm down. She didn't do this, and even if she had told us right away, it wouldn't have stopped what had already happened," said Mrs. Roman, as she stood up and pulled on Tyson's sleeve. It was one of the rare times I had heard her speak or say anything beyond the normal socialite pleasantries.

Tyson's face relaxed, but his eyes were still full of fire. "Sorry, I'm just on edge," he muttered.

"I think I may know who did it, too," I said meekly, hating to have to admit it.

The anger was back in his face, but he took a deep breath before speaking. "What makes you think you know who did it?" He sat back down in the chair next to his wife and grabbed a Styrofoam cup I was sure wasn't filled with coffee.

"When I got off the elevator and started walking toward Cal's room, I saw a nurse walk out. She was acting kind of weird, looking around everywhere. She even bumped into me as she rushed to the elevator. I thought it was kind of strange, but didn't give it a second thought till now."

Tyson eyes brightened. "That means we can go back and look at the surveillance video and find her."

He pulled out his iPhone and started dialing a number. "Let me speak to the sheriff, this is Tyson Roman."

Tyson got up and went into the hallway to speak to the sheriff. I sat in the chair, staring at the wall, not knowing what to say to Mrs. Roman. I looked her way, and she smiled at me like she always did, but didn't speak.

"Excuse me, I need something to drink," I said to her quietly and walked out the room in search of a soda machine.

My nerves were shot and my throat was

completely dry. Plus, I couldn't sit in the room with Mrs. Roman and stare at the ceiling. I needed to get up and move. Although some of the hurt inside had subsided, it was still there, weighing on my chest. Cal wasn't dead, but he wasn't safe yet either. I would have to wait however many hours it would take for the surgery and hope for the best.

I went to the elevator and headed for the hospital chapel I had seen when on the first floor. If there were ever a time to pray, this was it.

Chapter

15

AFTER SPENDING A COUPLE OF hours in the chapel, I went back upstairs. The waiting room was filled with Kythera members. I sat by a somber-looking Charlotte and Marcus. He had his arm slung around Charlotte, and she had her head on his shoulder.

Charlotte looked at me with her tawny eyes and motioned for me to sit down beside her. "I'm sorry about earlier at lunch. I just wanted to pretend none of this was happening. But obviously it is."

"It's okay," I said..

My stomach was in knots and I glanced at the clock every few seconds. I needed Cal to live. He was the first human I had ever felt a real connection to, who made me feel like I belonged. I didn't want to have to live without him. I needed

Wendy right now, too, but I was sure she wouldn't be allowed in the hospital. A grin crossed my face at the thought of Wendy clip-clopping through the ICU.

I looked up at the clock anxiously again, and started to bite my nails. I had never been a nail-biter, but I didn't know what else to do. Everyone was quiet and in no mood to talk. The tension was palpable as everyone paced, fiddled with magazines, or drank cups of coffee. Dad was sitting by Tyson, staring at the walls like everyone else. I caught his eyes and he smiled. Cal could be just like Trio after all.

Finally, a doctor walked into the room with green scrubs on and his mask around his neck. He searched for Cal's parents before speaking. "He's stable, but he's still in critical condition. The next twenty-four hours are crucial."

I felt a bit of relief knowing once again Cal had beat the odds. Tyson thanked the doctor, and Mrs. Roman started to tear up. I had to look away to keep the tears at bay myself. I couldn't stand to see anyone else cry.

"This is good. I know Cal, he's going to make it," said Charlotte, grabbing my hand. I looked at her and nodded.

"He has to," I said.

Everyone started chatting with one another, the mood suddenly happier. Several members slapped Tyson on the back as they exited the room. Crisis averted. Dad walked over to me and gave me hug.

"I guess you were right. I shouldn't doubt you, should I? You're the queen of lost causes."

I hugged him back. It was the first time since Cal and I had ran away since he had really spoken to me, or shown me any attention. It was nice to have my old dad back.

"Of course you shouldn't doubt me when it comes to people or horses I care about," I said playfully.

Dad put his arm around me. "Tyson said he's still in recovery and no one will be able to see him for a while—and even then, it will only be his parents. I've already told them to give you a call if anything changes. We'll come back in the morning, okay?"

"Okay," I said, as we walked out of the room, leaving the others behind. Things were looking up. Cal would survive—I knew it in my heart. Now that I knew he was safe, it was time to focus back on Marrow.

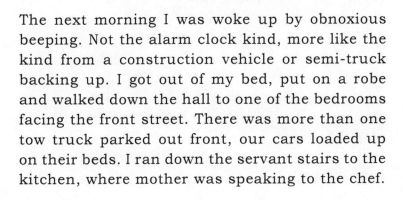

The next morning I was woke up by obnoxious beeping. Not the alarm clock kind, more like the kind from a construction vehicle or semi-truck backing up. I got out of my bed, put on a robe and walked down the hall to one of the bedrooms facing the front street. There was more than one tow truck parked out front, our cars loaded up on their beds. I ran down the servant stairs to the kitchen, where mother was speaking to the chef.

"What's going on?" I asked.

She excused herself and we walked into the family room so the chef couldn't overhear what she was saying. "They are taking our vehicles and replacing them with bulletproof ones."

"Oh." I sat down on the couch, reality setting in. I felt like the gilded cage was getting smaller by the minute.

"And there will be bodyguards following us everywhere we go. The ones assigned to us should be here in the next hour," she said as she stared at the notepad in her hand.

"So will they follow me around school, too? Am I allowed to drive?"

"Yes, some bodyguards will be going with you to school, but since so many Kythera members go to St. Mary's, they'll pick only a few to follow you around. They'll be dressed as school staff. As for driving, we would prefer if you would allow them to drive you around, but if not, then they will follow behind you."

"So we're getting Secret Service like the president or something?" I crossed my arms over my chest and slumped down against the couch.

"I guess so. Until they figure out who's behind Veronica's death and the attack on Cal, we can't afford to take any chances. We're all targets, as you know. And don't sit like that . . . it's not very ladylike."

I shot her a look. "You just told me we're going to be followed around like we're in witness protection because someone might try to assassinate us and you're worried about how I'm sitting in my own home?"

She rolled her eyes at me. "You're back to your old sarcastic ways, I see."

She started to walk back toward the kitchen, but I couldn't help but add, "So, does that mean you'll be followed when you go to meet Mr. Gray?"

She stopped dead in her tracks and turned to face me, the anger evident from the vein that always popped out on her perfectly smooth forehead. "Listen—"

"What meetings with Mr. Gray?" piped in Dad, who neither of us noticed had walked into the room. *Uh-oh.*

Mother stumbled and stuttered. "He's been helping me with a benefit for the Women's Club," she finally said.

His phone beeped and he looked at it, "I've got to go," he said quickly, and walked out of the room. Mother looked at me, her face turning a familiar shade of purple.

"I already told you to leave that alone. Why can't you listen to me?" she said.

"I just don't understand and I don't want to see Dad get hurt." I walked out of the room, my emotions starting to rise in my throat.

She didn't bother to call after me, and I practically ran to the front foyer, where Dad was standing, still staring at his phone. I felt sad at the thought of them not being together. Sure, my mother was difficult to deal with and my dad couldn't see the danger we were all in, but they were still my parents and I wanted them together. I'd said I didn't want to see Dad hurt, but it was really that I didn't want to be hurt by Mother's affair. My family might be screwed up, but it was still my family.

Dad looked up from his phone as I approached him.

"I'll be ready to go to the hospital in a minute, just let me change clothes," I said, as I started up the steps.

"Honey, I won't be able to take you. Something's come up that I need to take care of. But Brandon can take you," he said, as he texted on his phone.

"Who's Brandon?" I felt disappointed Dad wasn't going with me.

"He's your new bodyguard. He'll be here in fifteen minutes to take you to the hospital." He didn't look away from his phone once. I guess he was back to business as usual.

"Oh. You sure you can't go with me?" I asked hesitantly.

"Sorry, there's a business problem I've got to take care of. I'll catch up with you a little later." He glanced at me for second, returned to his phone, and walked out of the room.

I knew what that meant. He would get so preoccupied with work that he would forget all about the hospital and seeing me. I had come to expect it.

I continued up the stairs to my room. I walked over to my closet and pulled out a pair of black jeans and a dark blue tank top. I pulled my hair into a ponytail, put on a pair of black flats, and rushed back down the steps. Sure enough, a guy dressed in all black was patiently waiting for me at the door. He looked up at me, his Ray-Bans shining in the light of the foyer. He looked like a stereotypical bodyguard.

I jumped down the last two steps and walked up to Mr. Man in Black. "You must be Brandon. I'm Casper." I stuck my hand out for him to shake it.

"Yes, nice to meet you," he said, without taking his sunglasses off. He shook my hand, letting it go quickly.

He opened the front door and motioned for me to go out. Apparently, he wasn't going to be very talkative. I walked out the door, but stood on the porch, unsure which of the fleet of new black vehicles I was supposed to be driving.

"So, which one am I driving?" I asked, looking at Brandon, who was walking a few feet behind me.

He wasn't smiling, and there were several creases in his forehead, as if he was squinting behind his sunglasses.

"You aren't. I'm taking you to the hospital in the Escalade at the bottom of the drive," he said sternly.

"No, I was told I could drive and you could follow." I walked to the driveway and looked at the various new cars.

They still all had the red "K" on the back and "Kythera" on the wheel wells. I couldn't tell how they were any different, which I guess was the point. I spotted a black Maserati GranTurismo parked next to the Escalade.

I walked to the driver's door and opened it. "You can follow me in the Escalade."

Brandon smirked. "You can drive a stick?"

I leaned over the hood of the car. "Of course." I got in, the new car smell filling my nose. I noticed on the headrest a big red "K" had been stitched into the leather. *Great, people, let's make it even more obvious.*

I looked around for the keys, which were in the ignition. I had driven a stick before, but I couldn't drive it *well*. I looked at the steering wheel—*uh-oh*, it had the gear shift paddles. I had never used those before. It couldn't be that hard, could it? I cranked the car up and stared at all the controls and buttons for a minute, trying to figure out what I needed to do first.

I need to put it in reverse, I thought. I put my foot on the break and shifted it into reverse. I let go of the break and gave it some gas. Without warning I was in the street, halfway in both lanes. I looked around nervously for any vehicles coming toward me. There weren't any, but I still tried to hurry and get in the right lane. I put it into drive and tried to change gears with the paddles, my foot on the clutch. There was a loud grinding noise as I put my foot on the gas and the car jerked a few feet into the right lane. I put my foot on the brake. This was going to be the longest drive to the hospital *ever*.

There was tapping on my window and I rolled it down and Brandon leaned his head down. "You sure you don't want me to drive?" He was smiling and as much as I didn't want his help, there was no way I could get anywhere quickly or without tearing the car up.

Wordlessly, I opened the door and motioned for him to get in, then I walked around to the passenger side. I buckled my seat belt as he got in and adjusted the seat. Seconds later, we were off to a much smoother ride.

I walked into the ICU waiting room, half expecting to see the majority of Kythera's members sitting around anxiously for any word on Cal. But the room was empty. Brandon opened the door behind me and looked around the room as well. There were several empty coffee cups and crumpled-up newspapers on the table. The TV was on, and the local news was on with some late-breaking news. It immediately caught my attention because they were showing a photo of the white SUV I had followed from the Hunt Club.

I grabbed the remote and turned it up. "We're getting new information concerning a shooting, which occurred earlier this morning near downtown Charleston. Four men were shot at close range in their white Suburban. Two of the four victims have been identified, one of whom was fifty-year-old Michael Perry, a teacher at St. Mary's College Prep School. The other has been identified as local attorney Edward Whitaker. The identities of the other two victims have been not yet been released. Stay tuned for updates," said the pretty blonde anchor.

I stood frozen in shock. I should've known Tyson couldn't keep his word not to kill Mr. Perry, but I never dreamed he would act this quickly.

In all fairness, you could say he kept his word because Mr. Perry hadn't been found in a dumpster or the harbor, I thought sarcastically.

I had hoped Tyson wouldn't be out for blood after what had happened to Cal, because there was already too much blood on the ground. But I shouldn't have expected anything less. Tyson wasn't going to stop. He was out for vengeance now.

I turned the TV off, then I left the room and walked toward Cal's room. There was a man in black stationed just outside his door. He looked at me as I walked up.

"Name, please?" he asked, his voice crackly. He sounded like a heavy smoker.

"She's with me, Don," said Brandon from behind. It startled me when he spoke. I wasn't used to having someone follow my every move. The man nodded for me to go in.

As I opened the door, I saw Cal's mother sitting beside his bed, her hands wrapped around his.

She looked up at me and smiled. "Hello, Casper."

"Hello, Mrs. Roman."

I stared at Cal. He still looked peaceful, oblivious to everything that had happened. The heart monitor was beeping a steady rhythm in the otherwise quiet room.

Mrs. Roman got up and motioned for me to sit in her chair. "I need to get something to eat. Will you sit with him until I get back?"

I nodded and eagerly took the seat next to him.

"The doctors said he is doing remarkably well. He's improved a lot. He's not awake, but talk to him. I think he can hear us and they say it should help him recover."

She walked out of the room and I put my hand on Cal's. "You look so much better. Yesterday you looked like Edward Cullen, you were so pale. Not that looking like Edward is such a bad thing—he is hot, after all," I said, chuckling to myself. "I know if you were awake, you would argue with me about the whole vampire thing, but I can say whatever I want right now, can't I? Maybe if I bug you enough, you'll wake up and give me some sarcastic response."

I stopped talking for a moment, looking for any sign that he might be waking up. Nothing.

"I tried to drive a stick on the way to see you today and almost screwed up the car. I ended up in the middle of the street before I knew it. Good thing my new bodyguard, Brandon, was there to save the day. Yeah, you have one, too. His name is Don and looks like he should be competing in a bodybuilder competition. Something to look forward to when you wake up, I guess. No more late night trips out to the plantation to sit at the pond."

I rubbed my fingers lightly across the top of his hand as I spoke. Even though he didn't respond to my touch, I could still feel the electricity flowing between us.

"I miss you so much, and yesterday you gave me such a scare. I don't know what I would do without you . . ."

I was frustrated that he wasn't awake, but tried to focus and be thankful for the fact that he was still alive and that I could see on the EKG machine that his heart was beating a steady rhythm. I wondered if Tyson had already gone through the security footage from yesterday to find the mystery nurse who had run out of his room, who had triggered the nightmare that had unfolded afterward.

I squeezed my eyes shut, trying to force the thoughts of yesterday's events out of my head. I took a deep breath and refocused on Cal.

"I saw Lightning at the Hunt Club. I think he misses having you to throw around, so you need to get better so I can take you out there for another ride. I did find a little Shetland pony you can ride if you're too scared of Lightning. He even has a little cart you can sit on to let him pull you around the parking lot."

I pulled closer to the bed, and laid my head near his chest. I was afraid to put any pressure on him, knowing he had surgery yesterday, but I needed to hear him breathing and his pulse for myself.

His heart thudded loudly and I could've sworn it sped up when I got closer to him. I looked back at the monitor and it did register an uptick in his heart rate. I smiled, staring at his beautiful, angelic face. I stood up so I could whisper in his ear.

"I love you. I love you so much it hurts."

I kissed the top of his head, then I brushed my lips against his, hoping he was like Sleeping Beauty and would wake up with true love's kiss. But he still lay motionless.

The door opened and his mother walked back in. I got up from the chair and gave Cal a final kiss on the cheek. I moved the seat back so she could take her place by her son.

I looked at Cal's face again, and it looked as if he was trying to open his eyes. I moved closer to him. "Did you see that?" I asked anxiously.

I didn't move hoping to see him move again. Seconds later, his eyes fluttered, and then he opened them slowly.

"Cal?" I said in disbelief.

He moved his neck slowly to look at me. "Casper," he whispered quietly.

"Oh, my. Nurse, he's waking up! Get the doctor!" Mrs. Roman shouted out the door.

I brought my head down to his and looked into his ocean-blue eyes, tears welling up in my own. "I've missed you," I said, choking back tears.

"Not . . . as much as . . . I've missed you," he said slowly.

I laughed through the tears flowing down my cheeks. I wanted to grab him and hug him, but I thought I might break him and then he would be gone again. "I love you."

He gave me his normal half-smirk. "I know. I love you, too."

"Well, it looks like someone is feeling better," said the doctor as he walked in.

I moved out of the way and toward the door. I stared in amazement at Cal. His gaze met mine and, once again, the sparks between us went flying. I waved at him as I walked into the hallway. I stood in the hallway for a minute, trying to catch up with the emotions I was feeling. I had never been on such a rollercoaster in my life. One minute complete pain and despair to a feeling like I was floating on a cloud full of rainbows. I leaned against the wall, and looked up to say a quiet thank you to God that Cal had made it.

I looked back down to see Tyson coming down the hallway. He was still wearing the same shirt and tie from yesterday. He looked like he had been through hell. He glanced my way and but didn't say a word as he walked into Cal's room. He probably couldn't face me after so quickly breaking his promise not to kill my Calculus teacher.

Whatever, I was done trying to figure him out. All I could do was protect Cal, my family, and the horses, while hoping for the best.

I walked back into the ICU waiting room, where Brandon was sitting, reading the morning newspaper. I couldn't help, but notice the photo of Cal, dressed in a tux, smiling at me from the front page. I read the headline: *Roman heir dies at area hospital.*

"Why does it say that Cal's *dead*?"

Brandon didn't respond immediately as he finished reading a story. He finally peered over the paper, revealing his large brown eyes for the first time. "Oh, that? No one is supposed to know he's alive."

I sat down in a chair near him and crossed my arms against my chest. "Why?"

"They want Marrow to think they succeeded. Make them feel like they have the upper hand." He put the paper down on the table and picked up a steaming cup of coffee.

"Then why kill my teacher and everyone in the white SUV if you want them to feel secure?"

Brandon looked at me, a puzzled look on his face. "Who says that the K did that?"

I shrugged my shoulders. "I just assumed when I saw it on the news this morning. Who else would have targeted them?"

"I dunno, but it wasn't us."

"Huh," I said as I stared at the TV screen. Some crazy soap was on. Then again, maybe the soaps weren't that crazy after everything I had seen.

Chapter

16

I RETURNED TO SCHOOL THE NEXT day, and I had to pretend that Cal was dead. It wasn't an easy task because I was a terrible actress. But no one could know he had survived. Sure, the Kythera members knew he was alive and breathing, but they weren't asked as often if they were okay and how they were doing, since I was the one who was dating him.

I tried to tear up and act completely depressed, staring at the floor whenever I was in the hallway, but I don't think I was that convincing. Fortunately, other than the occasional, "How are you?" the students were focused on the shocking death of Mr. Perry. There was so much sadness in the school that I passed unnoticed most of the day.

As I walked into calculus, the feeling of sadness

around me intensified. I took my seat and looked around the room. Charlotte was sitting quietly in her usual seat. She looked at me as I sat down, giving me a quick nod. Marcus walked in, then Sarah, both with somber looks on their faces.

I thought about the moment I had seen Mr. Perry get out of the SUV and stare straight at me. Then something hit me, and I remembered the day that Mr. Perry had asked me to stay after class. Maybe it had been more than just a conversation about my grades slipping? I had told him that I was spending too much time at the Hunt Club and then they show up there. Was it not a coincidence at all that they had been there that day?

I looked up as a petite blonde woman walked into the room. "Hello, I'm Ms. Bellamy. I will be taking over Mr. Perry's class." She wrote her name out on the board. She didn't look old enough to be a teacher.

<hr />

The day ended with a school assembly in the gym to discuss the tragedies that St. Mary's had endured this week. Had it really only been a week? It felt like a couple of years had passed since Veronica's death at the club and everything that had happened since.

Large, blown-up photos of Mr. Perry, Veronica, and Cal sat on either side of the principal's rolled-in podium. He spoke highly of all of them and the sniffles of students echoed throughout the room. I tried to act sad. Of course I was upset about Veronica and Mr. Perry, but I was too focused on trying to wrack my brain as to who had caused Mr. Perry's early demise to show any kind of emotion.

If Tyson didn't do it, and no one else in Kythera had done it, then who would have been after them? *Please*, don't let there be a third group. I couldn't take it if there was another one.

It just didn't make sense how it happened.

Sarah nudged me, bringing me back to the here and now. I looked at her inquisitively and she pointed a couple rows down in the bleachers at Dev, who was staring up our way. He waved when I caught his gaze. I hesitated before waving back, remembering I had to be in mourning. I was a total failure at pretending.

"I believe he thinks he has a shot with you now that Cal's out of the picture," she whispered.

I turned to her, my eyebrows flying up.

"I don't know. He couldn't be thinking that already, could he? I mean, they haven't even had the funeral yet," I said with disgust.

I liked Dev and I couldn't help but feel something for him. We had so much in common and he was cute, but he just didn't hold a candle to Cal for me. I think that if Cal had never been in the picture, there would have definitely been something with Dev.

"True, but don't forget—you still have a job to

do. And Cal being gone will make it even easier to convince him," she said quietly.

"I guess you're right," I replied, leaning toward her.

Between all that had been going on, I had forgotten I was supposed to be recruiting Dev for Kythera. Obviously, I was terrible at the job, which I had known before Tyson had the crazy idea to appoint me to it.

Dev turned back around to face the principal as he spoke solemnly about the recent losses and how grief counselors would be available for any student who needed to speak with them. The assembly ended and the principal dismissed us for the day. We all slowly made our way out of the gym and I walked with Sarah to my locker.

"Charlotte and I will be stopping by this afternoon to see how you're doing," she said with a wink. I knew she meant they would be coming by the hospital, because that's exactly where I would be.

I nodded and told her goodbye as I got out my Spanish book and put it in my backpack to read some chapters for a quiz tomorrow. As I shut the door, a familiar face popped up beside me. Dev was smiling, but it was a sad, sympathetic smile.

"How are you holding up?" he asked.

"Okay. I guess I'm in shock. I can't believe he's gone," I said convincingly.

"If you need anything, give me a call?" he said, putting a hand on my shoulder. He had looked

ALL THE KING'S MEN

anxious to pounce earlier, but now he looked completely sincere. I nodded and he started walking down the hall, glancing back at me as he walked out the door.

I felt bad for lying to him, but what else could I do? I reminded myself it was to protect Cal and put an end to Marrow once and for all. Brandon had explained that not only would Marrow feel safer, but they probably wouldn't feel the need to attack us anymore. They'd killed the "king's" heir, a tough blow they didn't think Kythera would be able to come back from. I was still amazed how they were able to keep the hospital staff quiet. But he reminded me of Kythera's still-constant power to rule Charleston. How quickly I'd forgotten.

I closed my locker and looked down the hall, waiting for the "janitor" to walk by. Brandon, with his big, muscular frame, looked pretty ridiculous in his janitor's uniform. He didn't look happy to be carrying a mop and bucket, either. A girl walked by and gave him a look, for which Brandon "accidentally" got some dirty mop water on her shoes. She yelled in horror and a satisfied smirk crossed his thick lips.

I couldn't help but laugh, too, but I quickly tried to regain my somber composure as a group of jocks passed by. They looked at me curiously and I tried my best to look as pitiful as possible. Hopefully I wouldn't have to pretend Cal was dead for long.

Brandon finally caught up with me in the hall,

and wordlessly I started walking to the exit. He stopped to put the mop up, and follow behind a few feet. I got into the new black Lexus sedan Brandon had deemed okay for me to drive. He thought I couldn't break this one.

I pulled to the school exit and waited a few seconds, rubbing the skin under my eyes, while I waited for Brandon's gold Honda Accord to get behind me. I glanced in my rearview mirror and he gave me a nod to go ahead. It was weird having a bodyguard, but I had already fallen into step with the routine as if I had been doing this all my life. Maybe my subconscious had known all along that one day I would be in this dangerous situation.

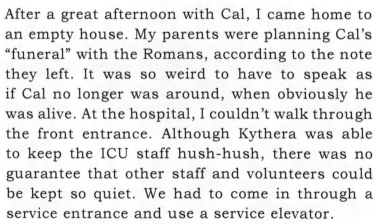

After a great afternoon with Cal, I came home to an empty house. My parents were planning Cal's "funeral" with the Romans, according to the note they left. It was so weird to have to speak as if Cal no longer was around, when obviously he was alive. At the hospital, I couldn't walk through the front entrance. Although Kythera was able to keep the ICU staff hush-hush, there was no guarantee that other staff and volunteers could be kept so quiet. We had to come in through a service entrance and use a service elevator.

Cal had been moved to an isolated operating room and only certain doctors had access. His bodyguard couldn't be stationed at the door

ALL THE KING'S MEN

because that would raise suspicion, but he was only a few feet down the hall at the nurses' station. Anybody who visited had to put on scrubs, hair caps, masks, and be accompanied by a doctor so we wouldn't raise suspicion. It was a tedious routine, but I had to admit Kythera's little stunt made me stand back in awe.

I sat my keys down on the table in the foyer and swung open the door to the kitchen. On cue, the back door opened and Brandon slipped in. I went to the fridge and dug around in the vegetable drawer for some chocolate, and pulled two Cokes from behind the grapes.

Brandon walked up to the counter, and I sat the Coke down in front of him. He pointed to the refrigerator. "I think you have a future as a spy, or at least a magician," he said as he popped the can open.

"I don't know about that, but I'm good at hiding things from my mother. I know she wouldn't go rummaging through the fridge, but if she did, I know she wouldn't be digging through the drawers. She doesn't snack, and if a maid is around, she would just ask them to get it for her." I unwrapped the chocolate bar and offered a piece to him.

He waved it away and chugged the Coke like he would probably do to a beer. "What if the chef or a maid found your junk food stash and told your mother?"

I laughed. "Ha, like they would risk being

accused of hoarding chocolate and Coke in the refrigerator. They're too scared of losing their jobs to rat me out."

"Sounds like I should be happy I wasn't assigned to her."

"Oh, yes, you should be very thankful." I finished off the chocolate and opened the can of Coke, still standing at the counter across from Brandon. "So, how long have you been a bodyguard?"

"About ten years," he said, crushing his empty Coke can and handing it me. I slid open a cabinet and threw it into the recycling bin.

"How did you get mixed up with Kythera?" I said.

"I take it you don't like being a part of the big K?" he asked, ignoring my question.

"Would you if someone had tried to kill you . . ." I counted dramatically on my fingers. ". . . three times, attempted to kill your boyfriend, and succeeded in killing Veronica, all because you're a part of some group?"

He sat back in the chair, and crossed his arms, his bicep muscles bulging under his tight black T-shirt. "Guess not. How did you get mixed up with them? Aren't you from Kentucky, some horse farm legend?" he asked.

"Cal," I said.

He raised his eyebrows, illuminating his big brown eyes. "And you're dating *him*?"

I shrugged my shoulders. "Couldn't help

myself, plus it wasn't just his fault. My dad had a hand in it and I still love him."

"Okay, but why get involved with the king's son? Wouldn't you try to distance yourself from them?"

I smiled. "Oh, I've tried—and Cal came along for the ride. He wants out, too. We got as far as Orangeburg before we were caught"

He rolled his eyes. "Oh, boy, I bet Daddy Roman just loves you."

"Of course," I said with a wink.

"So, now what?" he asked.

"Now I have to figure out who Marrow is, so at least if I'm trapped here, I can go outside without a bodyguard. Not that you aren't cool, but I really like to do things by myself."

He put his palms up. "I get it. But how do you plan on taking on a group who can go toe to toe with Kythera?"

"I've rattled Kythera—surely Marrow can't be much tougher?" I raised an eyebrow.

He shook his head and chuckled, his whole chest bouncing up and down. "I guess not. Just give me a heads-up when you decide to do something crazy."

I walked over to the refrigerator and pulled out bag of Doritos from behind the large container of organic yogurt. "How are you at horseback riding?"

He gave me a blank look. I opened the Doritos and started toward the servant stairs.

"I'm going to bed. See you tomorrow, Brandon," I called as I made my way up the stairs.

I laughed at the thought of Brandon on riding a horse. He would have to ride a Clydesdale for his large frame. Although the image was funny, would he seriously keep me from riding? I knew there was no way I would agree to stop riding—that would be like asking me to stop breathing. But how much of a fight would I be in for? *If* Brandon chose to try to keep me from it, he would find out quickly how I was like my mother.

As I walked into my bedroom, I heard the doorbell ring out in the hallway. I went to the top of the stairs and peered over the banister, Doritos bag still in hand. I couldn't really see anything but Brandon's shadow as he answered the door. As much as I didn't like having a bodyguard, I did enjoy never being alone in the house.

From listening to the conversation, it sounded like a delivery man of some sort. I looked at the grandfather clock in the hall. Who delivered things at eleven o'clock at night? Except pizza or Chinese, neither of which I had ordered.

I walked down the steps just as Brandon closed the door. Sitting on the little round table in the foyer was a gorgeous bouquet of red Calla lilies.

"Are those mine?"

"Yes," he said, and handed me the little unopened envelope from the bouquet. They had to be from Cal—he knew they were my favorite. I could remember him asking the first time we went to eat at the Italian restaurant the day I got here. After that, he would occasionally leave a single Calla lily on my doorstep, and I would get butterflies every time I found one. I looked at my name printed on the outside before ripping it open.

I pulled out the note and read it.

I'm so sorry for your loss. If you need anything, I'm always here.—Dev

"Huh," I said aloud as I stared at the card.

"What?" asked Brandon.

"How did he know red Calla lilies are my favorite?"

Chapter 17

I WALKED INTO SCHOOL THE NEXT morning hoping I would run into Dev, so I could thank him for the flowers and find out how he knew they were my favorite. He could've just gotten lucky, but that would've been a really big coincidence. I purposely walked down the science wing, where Dev had biology first period. Several girls gave me pitying looks as they stood next to their lockers. I tried to look sad, but I was running out of ways to look pitiful. I'd even Googled how to make myself cry. I had rubbed Vick's VapoRub under my eyes this morning which worked, until I got some of it into the corners of my eyes. I had to flush them out for a good five minutes. I wasn't crying, but my eyes were red and puffy, which was good enough to put on a show.

I caught a glimpse of Dev as he walked into his biology class. I looked up at the clock on the wall and knew I was going to be late for my own class, but I had to know how Dev knew about the flowers.

When I walked into his class, almost everyone was in their seats chatting with each other. I scanned the room and I found Dev sitting in the back. When he saw me, a goofy grin spread across his face and he waved me to the back of the room.

I walked between the desks, everyone staring at me. "Hey, thanks for the flowers," I said in a low voice, hoping no one would hear us talking. Unfortunately, the class got quiet.

"You're welcome. I thought they might brighten your day and all, given everything that's happened. The flower delivery guy tried to deliver them earlier, but no one was home all afternoon," he explained, answering my question as to why the delivery guy showed up so late.

"Yeah, we were over at Charlotte's house with her parents," I lied, praying he wouldn't bump into Charlotte today. I didn't think they had any classes together.

"Oh, well, glad you got them," he said, ending the conversation.

I stood there for a minute, trying to figure out how to ask him about the flowers without blurting it out. "I'm curious—how did you know red Calla lilies are my favorite?" *Oh, well,* I couldn't think of any other way.

"You told me the day you had dinner at my house, remember?"

I could see some eyebrows rise around the room. "I don't remember telling you that."

He shrugged his shoulders. "It was while we were on the back porch swing together."

I heard an audible gasp. I whipped around to see Lisa, a girl from my Renaissance literature class, her small mouth open wide as she stared at me. I had to stop this conversation now, before I turned into the girlfriend who cheated on her now-dead boyfriend. It was hard enough being the new kid. I didn't need to add anything else.

I looked at Dev for a moment, searching his face. He stared up at me with his deep brown eyes, and he seemed completely sincere. I must have told him that day.

"Okay, thanks again," I said with a smile, and walked out of the room without looking at anyone else in the room.

The bell rang and I raced down the hall to political science, but it took me a good minute to run with my backpack. I came to a halt at the door, and tried to walk in quietly, in hopes Ms. Epling wouldn't notice I was late.

"Thank you for joining us, Ms. Whitley," said Ms. Epling, without ever turning around from the board.

My face got hot as all the students looked up at me. I tried to quickly take my seat. I zipped open my book bag and pulled out my notebook. I looked across the room to see Alex staring at his paper, his pencil still against the page.

He hadn't been the same since Veronica's death, which wasn't a surprise. I didn't have any siblings, but if I did and one was killed, I can't imagine what that would be like. He hadn't shown up at the Kythera meeting this week, and he had been at from the hospital. Alex and Cal had been close—best friends, until I'd come along. Now, they barely spoke, and what happened to Cal was probably a reminder of what happened to Veronica.

Class went by fast. I felt like I had only been there for a few minutes when the bell rang. I was ready to jump and run out the door, but something made me stop and look at Alex as he slowly gathered his things.

I walked across the room to him. "Hey, Alex, how've you been?"

He looked up at me and smiled, but it wasn't anything like his normal confident smirk. "Okay, I guess. You still interested in finding out who the guy with the pin at Club Ultra is?" he asked, throwing me off-guard.

"Of course," I said, as we both started heading toward the door.

"I know a couple of the bouncers and they said the guy comes in every Saturday night and spends the whole time in the VIP room with his buddies. We could go this weekend and find out who he is," he said, his voice full of determination.

"Isn't that a bit soon?" I said softly.

"Why? The guy's probably responsible for what happened to Veronica. I want him found."

It didn't seem like Alex even realized he was talking loudly in a busy hallway, a bunch of nosy teenagers inches away.

"Yeah, but what happens when we find him? Are you really going to be able to go in there, ask for some names, and leave?"

Alex was quiet for a moment as we approached my locker. "I don't know—guess we'll see what happens when we get there," he said, not looking at me.

I got a sudden chill. "Listen, Alex, I get it. You're upset and you should be, but we can't walk into a room full of people and demand to know who they are. If they killed once, they could again."

Alex slammed his hand into the locker next to mine and got inches from my face. "And you don't think I'm as capable as Cal to take care of them?"

I was genuinely scared as I looked into his eyes—they were almost black. I tried to scoot away, but my back was already against my open locker. "I—"

"Hey, back off!" shouted Dev as he came up behind Alex. Dev pulled on Alex's shoulder, which was met with a swing from Alex. Dev dodged it, and easily brought Alex to the ground.

I looked around to see that everyone had

stopped in the hallway and were staring at the two of them wrestling on the ground. The principal broke in and grabbed both of them up, pushing them toward his office.

I stood in the hall, clutching my textbook, stunned by what had just happened. Finally, when the crowd of students started to break up, I felt like I could move again. I closed my locker and hurried to class.

Brandon came strolling by with his mop bucket and gave me a worried glance. He mouthed the words, "Are you okay?"

I nodded and walked into class, completely freaked out about what had just happened.

After the fight in the hall, I was bombarded with questions about what had happened by Marcus and Charlotte. They wanted to know what Alex had said and what he had done. When I told Marcus how Alex had scared me, he became visibly angry.

I didn't even stop at my locker once school was out, afraid the interrogation crew would find me and start asking me even more questions. I had homework from political science and Spanish, but it was just going to have to be late. I couldn't take any more questions from them, because I just wanted to forget what happened.

I had made it halfway to my car when I realized I needed to wait for Brandon. I turned around and stared at the crowd exiting the building, which included Charlotte and Marcus, walking hand in hand. I looked around the parking lot for a quick escape and spotted Dev near his truck. I made a beeline for him, hoping to wait long enough for Marcus and Charlotte to get in their cars and leave.

"I've had to tell you thank-you a lot lately," I said as I walked up to him.

He smiled at me as he threw his stuff into the passenger seat. "I'm okay with that. Does that mean you are in my debt?" he asked, slamming the creaky truck door shut.

"I guess technically I am, but I'm hoping you won't hold me to it."

He leaned against his truck. "I won't, except for maybe a horseback ride?"

"That's sounds okay to me," I said.

"I gotta ask, what was up with Alex?"

I sighed. *More questions?* I felt obligated to answer since he had come to my rescue.

"He's having a hard time with the death of his sister and now Cal," I said, leaning against his truck, trying to remember to put on a pouty face about Cal. I already had probably looked too happy, but it was just really hard to remember to be sad about him when I was the exact opposite.

"He's got a lot on his plate, but so have you. No reason for him to get in your face about it," he said calmly, shifting a little closer to me.

"Yeah, but he's translating his feelings into anger. He wants to find whoever killed his sister, which I get. He thinks the person or people who were responsible for it will be at Club Ultra again Saturday. He wanted me to go with him, but I don't think it's a good idea for him to go. He's kind of unhinged. Who knows what crazy thing he would do if he found the killer?" I said, spilling my guts. He was just so easy to talk to about anything.

"How does Alex know who killed Veronica? The police don't even know."

I hesitated for a moment, "I . . . there's . . ." I stuttered, as I looked around the parking lot. Lisa was staring at me again, a look of disapproval on her heart-shaped face.

"What's the K gotten themselves into now?" asked Dev, whispering it into my ear, very aware that Lisa was still gazing in our direction.

Her eyes widened and she scurried off.

It took a second for what Dev had said to sink in. "Wait, you know about them?"

He laughed. "They aren't exactly secret. The marked cars and the tattoos are a dead giveaway. Your tattoo is one of the nicest ones I've seen."

"I guess it is dumb to think it's a secret, but why didn't you say anything if you knew I was a member?"

He nodded. "Because I didn't think it mattered. You were nice and we share a lot in common. Cal and I used to be pretty close until he tried to get me to join. I know all about them."

I felt a sense of shock. Tyson hadn't mentioned that Cal had tried to recruit Dev. Come to think of it, neither had Cal.

"Oh, I had no idea," I said.

"I thought they had sent you to try to recruit me, which would have been way more effective. But then I realized you were just trying to be my friend . . . maybe more."

Guilt settled in my stomach. "Oh," was all I could say.

"So, what makes Alex think he knows who killed his sister?" he repeated.

"When they found Veronica, they found a gold pin near her body, and I had found out earlier that it's a symbol for another group. That's why I'd wanted to go to the club that night, because Alex said he had seen a guy wearing the pin I had described at the club. Alex talked to one of the bouncers and he said the guy is a regular that always hangs out in the VIP room."

"And he got mad at you because you didn't want to go back?"

I nodded. "I just don't think it's a good idea—at least, not for Alex. He's still too angry, and especially after the way he acted today, I don't know what he would do at the club."

"But you want to go?"

I looked at him, a smirk on my face. "You think you've already gotten me figured out?"

He shrugged. "You're easy to read, or maybe we're just that much alike. If you want to go, I can go with you. I don't want you going by yourself."

"You would? That would be great."

"I'll come pick you up at your house around

ten o'clock Saturday night?" he said, looking down at his watch.

"Great," I agreed.

Dev started walking to the driver's-side door. "I've got to get home, but you're more than welcome to come along if you want. We could go for a ride?"

"Thanks for the offer, but I think I'm going to go see Wendy. She always makes me feel better when I've had a bad day," I said, trying to ignore the warm, tingling feeling coursing through my body as I looked at his handsome face.

"Understand. Maybe later this week?"

"Definitely," I replied, and took a couple steps back from his truck.

He got in and cranked the truck up. It sputtered to life, a cloud of smoke trailing behind him as he pulled out of the parking lot. I really hoped that Dev knew this wasn't a date. That it was just a couple of friends going to the club to find a killer.

As he disappeared, it finally sunk in what I had agreed to do with Dev, and I got a little nervous. It was dangerous to go back to the club, but I was more worried about how was I going to keep the "janitor" from finding out.

18

I LOOKED UP AT THE ANTIQUE clock on the mantel in the library, each minute ticking closer to the time that Dev was supposed to pick me up. I still hadn't told Brandon, not that I had planned on telling him, but I still didn't have any alibi for why I had suddenly disappeared.

How do you get rid of a bodyguard?

It was something that I had never thought about—until now. There was no way he would agree to let me go anywhere with Dev in his beat-up truck, which was obviously not bulletproof. And even if he agreed to let me go somewhere with him, there was still no way he was letting me go back to the club. Why couldn't he like parties like my parents, so I wouldn't have to tell him anything at all?

I couldn't climb out the window like I had

with Cal. I chuckled at the memory of the lattice falling down and the poor gardener who had to take the blame for it. I also couldn't forget the way Cal looked on his motorcycle or without his shirt on. But thinking about that wasn't going to solve the bodyguard problem.

As if he could hear my thoughts, Brandon walked into the room and took a seat opposite me in one of the wing chairs. "So, are you finally going to tell me what happened with Alex in the hall?"

"What are you talking about?" I asked, trying to buy a couple of seconds to come up with a lie. Brandon had tried several times this week to talk to me about it, but I would make up some excuse about my mom needing my help or that I was in a hurry. I knew I couldn't hold him off forever, but I could try, *right*?

"You know, the fight in the hall? I don't think you would have forgotten about it that quickly," he said, crossing his arms over his chest.

"Oh, that. It wasn't anything, really. He was mad because he got a bad grade on a test I helped him study for." *OMG*, that was the worst lie I had ever came up with in my entire life.

"Really?" he said, not convinced.

"Yes. You know Alex, he's a hothead," I added nervously, picking up a book from the coffee table and thumbing through the pages. I didn't look at Brandon, but I could feel the sweat starting to break out on my forehead.

"I would've figured you would be getting ready to go out somewhere. Don't most girls spend a couple of hours getting ready for a night out on the town?" he asked, totally changing the subject. I was relieved.

I rolled my eyes. "You really think I'm one of those girls?"

"No, but I didn't think you were the kind who moped around either."

"Who says I'm moping? I'm just lost in thought." *Thoughts about how to get rid of you,* I said to myself.

"So, what are you thinking so hard about? That Dev kid?" He crossed his arms, and I couldn't help but laugh.

"I don't have those conversations with my dad and I'm not having them with my bodyguard," I said, sitting up and staring at him. He didn't move.

"Yeah, but the difference is I have to know where you are every minute of the day and who you're spending it with and if they might get you into trouble. My résumé won't look good if I end up with a dead client."

"You think Dev will get me into trouble?"

"He's a nice enough boy, but I don't know much about him. And he's not a Kythera member."

"*Ugh,*" I said, and sighed heavily.

"I know you want to get away from them, but right now you need to stick to them like glue. They are the only people you know who for sure don't want to kill you."

"I wouldn't be too sure about that. I can think of a couple of members who might want me out of the picture," I said with a smirk.

He smiled, but it wasn't a friendly, nice-to-see-you smile. It was the kind that meant he wasn't playing around. He stood up. "Then you should be on your best behavior, shouldn't you?"

With that, he walked out of the room and vanished somewhere into the house. This was going to be even more complicated than I'd thought. Maybe I didn't need to get away from Brandon completely. If I could just get a ten-minute window to get out of the house, that would give me a good enough head-start. Brandon didn't know anything about what Alex had said to me in the hall, thanks to my "clever" lie about some stupid test that I was a hundred percent sure he didn't buy. Either way, he wouldn't figure out right away what had really happened, and put two and two together, would he?

With a plan slowly forming in my brain, I got up and went to my room. I opened my closet and looked for a pair of black jeans and a nice top. It wasn't really club-appropriate attire, but I couldn't be too careful that Brandon would see me leaving. A short, sparkly dress would be a dead giveaway. Not that I even owned such a thing, or would wear it if I did.

Adrenaline started pumping through my veins. I knew what I was doing could turn out very bad, but I had to know. I had to know for me, for Wendy and Cal. I felt a pang of guilt because I hadn't told Cal what I was up to today. When I saw him earlier, he had asked me what I was doing tonight, and I'd said I would be watching *The Golden Girls* reruns and working on a paper. He thought it was a pretty boring plan, but not unexpected from me.

He had looked so much better today. His skin had some color and he was talking energetically and even smiling again. He probably wouldn't approve of me going with Dev, but I had no choice. I knew I couldn't go alone. I knew I could've called Marcus, but going with Dev felt like the right decision. Marcus would probably be furious, too, if he found out what I was up to at the club.

I threw on my black jeans, a white top, and a pair of black flats. I picked up my cell phone. It was ten minutes till ten. I had just enough time to get my purse and try to do something with my hair. I stared at the frizzy black mess around my face. I pull my hair up into a messy ponytail, because it was about the only thing it was willing to do in the heavy humidity.

My phone beeped and I looked at the text from Dev that said he was out front. I quietly left my room, shutting the door slowly. I peeked over the stairs and I didn't see or hear Brandon. In the short time that I had known him, he had developed a pretty predictable routine. He spent his afternoons while I was at home watching CNN for a couple of hours, then reading in the library until bedtime, then walked upstairs to his bedroom on the third floor. He probably didn't suspect that I would sneak out. My parents never knew when I did, so it's not like they could've warned him.

I decided to head down the servant stairs so I could make sure that CNN was, in fact, on, before sneaking through the quiet swinging door in the kitchen to the front foyer. Sure enough, I could hear the news anchor talking about the stock market and the latest political news. But then I heard the creak of the wood floors and I ducked behind the kitchen island. Brandon came to the island counter and stopped. *Uh-oh.*

I tried to stay completely still and held my breath. He stood there for a minute, and I could hear some papers rustling. He must have picked up the newspaper. Thankfully, his phone rang, and I could hear his heavy footsteps going back into the family room. I crawled across the floor and through the kitchen door, catching it so it wouldn't swing back and forth too hard. Once I thought it was safe, I got back up and started slowly walking to the front door.

I pulled it open and walked out onto the porch, careful not to make too much noise as I locked it. Dev was driving his parents' Lexus, which surprised me—but I was grateful, because his rumbling truck could've tipped off Mr. Bodyguard.

"Ready to do this?" asked Dev, as I sat down in the passenger seat.

"Yeah, let's go."

The club didn't look any different—not that it should've, but I still expected a more somber atmosphere. A murder *had* taken place outside, but that was old news already. But the club crowd was as rowdy as ever, the parking lot filled to capacity. I had to pull some strings to even get in, which meant flashing my tattoo.

I asked the bouncer where the VIP room was and he pointed to the back of the building. The bass-filled song that was playing was already making my ears hurt as we weaved in and out of people. Finally, we made it to the bright gold door, with VIP stamped on it.

As I put my hand on the door, Dev pushed in front of me, motioning that he would go in first. I nodded, as he opened the door. I was hit with the strong smell of liquor and sweat, which stung my nose. At least it was quieter than outside, the music only background noise to the conversations going on. The room was barely lit with red lights. Plush red velvet lounge booths stretched along the walls, and small coffee tables were in front of them, all covered in beer bottles, shot glasses, and half-empty glasses of champagne.

The room was crowded, people literally sitting on top of each other. I grabbed Dev's forearm as we walked deeper into the room. He looked back at me reassuringly as he found a small space for us to sit. Immediately, a waitress walked up to us and asked us what we wanted to drink.

I was about to say we didn't want anything when Dev piped up and ordered a shot of tequila and a glass of champagne. I looked at him, totally confused.

He leaned in and whispered, "We've got to blend in. Just sip it."

I nodded again and started looking around the room. I kept my gaze floating between all the guys in the room, searching for the gold pin that was burned in my brain. The waitress returned with our drinks and flitted off to another group.

Dev picked up the shot and downed the whole thing. "Wow, didn't know you were a drinker," I said, as I picked up my own glass of champagne and sipped it.

"I'm not, but you don't exactly sip a shot."

"True, but why didn't you order a beer or something?"

"'Cause I can't stomach the taste. At least with a shot, it's over really quick."

I laughed. "Yeah, but you aren't going to feel too good later."

The door swung open and a couple of guys walked in. They were dressed casually in jeans and leather jackets, but they immediately caught my attention because one was wearing a gold pin. Marrow's pin.

"Hey, look," I said to Dev, and his gaze immediately followed mine.

We continued to watch as the guys sat down and were immediately surrounded by girls in short, tight dresses. I couldn't see them anymore. I got up from where I was sitting and walked toward them. Dev shouted my name as I walked over.

My heart was thumping so loudly that it was like the bass music was in my chest. I just kept thinking I had to do this and find out who these people were.

I made my way through the crowd so I could see the guys up close. I pushed a girl in a sparkly silver dress out of the way, and squeezed myself down onto the seat next to the guy with the pin. They all turned to look at me, curious grins on their faces.

"Well, hey, beautiful, what are you drinking?" asked the guy with the pin. His voice was nice, reminding me of Channing Tatum. He kind of looked like him, too.

"Champagne," I responded confidently.

With a snap of a finger, he had the waitress bring me a glass, a confused look on her face.

"I've not seen you around here before. New to the club scene?" he asked, as the waitress set our drinks down.

"Yes," I said, barely getting the word out.. I froze—my confidence was starting to fade.

"What's your name?" he asked, trying to keep the conversation going. He was obviously interested, which was good, except I didn't know how to really use it to my advantage.

"Bella," I spit out quickly. Your name is a question you should definitely not hesitate on.

"Pretty. My name's Cameron," he said, his light eyes sparkling. The strange red light made it impossible to really tell the color.

"Nice to meet you," I said.

He scooted a little closer, which made me uncomfortable, but I didn't budge.

"You want to get out of here?" he asked, out of the blue.

"I don't make it a habit to leave with strangers. I don't even know how old you are or if you're from Charleston."

I looked around the room casually, looking for Dev. I finally found him standing in the corner, staring in my direction. I quickly looked back to Cameron, afraid he would notice my gaze on Dev and get spooked.

Cameron laughed. "Okay. I'm twenty-one and I live in Charleston, but I'm not originally from here. I'm going to the Citadel."

"Impressive. Where are you from originally?" I felt my nerves subside again as the conversation continued. He wasn't too difficult to talk to, as long as I didn't think about what he had done to Veronica.

"Boston. Are you from Charleston?"

"No, I'm from Orangeburg. I've been to Boston a couple of times." I turned my gaze to his pin and reached out to touch it, bringing my face a little closer to his. "Cool pin, what's it for?" I lifted my eyes to his, a smile on my face.

He smiled back, holding my gaze. "It's a family thing," he said casually.

"So your last name starts with an M?"

He moved a little closer to me and I was afraid he was going to try to kiss me. He was so close now, I couldn't focus on anything but his face.

"No," he said with a smirk.

"Oh," I said, confused.

He closed the distance between us and his lips were on mine. I wanted to resist, but I tried to keep my cool. I had to admit it—he wasn't a bad kisser.

He finally released me and moved his lips to my ear. "You know exactly what it stands for, Casper," he whispered. A chill went up my spine, but I was afraid to move.

"Be glad you're too pretty to kill," he said, and backed away, a twisted sneer on his face. He got up, and his group followed him out of the room.

Dev rushed over to me the minute they were out of sight. He sat down and grabbed my shoulders. "What happened? You let that creep kiss you?"

I was dazed and out of it. It took me a minute to process what Dev had just asked. "I . . . he . . . I didn't want to spook him, so I went with it."

"What did he say?"

I gulped. "He knew exactly who I was and he told me to be glad I'm too pretty to kill."

Even in the dark red light, I could tell Dev's face had paled, which made my stomach churn. This had been a very stupid mistake.

Chapter

19

WHEN I GOT IN THE car with Dev, all I could do was fiddle with the seat belt, rubbing the smooth fabric between my fingers. I couldn't wait to get home and be near the protection of Brandon. My skin had been crawling since we left the club, and I felt so exposed and helpless. For the first time, I really felt like I needed a bodyguard. I didn't plan on trying to escape ever again—and I prayed neither my parents nor Brandon knew what I had been up to tonight.

"So, did he tell you his name?" Dev asked, breaking the awkward silence.

I kept staring out the window at the dark houses lining the deserted streets. "He said it was Cameron, but I don't know if he was telling me the truth."

I could see Cameron's eyes, the mischievous glint that sent shivers up my spine when he had revealed that he knew who I was all along.

"How do you think he knew your name?" asked Dev.

I shrugged my shoulders. "The same way they've known things about us all along. Someone's telling them . . ." I paused, trying to decide if I should tell him everything that I was thinking. "Mr. Perry was one of them. He got out of one of their SUVs when I followed from the Hunt Club," I finally said.

"What!?" Dev looked at me.

"That has to be who was giving them information."

"And now he's dead. Did the K kill him?"

"No, that's the part I can't figure out. If Kythera didn't, then who did?"

Dev clenched his jaw and kept looking straight ahead.

"What?" I asked.

"Maybe *they* killed him, because you saw him and it blew his cover."

It suddenly felt like my heart dropped into my stomach. "Would they kill one of their own members?" I whispered, not really asking Dev, because I knew what he had said was true.

"I don't think we should try to go back there again," he said, the fear evident in his voice.

"Me either."

The minute we pulled into the driveway I knew

I was in trouble. My parents, along with their bodyguards and Brandon, were standing on the front porch. All the lights were on in the house, and they were staring at me as I got out of the car. Dev pulled out without saying goodbye, probably not wanting to face the onslaught of questions that was coming.

I walked slowly toward the front porch, looking down at the damp grass and avoiding any eye contact. *Is there any way I could just sneak in?* I thought playfully.

As I tromped up the front steps, my mother walked to the edge of the last step blocking my path. I was forced to look up at her. Her face was deep red, and her blue-gray eyes were flat and expressionless.

"Where the hell have you been?" she asked. I was shocked at her choice of words. Mother had always said it wasn't very ladylike to curse.

"I went out with Dev," I said calmly, even though I was a mess on the inside, terrified to tell them what I had learned.

"And you didn't think to tell anyone?" She crossed her arms across her chest, the Tiffany charm bracelet tinkling against her black dress.

"It was no big deal," I said, shrugging my shoulders.

"No big deal? You have a bodyguard now for a reason, and you just decided to leave? He called me the minute he saw that you were missing, which was only seconds after you walked out the door. We've had a search party looking out for you ever since." Her words were biting and she didn't move an inch, forcing me to have to look up at her from the step below.

"There was no need. I'm back and everything is fine." I attempted to walk by her, but she grabbed my forearm. I looked back at her, anger filling my face.

"You are not allowed to move an inch without Brandon till we say so, understand?"

I looked at Dad, but his gaze wasn't even on me. He was looking aimlessly across the porch.

"What do you care anyway? You sneak off from your bodyguard all the time. Don't you have somewhere else to be right now?"

Her eyes widened, the rage in them evident, but there was also a look of hurt. "You have no idea what you are talking about," she said coldly.

"Then why don't you tell me and Dad?"

She paused, Dad's full attention on us both. Suddenly, she pulled me forward into the house and away from everyone else. "Hey!" I yelled as she continued to drag me into the dining room.

She let me go and got up in my face. "Don't you ever do that again! You hear me? I'm your mother and you're not going to talk to me like that."

"I can talk to you however I like. I'm not the one having an affair," I said with malice in my voice.

A second later, I felt a stinging slap across my face. I shut my eyes, tears threatening to surface. My mother had *never* hit me.

"Oh, no! I'm so sorry, Casper. I shouldn't have done that. Please," she said, grabbing my shoulders.

I backed away from her. "What's wrong with you?"

My mother looked like she was on the verge of tears, her perfect world crumbling around her. Charleston was bringing this family to its knees.

"You have to promise you won't say anything— not even to your father," she said quietly, looking at the closed door behind us.

My face still felt numb, but I managed to nod.

"I'm not having an affair, but it was just better for us both to look like we were instead of what we are really up to."

I raised an eyebrow. "What?"

"You are not the only one desperate to get out of this group. After I found out about what happened to Jacob at the Romans', I'd had enough. I went to your father, but he still won't budge. He thinks this group is the only solution. I ran into Mr. Gray at the Country Club and he wants out, too. We've been working together to find a way out, but we agreed it would look better if we were simply having an affair. Your father, Mrs. Gray, Marcus . . . none of them know what's really going on."

I just stood there, speechless. I felt so many emotions. I was angry she had hidden it from me. I felt terrible guilt because of the way I had treated her when she was just trying to help. I felt sadness because we both felt stuck in a situation we couldn't get out of.

"I had no idea," I whispered.

She breathed out deeply. "That was the point. I didn't want to get you involved because then you would be in danger."

"Huh, funny." I leaned against the dining room table.

"What?"

"We're in danger because of another group trying to get rid of us and we're in danger from our own group because we want out. It's just ironic."

"I guess it is. But listen, you can't say a word to anyone, not even Cal," she said.

I nodded. "I won't."

She looked at me, and I felt a kinship with her. Most of the time, we were at odds with each other, with very different ideas of how life should be. It was nice to be on the same page for once.

"And I won't tell Brandon you were at the club," she said, raising a perfect eyebrow.

"How did you know?"

"A mother knows these things," she said with a wink, and walked out of the room.

Tonight had been bizarre, with so many twist and turns—I felt like I was on one of the roller coasters at Kings Island, where my old high school had always gone for our end-of-the-year trip. I could remember getting off one rollercoaster, feeling light-headed and disoriented. That feeling was becoming a way of life.

I walked out of the dining room and toward the front staircase. I could hear my parents arguing through the closed pocket doors of the front room. I felt another pang of guilt, knowing I probably caused the argument. I should have kept my big mouth shut, but I was just so upset and confused.

Maybe tonight was a reminder for me to keep out of the middle of things. I had gotten dangerously close to the enemy and now I might have destroyed my parents' relationship for good.

I walked up the stairs slowly, my hand running along the smooth rail. I abruptly stopped at the top of the steps when I saw Brandon's unsmiling face standing in the way of my bedroom door. His arms were crossed over his massive chest, his biceps bulging.

Uh-oh.

"If you pull a stunt like that again, you'll be wearing an ankle bracelet like Lindsay Lohan."

I smiled, but quickly erased it. It was funny to think that Brandon even knew who Lindsay Lohan was, let alone for him to use her name in a sentence.

"Yes, sir."

"Where did you go with that boy? You're not allowed to go with him anywhere again."

"Club Ultra," I said, no hint of remorse in my voice.

His mouth dropped open. "You went there? Why!?"

I let out a deep breath. "To find the guy who probably killed Veronica."

He put his hand on his forehead. "You're kidding, aren't you?"

I shook my head.

"You've lost your mind. If that's who killed Veronica, what makes you think he wouldn't kill you?"

"He said I was too pretty to kill," I admitted, blushing because I knew how dumb it sounded.

"You spoke to him? What's his name? What did he look like?" Brandon's fury turned into an inquisition.

"Cameron and he looked like Channing Tatum," I said.

"Who's Channing Tatum?"

I rolled my eyes. "You know who Lindsay Lohan is, but not him?"

He didn't say a word. He wasn't in the mood for games.

"He was kind of tall, dirty blond, and maybe blue-eyed. It was hard to tell in the light."

"Did you get a last name?"

"No, but I'm not even sure his real name is Cameron. He knew my name was Casper, even though I gave him another name. Who's to say he didn't give me a fake one, too?"

"True. Do you think he'll be back at the club?"

"Apparently, he's a regular."

"Good," he said as he moved away from the door.

"So, are you still mad?" I asked as I opened my door.

He looked back at me. "Yes, but good work." He let a half-smile slip as he walked down the steps.

The air I breathed with every long stride Wendy took beneath me was warm and heavy with humidity.

I needed to ride. I needed to forget all the problems that seemed to be piling up on my shoulders and just . . . let go. The fields surrounding the Hunt Club were quiet and still except for the pounding of Wendy's hooves against the hard ground and her even breathing. I held onto the reins, but closed my eyes and let the freedom sink in.

These were the moments that I lived for—without them, I probably would've been crushed. In the distance, I could hear guns going off, but they barely registered in my mind. I was sure it was a group of hunters after some doves. Wendy slowed down and I opened my eyes to see a stone wall in front of us that was about four feet tall. It must have been the property line for the Hunt Club. I felt the urge to jump over the wall, but I also felt fear. Wendy wasn't a jumper; she came to a complete stop a few feet before we reached the wall.

"Don't want to jump, huh?" I asked her, bending to pat her on the neck. "Can't say I'm ready to do it either."

I had been a competition jumper until I'd had a bad fall. I hadn't attempted it since then, but had been working my way up to it before we'd moved. As I stared at the wall, I knew I wasn't ready to jump over it yet.

"Maybe next time," I said to her, turning her away from the wall. I flicked the reins and she began walking. I held the reins lightly, letting Wendy move as she pleased. Without any encouraging, she started to run across the open field. She loved the feeling of the wind in her mane as much as I did.

We finally reached the Hunt Club and stables. Wendy walked slowly past the Hunt Club buildings and the parking lot. I couldn't help but look at all the white vehicles. Were they Marrows? Did everyone think about Kythera when they saw a black vehicle?

I guided Wendy into the barn, and turned her over to one of the horse hands for her to be groomed. I gave her a final pat on the muzzle and a kiss before walking out, feeling much more alive than I had hours ago.

As I walked out of the barn, I noticed a white Bentley pull into the parking lot. Seconds later, Cameron stepped out of the car and leered at me. I froze. I looked around, and there were several men sitting on the front porch with their customary pipes, so at least there were witnesses. Brandon was still inside, where he stayed while I was riding. Apparently, he was allergic to horses. He knew I wasn't giving up riding, so he had compromised.

Cameron was wearing a pair of dark blue jeans, a white polo shirt, and sneakers. Not hunting and *definitely* not riding gear.

What is he doing here?

"Weird bumping into you out here," he said with a smirk.

"Why are you here?" I said flatly.

"Can't a person just want to come out to the Hunt Club?" he asked, his light eyes sparkling. In the sunlight, I could see that they were green.

"Usually they have riding gear. Or a gun."

He smirked. "Who says I don't have one?"

My mouth went dry and I glanced back once more at the building. Still no Brandon in sight. I turned back to Cameron, who was still smiling from ear to ear. Then something overtook me and I got a shot of courage.

I walked up to him. "Do you think you're cool or something? Because you're not. You don't scare me."

He looked at me for a long moment. "You should be scared. Veronica was."

A chill went up my spine, but I tried to hold my courage. "If you haven't figured it out yet, I'm nothing like her."

He laughed. "Oh, I've figured it out all right. You've got a lot more guts. You're a firecracker."

It was disturbing how easily he admitted to killing Veronica. "If you wanted to kill me, you would have already done it."

"You're right. You're more valuable to us alive."

I heard the door of the Hunt Club open and I instinctively turned to look at who was coming out. It was Brandon. As soon as he saw I was talking to someone, he looked alarmed. But I waved to him and smiled, as if I were only talking to a friend. I didn't want him coming over here if Cameron was willing to give me information.

I turned back around, putting my hands on my hips. "Why am I valuable?"

"Because we want you to leave Kythera and join us."

"Are you kidding me?" I asked. *What the hell?*

"No, not at all."

"You might as well forget that one," I huffed.

"I thought you might say that, but with the prince dead and the kingdom falling apart, you won't have much choice soon." He started to walk back toward his vehicle.

"If Kythera's gone, then I'm out of all this mess!" I shouted.

He stopped and smirked. "When Kythera's gone, you'll be one of us, or you and your parents will end up like your prince and his hot ex-girlfriend."

He turned back toward his car and confidently walked up to the driver's side door. He glanced at me once more before getting in and speeding down the gravel road.

Chapter

20

THE CRUNCH OF THE GRAVEL under Brandon's unmistakable heavy footsteps filled my ears, but I didn't turn around.

"Who was that?" he asked.

"Channing Tatum," I said quietly, still deep in thought.

I never imagined that they would want me. I hadn't seen that coming. What did I have that was so valuable? Tyson had explained my father's connections were worth more than the money we had. It was true that owning and breeding some of the best horses in the world put us in contact with a lot of powerful people, including the Queen of England and several Middle Eastern sheiks—they all shared a love of horse racing. The Queen had even been to Ghost Hill Farms while she was in the U.S.A. to buy thoroughbreds at Keeneland. We'd had a couple of sheiks over for dinner, but that wasn't a big deal to me. I had grown up seeing these people come to our home, and it seemed perfectly normal.

I hadn't known how valuable those connections would be to people looking to gain power.

"What did he want?" asked Brandon, breaking my thoughts.

"Me."

"What?"

I finally turned to look at his confused face. "They want me to join them."

"You're kidding, right?" he asked. From the look on my face, he should have been able to tell I was dead serious. "What did you say?"

"No, of course."

He bit his cheek, as if he was thinking. "Maybe you shouldn't have said no so quick."

I looked at him, my mouth dropping open. "What do you mean?"

He shrugged his shoulders. "Maybe it's just what we need to figure out who they are and to get rid of them. They've obviously bought that Cal is dead and Kythera's in trouble, or he wouldn't have been brave enough to ask that. So maybe you should join."

I was speechless—but when I started thinking about it, he did have a good point. What better way to get information? And to prove to Tyson that I was the one who got it, which meant he would have to sign Wendy over to me. But it was also a big risk.

I thought about last night at the club, the fear I had felt. But what choice did I have though? Cameron had threatened not only me, but my parents. We were all dead if Marrow wasn't stopped.

"Okay, so how do we do this?" I asked, now totally on board.

"We've got to run it by Tyson first, but I think he'll go for it," he said, as we headed toward my black Lexus. I nodded in agreement.

Minutes later, we were back at the hospital. Brandon had called Tyson to tell him that we needed to talk to him, so we knew he was already here. We pulled into the staff parking lot in the back and went into the maintenance entrance. We pulled out our scrubs, caps, and masks from a junked-up janitors' closet before taking the elevator to the fourth floor. We took the familiar route to the operating room, where Cal was now sitting up in his hospital bed, watching a movie on his iPad.

When he saw us walk in, he immediately smiled. I pulled my mask and cap off as I rushed over to give him a hug. As I closed my arms around him, I made sure to only squeeze him lightly. He was doing so much better, but I was still afraid I might break him and he would be gone forever.

I let him go and he leaned up to give me a long kiss. It felt so good to feel his lips on mine.

"Ahem," said Tyson, which reminded me that there were other people in the room.

We parted, but Cal grabbed my hand and held it firmly in his as I sat down on the edge of his bed.

"So, what do you have to tell me?" asked Tyson getting up from his chair.

I looked at Brandon, who nodded for me to go ahead. "I've met the guy with the pin from the club. He says his name is Cameron, but I didn't get a last name. I tried finding him on Facebook and on the Citadel's website where he said he goes to school, but there wasn't a Cameron listed for the Citadel and he wasn't listed on Facebook either. I'm not sure if that's really his name or not." I felt Cal's grip on my hand tighten. "He came to the Hunt Club this afternoon to find me. He wants me to join Marrow."

The look of shock on Tyson's face was surprisingly satisfying. He started to pace the room. "Do you believe him? Why does he want you?"

"I believe him, because he could've easily killed me at the club last night."

"You went back to the club!?" interjected Cal. I looked at his face. His jaw was tight.

"Sorry, but it was either me or Alex, and Alex would've killed him and then we couldn't get any information from him."

"You still didn't answer why he wants you," said Tyson.

I looked back at him. "He said I was more valuable to him alive than dead. He said I could either come willingly or I would end up like Veronica and Cal."

"You can't let her do this," Cal said, his voice full of anger.

"You think you can handle it without messing it up?" he asked, ignoring his son's plea.

"Yes," I answered.

"You can't do this. Please, Casper, they're dangerous. If they figure out what you're doing, they'll kill you," pleaded Cal.

I looked at him. "I've got to do this to save all of us. You risked your life to save mine—now it's my turn."

He shook his head and forced his eyes shut. "No, you can't," he said.

"Sounds like a good plan to me," said Tyson.

"This is insane," said Cal.

"Just make sure you work with Brandon on this," added Tyson.

"And if I do this, you'll give me Wendy, right?" I asked, hoping having witnesses would mean he would keep his word.

"Yes," he said sternly.

I let go of Cal's hand and gave him another hug. "I love you," I whispered in his ear.

"Casper, don't do this. It's too risky," Cal said as I let go.

I walked back to the door, where I put on my mask and cap again, and waited for Brandon to follow.

"Casper!" Cal yelled.

"I'm sorry," I said, and we walked out of the room.

I hated to leave things like that between us, but I had no choice. This was the way out for all of us. If it had been the other way around, Cal wouldn't have hesitated to do the same thing. He *hadn't* hesitated on the roof, with bullets flying past his head. Surely I could handle it.

As the nervousness built in my stomach, I said a little prayer.

The next difficult task would be to tell my parents what was going on. *Oh, hey, Dad, I'm joining the other group and hoping they don't kill me.* I wondered what Mother's reaction would be now that I knew she was trying to help us get out of Kythera. Sure, my plan wouldn't get us out, but at least we could focus on getting our lives back without worrying about whether we would survive at all.

Brandon pulled the car into the driveway and told me to go on in while he made a couple of phone calls. The house was dark, but I was sure they were both home. After their fight last night, I doubted they had gone to any parties or functions. My parents had never fought a lot— but when they did, it was always epic. I could remember one time, when I was eight years old, they had yelled so loudly I could hear them from the barn. I also remembered the sound of crystal breaking against wooden floors. I had been so terrified, I had stayed in the barn with the horses all afternoon, lying in the straw next to our newest foal and talking to them as if they were able to talk back.

Even though I was no longer a little kid, their fights still scared me. I hesitated to open the front door, waiting for the searing heat to hit me like a ton of bricks. That was the other thing I hated about their fights—the tension seemed to linger in the air for days.

The house was quiet and I could see some light coming from the back. I walked into the dark kitchen and noticed the dim light coming from the library. It had to be Dad, typing or writing emails.

I opened the door. "Hey, Da—" I stopped midsentence when I realized it was Mother. "Oh, I thought Dad would be in here."

She was sitting in the wing chair, no book in her hand or anything else. She had just been sitting there, staring at who knew what. She smiled slightly, but it quickly faded. "No, he's not in here," she said quietly.

This was worse than when they normally fought. She was never this calm after a fight, which made me very nervous.

"Where is Dad?" I asked.

"He's packing his things and staying at a hotel."

I felt the blood drain from my face. "Why's he leaving?"

"Because of the affair."

"But you didn't really have an affair. Why don't you just tell him the truth?" I begged.

"Because he wouldn't believe the truth. He still believes in Kythera." She picked up a glass of wine from the coffee table and took a sip of the dark red liquid.

"So you're just going to let him leave?" I asked, my voice cracking. I was on the verge of tears as I rushed through the kitchen and up the servant stairs. I ran down the hall to my parents' room. Sure enough, Dad was throwing his shirts and suits into a large suitcase. He looked up at me, the sadness evident in his face.

"You can't leave," I said, crossing my arms over my chest.

"I have to," he responded, as he pulled a jacket off a hanger and folded it neatly on the bed.

"She didn't really do it," I pleaded.

"And how do you know that?"

"I just know. You have to believe me," I said, not willing to share Mother's secret either.

He continued packing and I felt like my world was falling apart for the millionth time. When would the emotional rollercoaster end?

I walked over to the bed and tried to move in front of him, but he simply stepped aside and kept packing. "You can't leave me," I said.

I felt like I was five all over again. I went through a phase where Dad couldn't leave the house for work without me giving him a kiss on the cheek.

I remembered one day when he had pulled out of the drive without me knowing; I had run out into the driveway, tears streaming down my face, screaming for him until he'd turned around.

I wasn't screaming now, but I felt like it. I was almost eighteen, but I still needed my dad.

"I'm not leaving you. I'll still be here," he said reassuringly.

I stayed quiet for a moment, trying to think of what I could say to get him to stay. As he pulled out the last shirt, I started throwing his clothes out of the suitcase onto the floor.

"Casper! Stop that!" he said in a stern voice.

But I continued. I was so angry and frustrated with everything that had happened—I couldn't take anything else.

"Casper, stop right now," he said. I dropped the shirt in my hand and looked at him.

"Why? So you can leave? So you can run and hide? That's not what you taught me. Weren't you the one who told me to get back on the horse when I would fall? To have courage? Where's yours?"

He stared at me clenching his jaw. "This isn't the same thing. Your mother cheated on me. I would think you of all people wouldn't defend her."

His words were especially stinging. It was like he was suggesting that I didn't love my mother just because I didn't always understand her.

"If she really had, then I wouldn't defend her. But she didn't. I can't tell you what's really going on, but you need to trust me. It's not what you think."

He bent over and picked up a shirt and pair of pants off the floor. "I have to go. I'll see you later," he said, and walked out the door.

I fell on the floor and cried like a toddler. I knew it didn't make since, but I was learning no one could ever know how much they needed someone until they left. I knew he was leaving because of what he thought Mother had done, but how could he walk out on *me*? What had I done?

Then I started thinking about all the ways I had disappointed him this year. Running away, causing problems in Kythera. Maybe that was why it was so easy for him to walk out.

I cried into one of his shirts that still smelled like him, curling up into a ball on the floor. I was mentally exhausted and broken. How much more could I take?

I felt Mother's hands around me, and that only made me cry harder. I got up and let her hold me in her lap, which felt a little weird since that was something that Dad would've done for me when I was scared of the boogey man under my bed. That thought made me cry even harder.

After a few minutes, I was able to lift my head up and look at her. Her own eyes were streaked with tears, and her usually-perfect mascara had left black rings around her eyes.

"Why didn't you just tell him the truth?" I asked, my voice hoarse and hollow.

"Because what we're doing is more important right now. Saving your future is more important than anything right now," she said, fresh tears in her eyes.

"But what about Dad?"

"He'll come around. You just have to believe and continue to be brave. You've taught me so much these past few months. You're such a courageous girl. Do you know how proud I am of you?"

I scoffed. "What have I done that's so brave?"

She lifted my chin with her hand. "You saw what was right and what was wrong and you were willing to stand up for what you believed in. How many people would have been willing to stand up to something like Kythera and fearlessly fight for what's right? Not many people—definitely not someone your age. You've inspired me. You're an amazing daughter. Don't stop fighting. Your freedom is worth it."

"But I didn't do it alone. Cal came with me. And he's the one who risked his life for mine over and over again."

"But *you* gave him a reason to fight—he told me so. That's why I was willing to go against Tyson and bring him back from the boarding school. I could see it in his eyes that he loves you, and that you gave him that same courage to stand up. " She took her hand and wiped away the tears on my cheeks. "You're a strong young woman who can do anything you put your mind to."

I leaned my head against her shoulder and breathed deeply. "I love you, Mom," I said.

"I love you, too, sweetie. It's all going to be okay," she said quietly, rocking me in her arms.

Was I really that courageous? Could I stand up against them? This wasn't a game or some movie—it was real life and it could easily end tomorrow. But we weren't ever promised tomorrow, were we? I knew that tomorrow might never come—so didn't I want to know I spent my last moments standing up for what was right and what I believed in?

Finding out who was in Marrow wouldn't get me my freedom, but it would put me one step closer to having it. I couldn't stop now.

Chapter

21

M Y DECISION MADE, I WALKED confidently into Club Ultra, once more looking for Cameron. Brandon had dropped me off and promised to be waiting for me in the parking lot. He gave me a special cell phone and told me to hit number two if I felt like I was in trouble.

The club didn't faze me anymore; the loud music was just a little annoyance in the back of my mind. I walked through the door of the VIP room and searched for Cameron. He was easy enough to spot with the group of scantily-clad girls surrounding him and his friend. *He's cute, but not that hot*, I thought to myself.

Once again, I walked through the group of girls, barely noticing them standing there. Cameron looked happy to see me and motioned for me to take a seat next to him. I sat down and faced him.

He leaned toward me. "Had a change of heart?"

I nodded.

"I'm surprised you gave in that easily—but, then again, you seemed like smart girl."

"Oh, I'm very smart. Now that you've gotten what you want, you have to do something for me."

He put his arm around me and I hoped that he couldn't see how much that disgusted me. "Anything you want, you can have it," he said, raising a blond eyebrow.

"Is your name really Cameron?"

He looked amused. "Yes. Surprised I gave you my real name?"

I shrugged. "A little. So what's your last name?"

"Maxwell, but I did fib about my age. I'm actually twenty-six."

I scooted away, not caring if he noticed. "Wow, you're a lot older than me."

He laughed. "You make it sound like I'm forty or something." A waitress brought over a glass of champagne and a bottle of beer and sat them in front of us.

I had no intentions of drinking tonight. I wasn't a drinker to begin with, and I didn't plan on becoming one. "I guess it's not that old, but still. I thought people didn't start lying about their age until they were thirty."

He picked up the bottle of beer and motioned for me to pick of the glass of champagne. I did, but I just held it in my hands. "It just felt wrong to tell you the whole truth. Now, let's get to why you're really here. You've decided to join the winners in all of this, but are your parents on board?"

"Yes," I lied.

I had gotten all caught up in Dad leaving last night—I hadn't even told them about my plans. But I really didn't need them to approve. Tyson was the one in charge of our money now, and he was the only one I needed permission from to do this.

"Good, so we'll set up a time to sign the papers and get everything in order. In the meantime, welcome to Marrow."

I looked at him, confused. "That's it?"

He laughed loudly, throwing back his head. "What? You thought we would brand you like Kythera and have some ceremony? We're not like that. We're more modern than Kythera with its archaic rituals. I mean, unless, of course, you're into tattoos or ceremonies. We can have it arranged."

I sighed with relief. "No, that's okay."

I was surprised but thankful it didn't require getting another tattoo. I didn't want to go through the pain of another one, not to mention the pain of having a tattoo removed.

"I don't have to get the Kythera one removed, do I?" I asked, panicked. It hadn't crossed my mind till now that leaving Kythera might mean having to get rid of the tattoo. Wait, when this was all over, would I have to re-do the Kythera tattoo?

He shook his head. "No, I kind of like it."

Creep, I thought to myself.

"So, drink up, we need to celebrate tonight," he said, nudging my shoulder.

I reluctantly brought the glass to my lips and took a sip, but as he turned his head to talk to someone else I spit it out on the floor. Unfortunately, it landed on the strappy high heel of the tall blonde standing in front of us. She let out a squeal and looked at me and sneered.

Fortunately, Cameron had become too absorbed in a conversation with the guy sitting next to him to notice. I shrugged and mouthed, "Sorry," to her.

Now what?

I looked around at all the unfamiliar people, unsure of what to do. I was an introvert, and no matter how many parties my parents had forced me to attend, I hadn't learned the art of small talk.

Now that I had Cameron's full name, I had something to go on. Maybe I should get some information on the guys he was talking to, but I hesitated when I noticed none of them were wearing a pin. Chances were that I would be wasting my time. I looked around at the girls who were gyrating against each other, their dress straps slipping down their shoulders. They probably weren't wearing pins either, not that I was getting in the middle of that to find out.

Cameron turned back around toward me. "You look bored. The club scene not for you?"

"Not really."

"Then let's get out of here. We can go back to my place if you want?"

"No, that's okay," I tried to say politely.

A kiss with this jerk was one thing, but anything else was unacceptable—not to mention illegal. I wanted out of Kythera, but I wasn't willing to sleep my way out. I liked to think I was smarter and respected myself more than that.

"Are you hungry? We could go to a restaurant or something."

"Yeah, that sounds great," I said.

At least that would be someplace public— but then I realized that Brandon was out in the parking lot and we hadn't discussed me leaving the club. Should I really trust Cameron and get into a car with him? How did I know he really bought that I wanted to join them? He seemed smart, and it had to cross his mind that I might be playing them.

Cameron got up and grabbed my hand, helping me to my feet. If I backed out now, it would look obvious what I was doing. So, I let him lead me out of the club and into his shiny white Bentley.

We ended up on Queen Street, where we parallel-parked and walked over to Husk. I was kind of excited, because I had wanted to try this restaurant since moving to Charleston. Cal had promised to take me, but that had been before we had run away and he'd gotten shipped to boarding school. I was sad I wasn't going with him.

The two-story restaurant looked like the plantation-style homes that could be seen throughout the city, with a porch on each floor that ran the width of the building. It was pristine. White and black shutters hung on either side of all the windows. Like our own historic home, it had a small front yard, guarded by a fence.

The place was buzzing, with people talking loudly outside. I couldn't imagine what the inside would be like. Cameron paused on the front porch and walked over to a guy who immediately gave him a big hug. I didn't know if I should walk up to them, or kind of hang out in the shadows. I was starting to wish I had paid more attention to my mother when she droned on about social etiquette.

Cameron looked back at me. "Come meet our newest member," he said, walking the man over to me.

He was tall and middle-aged, with graying hair and rimless glasses. He was wearing a checked button-down and yellow bowtie. When he approached me, his eyes widened with surprise. "I know exactly who you are. You're Casper Whitley. I've heard so much about you," he said, smiling widely.

I shook his hand. "Nice to meet you?" I said, confused as to he was.

"My name is Henry Porter. I'm the President

of Marrow here in Charleston. I'm glad you've decided to join us. I'm here with the papers to complete the process," he said, waving a manila envelope.

Wow, they don't waste time. When had Cameron even had time to call him? Had they already known that I had been planning to join? I hadn't known this was going to end up being a meeting with the president, but if I'd really thought about it . . . it was a smart idea. I should've known they wouldn't trust too much information with me until they had my signature or writing in blood that I was pledging loyalty to them.

"Great," I said enthusiastically.

They gave each other looks. Were they surprised? They could've thought this would throw me for a loop, but I had already gotten permission from Tyson. He knew *exactly* what I was doing and we were prepared for this moment even if I hadn't expected it to happen so fast.

Cameron led us all to a table on the porch, where he pulled out a chair for me to sit.

"Now, there are several things that need to be signed so we can finalize everything. Tyson's already been called, and although he wasn't happy, he said he would sign the papers as soon as he got them."

"Wow, he let me go that easily?" I said, pretending to be shocked. Henry's huge grin was enough for me to know that my acting skills were getting better.

"Your signature is only a formality for us, since you are a minor. When you are eighteen, you'll have to sign a few more things."

He slid some papers in front of me and I looked them over.

"They're standard forms, kind of what you probably saw with Kythera. You, as the sole heir of your parents' property pledge and sign over all rights you have in their property over to Marrow," said Henry, as he pointed at the signature line.

I signed quickly, and he slid another paper toward me.

"This one says that Kythera will relinquish any rights to your property, real and otherwise, to Marrow."

Once again, I signed.

There were a couple of more papers I was required to sign, but they were all legal mumbo-jumbo, and I didn't even listen to what he was saying as I scribbled my name.

He folded the papers and stuck them back into the envelope. "That should do it. Welcome to Marrow, Miss Whitley," he said.

Cameron, who had been sitting quietly beside me, threw an arm around my shoulders. "Welcome to the club. You've made the right decision," he said confidently. "I do have to ask . . . what made you so willing to leave Kythera? They don't let go of members so easily."

"I'm sure you know I've already tried to get out."

"Oh, yes, we heard all about it. You even convinced the prince to come with you. We were interested in you before that, but someone so brazen against a powerful group like Kythera is a rare and powerful asset."

"Well, now I'm your asset," I said coolly.

They both chuckled and Cameron signaled the waitress and asked for three glasses of champagne to celebrate. As they looked at each other, so smug and confident, I couldn't help but take pleasure in knowing what they didn't.

As soon as our plan had been set in motion, Tyson had signed all rights to our property into a separate company Tyson's attorney had set up for this purpose. I had no right to sign those papers and neither did Tyson. We had given them *nothing*.

<hr />

I sat next to Cal's bed. I could feel the tension in the air. He was still mad at me for agreeing to become a member of Marrow. I could see it in his face, the way he tightened his jaw anytime he was unhappy. He was clenching his teeth, trying to hold in his feelings.

"Are you going to ever talk to me or not?" I finally asked, tired of the silence.

"Eventually." He picked up the remote of the TV that had been wheeled into his makeshift room, and started flipping through the channels.

I sighed. "What choice did I have? Do you

really want to live in this room? You know you can't leave here until they're gone. Not after we told them you're already dead."

He finally looked at me. "I know that, but there could've been another way. Kythera didn't need to send you in there to do its dirty work. They're putting you in a lot of danger. What if they figure out what you are really doing? Then what? I couldn't stand to lose you," he said, and I felt a pang of guilt.

"But you've put your life on the line so many times for me. Why isn't it fair that I do the same?"

He was quiet.

"Exactly," I said, happy I had won the argument.

"Have you enjoyed watching me in the hospital? Do you like the memory my heart stopping?" he asked.

"Of course not."

"Then why do you want to do the same thing to me?"

Ugh, I hated that he could always come up with a very convincing argument. When was he just going to let me win already?

"Because if you hadn't gone after those guys on the roof, I wouldn't be here at all," I finally said.

He was trying to hold back a smile. "True, but . . ."

"Listen, can't you just accept that I'm not a damsel in distress? That sometimes I can take care of myself?" I pouted, hoping he would finally see my way.

He couldn't contain it any longer and a smile broke out on his face. "You're definitely not a damsel in distress—at least, not all the time."

I leaned up and kissed him on the lips. "I *am* the one who can come in riding a white horse, after all. You ride the little pony, remember?" I said, as I kept my face close to his.

He stared at me, shaking his head. "That's for sure."

"I love you," I said, my heart speeding up just at saying the words.

"I love you. Be safe, my knight in shining armor," he added playfully.

"Always." I kissed him again, this time long and deep.

"Ahem," coughed Tyson as he walked into the room. I couldn't wait until Cal could leave and maybe we could kiss without his dad walking into the room all of the time. We pulled apart, both our cheeks turning red. I sat down quickly and tried to act like nothing had happened.

"What did you find out last night?" he asked, sitting in the comfy chair on the other side of the room.

"I've got some names, and as far as I can tell, they've bought that I want to be a member."

He raised an eyebrow as if to say "And?"

"Cameron Maxwell is the guy from the club I met, and he's a lot older than I thought. And I met Henry Porter, who's the president."

Tyson's eyes lit up with recognition. "Henry Porter? I know him," he said in disgust.

I looked at Cal and we both shrugged our shoulders. "Who is he?"

"He used to own a construction company that we always bid against. I drove him out of business," he responded, almost talking to himself. "Did he say anything about me?" Tyson looked directly at me.

"No."

"Did they already have you sign the papers?"

"Yes."

He laughed. "They didn't waste any time, did they? When's the next time you are supposed to meet them?"

"Tomorrow, after school. Cameron is picking me up to take me to meet some of the other members."

"Good," said Tyson.

"Brandon will be following her, won't he?" asked Cal.

"I think they will be too suspicious. They've proven to be resourceful." Tyson got up and straightened his tie.

"So you're going to let the monster who killed Veronica leave with Casper without protection?"

I hadn't been nervous until this moment. I had assumed Brandon would be going with me. Now I would be completely on my own, and I wasn't sure I could do it. It was easy to be brave when I knew a trained bodyguard was following behind me.

"What choice do we have? They like her, for

whatever reason, and think she's valuable, so I doubt they would hurt her now that they think I've signed everything over to them." Tyson had no emotion on his face, as if this was strictly a business deal.

"I don't like it," Cal said.

"Please, let's not go through this again," I whispered.

He looked at me, but his eyes were still deep blue and full of anxiety. "Fine, but you better call me the minute you get back," he said, crossing his arms over his chest.

"I promise," I said.

"Now, I've got some business to discuss with Cal, if you don't mind?" Tyson said, and all but shoved me out of the room.

Something didn't feel right, but I didn't know what. Tyson was always so businesslike with me—and even his son—but he was even more emotionless than usual. After all, he was throwing me to the wolves, yet he didn't seem to care about anything but what I could bring back. But I guess that *was* typical Tyson.

Chapter

22

ORMALLY, AT SCHOOL I WAS watching the clock, because I couldn't wait to get out, but today I was hoping I could slow time down. Why did the minutes always seem to fly at lightning speed when I didn't want them to, but any other time it was like watching a snail crawl across the floor?

The bell rang and the day was over. I gathered my books, and walked slowly into the hallway. I bumped into David, a quiet guy who always sat in the back of Renaissance literature. He gave me a dirty look, but I didn't even say sorry.

The minute I stepped out of the room, Marcus was waiting for me. He looked me up and down. "Are you okay? You've been acting weird lately."

I looked up at him, not sure what to say. "I'm fine. Just got a lot on my mind."

"Have you found out any more about our parents and *you know*?" he asked, his eyes wide and his thick eyebrows raised.

"No, I haven't." I wanted to tell him the truth so much, but I couldn't betray my mother, not when we were starting to get along.

"Oh, okay," he said, looking at the ground.

"I haven't found anything else, but I think it will work out," I said. I hated not to give him something.

He nodded. "So, how've you been? You've been scarce the past few days. What are you up to?"

"I've just been at home. Just don't feel like hanging out right now." I readjusted my backpack, which felt like a ton of bricks. Marcus saw me struggling and lifted it off of me.

We walked down the hallway and he held my backpack while I opened my locker. "You know, you can tell me what's really going on. You're like my sister," he said, leaning against one of the lockers.

"I know, but it's just something I have to take care of myself," I said as I pulled out my calculus book. "But I'll give you a call tonight. If I don't, call me, okay?"

"What are you up to?" he asked, concern on his face.

"Nothing, just make sure to call me." I closed my locker and took my backpack from him, then marched out of the building and into the parking lot to wait for Cameron.

As I walked down the sidewalk, I saw Dev sitting on the bench. He beamed as soon as he saw me. "Hey! You want to go riding today?"

I shook my head. "I can't. I have other plans."

"What kind of plans?"

"With Cameron."

Dev's face instantly went blank. "You're kidding right? Why would you go anywhere with him?"

"Because I have to."

At that moment, the now-familiar white Bentley pulled up to the curb.

Cameron rolled down the window, "Ready to go?" he asked.

Wordlessly, I opened the passenger door.

"I'll give you a call later, promise."

"Casper, wait!" yelled Dev, but I was already in the car.

As we drove by, I could see the stunned expressions on Marcus and Charlotte's faces as they walked down the front steps. I felt like I was seeing them for the last time. But I had to think positive. I was strong, and a survivor. Alicia Keys's song, "Girl on Fire" started playing in my head. It was the only thing keeping me calm.

We turned onto Concord Street, near Hazel Park playground, and drove to the end, through an open gate. I could see about a hundred feet out on the water was a beautiful house. It literally was on the dock, nothing but water underneath the massive, three-story structure. Beyond the house, a large yacht swaying in the waters.

Cameron parked in front of a three-car carriage house, which was on land. I opened the door and got out, and he motioned for me to follow him out onto the dock. I had never seen a house like it, completely over the water. We walked into the double front doors and up the large staircase to the third floor. The view took my breath away. The whole back of the house was floor-to-ceiling windows, and all I could see was the yacht framed by the dramatic backdrop of blues sky, white clouds, and ocean.

"Wow, who lives here?" I asked, walking over to the windows and staring out, a sea gull swooping down to the water.

"Me," he responded.

I twirled around, my nerves becoming unsettled. "You? By yourself?"

He nodded as he walked behind a bar and pulled out a couple of glasses. "Just me. Crazy, isn't it? And you thought Kythera had money."

I turned back to the windows, so he couldn't see my satisfied smile. He was so full of himself. I wanted to throw it in his face that Cal's home was triple the size of this one, even if it wasn't suspended over the ocean.

"I guess Marrow has plenty of money."

He walked over to me and handed me a glass of dark liquid. I took a whiff and it definitely was whiskey or scotch. I had no intention of drinking it.

"So, how did you end up in Marrow?" I asked.

"I just kind of fell into it. I'd dropped out of high school in Boston, and was working at a fast food joint when the president of Marrow saw me. He liked me for some reason, and made me an offer I couldn't refuse."

"What did you have to do to get here?" I said, pointing at the house and the yacht.

"Worked my way up. I started out as an errand boy, and then I took care of the dirty business and I was good. After that, they promoted me to recruiter, and now I'm like the vice-president of Charleston," he said, taking a sip from the crystal glass.

"Where's your parents?" I asked, studying his profile as he stared out the window.

"They died when I was thirteen. I lived with my great-aunt for a while, but we didn't get along. I got my own place at seventeen. Now look at me." He raised both hands in the air, the liquid in the glass sloshing around.

"When you say you took care of the dirty business . . . does that mean getting rid of people?" I asked. I couldn't bring myself to say the world "kill."

"Yeah, but that's behind me. I've made it to the top."

"But what about Veronica?" I asked.

"You think I killed her? Nah, I'm above that now. I was just messing with you," he said, as he bumped into my shoulder, spilling what was left of his drink onto the wood floor. The alcohol was starting to take effect.

"Damn, I'm out. You need anymore?" he asked as he walked over to the bar.

"No, thanks," I said. I walked over to the bar and sat down on one of the stools. "So, why did you bring me here?"

He shrugged. "I don't know. You're kind of fun to hang out with, and you're pretty." He poured another drink, but stayed behind the bar.

"Oh,thanks,"I said nervously..

"You think someone like you would ever go out with someone like me?"

"You're a lot older than me, and I'm not looking for a relationship," I said quietly, hoping he wasn't an angry drunk.

He hung his head low as he looked at the ground. "I figured. You were dating the prince, weren't you?"

Why couldn't they ever say Cal's name? "Yes. I loved him."

"Could you ever love someone like me?" he asked, taking me by surprise.

"Why do you keep saying someone like you? Someone older?"

He laughed. "No, I mean someone without the best background. I'm no blue-blood like your boyfriend or you. I'm from the streets and not from money." He gulped down the second glass of alcohol.

"That wouldn't matter to me. I don't care where a person is from. My dad's family made their money. They were poor when my grandfather scraped enough together to buy his first thoroughbred. Before that, they lived in a two-room house. My grandfather started out with nothing and built a horse-racing empire. Not having tons of money wouldn't bother me, but it would depend on how the person had made their money," I said, studying his expression for any kind of emotion.

"Huh, I didn't know that about your family. So, because I joined Marrow the way I did, you wouldn't go for a guy like me? That's pretty ironic, considering your Roman boy toy," he said with sarcasm.

"But Cal wanted to leave it all behind," I pointed out cautiously.

Cameron poured himself another drink. "You think his dad would ever let him leave? You're better off believing in fairy tales if you think he would've escaped Kythera. The only way that was happening is if he was gone—which he is."

"How did you all get to him? Did you pay off a nurse or something?"

"We paid her off. I found someone like me, struggling, who needed the cash. We paid her very well to pump some stuff into his IV and leave."

"Was she a member? Is she still around?" I asked, trying not to sound too anxious.

He looked up at me, his eyes roaming over my face. "What does it matter?"

"It doesn't—I was just curious how you pulled it off. It took a lot of guts," I said, but my voice was uneven. I hoped he was too drunk to notice I was fibbing.

He took another sip of his drink and sat it down on the bar. "Are you wearing a wire?"

I looked at him, unable to move. Then he laughed.

"Just kidding! You're one of us now, nothing to worry about."

He walked around the bar and put his arm around my shoulders, shaking me back and forth. I started looking around for a way out—or at least something to hit him with if I needed it.

"You must have been the mastermind behind the whole plot, right?" I hoped that stroking his ego would get him to tell me who the nurse was and would bring the focus away from me.

"Of course. I was for Veronica, too. She made it so easy. I sent someone in to flirt with her and she followed him out into the alley. She thought they were going to make out or get to second base. Stupid girl. Cal was a little harder, especially in the ICU, where nurses were always coming by. I had to take some time to find the right one, the one who looked desperate. Once I found her, I just had to throw enough money at her and she caved. She went in and did her thing and now she's living it up somewhere in the Caribbean. And I got a nice bonus for pulling off the whole thing," he said, pointing toward the massive yacht at the end of the dock.

He kept one arm around my shoulders, and I

could feel my skin begin to crawl. I really wished I had a way to call Brandon at this moment.

"Wow, that is amazing. Love the boat, by the way. I think I'm going to get another drink." I moved away from him and to behind the bar.

"But you didn't even finish that one," he said fake pouting.

"I'm not really a scotch drinker."

"Oh, I forgot. Your kind likes champagne. It's in the wine fridge underneath. A big bottle of Cristal just for you, babe," he said with a wink.

I hated being called babe, honey, or any other stupid pet name. I bent over to get the bottle out, even though I had no intentions of drinking it, either. As I got up, I could see that he had moved behind the bar as well. This was going to be tougher than I thought.

He moved closer, aiming to get close enough to kiss me, but I moved back some as I pretended to look for something—anything. He was still determined. He moved closer, pulling me to him. There was no way for me to get out now. He bent down and pressed his lips against mine, but I refused to play along this time. I held my lips together, tight and unmoving.

He stopped and looked at me. "What's the matter, babe?"

"I'm just not ready for this. Cal's not been gone that long and I really did love him."

"But you kissed me at the club!"

"I was drunk. I just can't handle this right

now. The memories are too painful," I said, willing myself to tear up.

I started thinking about the mess my life had become and how it would feel to lose the horses. Then I let myself drift into the memory of collapsing onto the hospital floor when I thought Cal was gone for real. I thought about the total emptiness and the total ache that overtook every inch of me.

Within minutes, I was so worked up, the tears were pouring down my face. Cameron quickly let go of me, clearly unsure of what to do with an emotional female. He led me to the couch, sobering up quickly.

"Sorry, I didn't know," he said, as he patted me awkwardly on the back. "I'll take you home."

I continued to cry, unable to turn off the waterworks. "No, I can call someone," I said quietly, my voice crackly and sad.

"Okay," he said, and quickly got up.

I breathed out a sigh of relief as I tried to get the tears under control. I called Dev, because a Kythera member or Brandon would look suspicious. Dev was the only safe person I could think of to call. He said he could be there in five minutes.

Cameron returned with a paper towel, which I assumed was supposed to be a tissue for my runny nose. I took it and blew hard, hoping he sound would repel him further. He was now on the other side of the room staring out the windows awkwardly.

Thank goodness I could fake some tears today. Why couldn't I do that any other time I needed it? Either way, it had worked, and I had gotten myself out of a difficult situation without having to hit Cameron over the head with the giant bottle of champagne. That would have given me away, but I was prepared to do it. I wasn't about to let some slimy guy take advantage of me just because he thought he could.

I was getting the feeling that because I was now a member of Marrow, Cameron thought that meant I was his property.

I looked at him. He was still staring out the window, his drink untouched in his hand. Part of me felt sorry for him. He had had nothing and Marrow had given him everything he had wanted. If I had been in his shoes, would I have done the same things for the money and power? He had been my age when he'd found his way into Marrow. Could I run "errands"—which were probably drugs or something else illegal? Could I then kill to further my own agenda?

As sorry as I felt for him, I couldn't see myself choosing the same path. No matter the amount of money, taking lives wasn't worth it. Not for Marrow, not for Kythera.

⬦

Dev walked me to my front door, and we stood there for a minute. "Thanks for the ride home," I finally said, breaking the awkward silence.

"What have you gotten yourself into, Casper?" he asked, shaking his head.

"Nothing I can't handle," I said curtly. It was none of his business, and I wasn't having this conversation today for the second time. I had gotten enough from Cal.

"That guy looks like he's almost thirty. Why were you at his house?"

I had no good reason, so I shrugged.

"Are you going out with him? So soon after Cal?"

The words stung, and I felt a bit of rage. "No, I'm not dating him, but it wouldn't be any of your business anyway if I was. Funny you would mention Cal when you couldn't wait to pounce after he died," I said angrily.

I looked at his stunned face. I instantly felt bad, but I had had enough from everyone.

"Sorry, I was just worried about you." He started walking back to his truck.

I sighed heavily and followed after him, "I'm sorry. I shouldn't have said that—but I can take care of myself, I promise. I know what I'm doing," I said, grabbing his forearm.

He looked at me, and I couldn't help but feel a little spark between us. "I hope you do, because I would hate to see something happen to you."

He grabbed me and gave me a hug. It felt so good to be near him, but I quickly broke away, knowing it was just me wishing he was Cal. Dev got into his beat-up truck and drove out onto the busy street.

I looked up at the house again and I had a sense of déjà vu. It wasn't too long ago I was looking up at this big old house that had become my prison, wishing for the day that I could escape. Now I was hoping that its walls could protect me from the evil lurking outside.

Chapter 23

THE NEXT COUPLE OF WEEKS flew by. It felt like the weather changed overnight, the nights had becoming cooler—but it was a welcome change. Thanksgiving was just around the corner, which meant a break from school. I couldn't wait. I stared out my bedroom window at the giant oak trees in our small backyard. They had lost a lot of their leaves, and their twisted branches were bare except for the thick, gauzy blanket of Spanish moss. They looked eerier than ever.

I looked at the clock on the mantel and it was almost time to go. Tonight I would be meeting with Henry Porter and Cameron to officially talk about my role in Marrow. I wasn't excited about it, but at least this was the beginning of the end for me. Today I would be wearing a wire and I was somehow supposed to convince Henry and Cameron to confess to killing Veronica. I had no idea how I was going to do that, but I had to figure it out soon.

The minute Tyson had found out Henry and Cameron's names, he had wanted to go ahead and kill them, thinking the blow would be enough to get rid of them. Fortunately, Mr. Gray had convinced him to take another path. He'd said if we could get them to confess to Veronica's murder, then we could take that to the police and have them prosecuted. The media would have a field day when it was revealed a secret group had killed her, which would, in turn, splash Marrow's name across the front page. Journalists would start digging—and the more information that was revealed, the quicker the whole organization would collapse.

I was hoping it would work, because I was tired of the killing, even if they were the "bad guys." I grabbed my purse and cell phone, and took the servant stairs down to the kitchen, where my mother and a detective were waiting on me.

Detective Holden placed the wire on my body, taping it on my chest between my breasts. It was awkward to have to take my shirt off in front of him, especially as my mother stood by and watched.

When he was done, he checked to make sure it was working and told us we were good to go. After he left, I turned to look at my mother. She was wearing red skinny jeans and a crisp button-up blouse. She was out-of-character casual, which could only mean she was super worried. Her outfits had always been a great way to tell her mood. She literally wore her emotions on her sleeves.

"Everything is going to be fine," I reassured her.

"It has to be," she said.

"I'll be back in no time and this will all be over."

She walked over and gave me a hug. "I love you," she said as she squeezed.

It felt so nice to be near her, to smell the faint scent of Chanel Gardenia on her hair and to feel her arms wrapped around me. But there was some sadness, too, because Dad wasn't here. Hopefully, after all this was over, Mother could tell him what had really been going on and he would come home.

I let her go and waved at her as I went out the back door and walked around the house to the driveway the driveway, where I got into a red Audi. I would've thought that by now Marrow would've delivered a bunch of white vehicles to our house, but they hadn't. My mother had rented a vehicle, so they wouldn't see me rolling into their driveway in a Kythera car. Part of me thought they'd like for me to be driving the car with a red "K" on it, because it would be a slap in the face to Tyson, knowing I had left them.

I made the short drive to Cameron's house and pulled up to the carriage house. I looked down the long dock at the house, which was glowing brightly against the dark, inky waters. There were several cars in the driveway, which meant Cameron and Henry were not the only ones at the house—that could make things much more difficult, but I wasn't going to think about it. I was going to think about how this could end all the hiding. Cal could come back and be a part of my life beyond the walls of his suite at Charleston Place, where he had been staying since being released from the hospital. He had not been allowed to leave his room these two past weeks, and I had not been able to find too many excuses to visit Charleston Place that Henry or Cameron would buy. I made up that a relative from Kentucky was in town and that had bought me some time that I needed with Cal.

Keep it together, I told myself, *and Cal will be home soon.*

I walked down the dock, the cool, salty night air clinging to my arms. I got to the front door and hesitated. I closed my eyes for a moment and tried to focus on what I needed to do. I breathed in and out deeply, opened my eyes, and rang the doorbell. Seconds later, a girl in a short, glittery dress answered the door.

Her hair was in disarray and it was obvious that she was loaded from the strong smell of alcohol reeking from her body. She took a few steps in her six-inch heels, propping herself against the door as she motioned for me to come in. There was loud music blaring from the third floor, and I could hear people screaming and laughing. I'd had no idea this was going to be a party. I felt underdressed in my jeans and black T-shirt with three-quarter sleeves, but I doubted one of my prim and proper party dresses would fit in either.

I climbed the stairs, dodging a couple who were running down the steps barefoot. I turned around to see them head into one of the bedrooms on the second floor. I finally made it to the top of the steps of the third floor. The room was packed, and there was a DJ in the corner.

The lights were low and hundreds of candles were burning all around the room, making the already warm space almost unbearable. I broke out in a sweat as I made my way in a circle around the room, looking for Henry or Cameron. With all this noise, how was I supposed to get a confession clearly on the microphone taped to me? I made a couple of circles, but couldn't find either one of them. I finally looked out the windows to see them talking out on the large deck. They looked like they were in a very serious conversation, but I didn't care if I eavesdropped.

I opened the sliding door, and closed it quickly blocking out most of the noise from inside. The chilly sea breeze caused goose bumps to form on my bare arms. They turned around to see me, and both of the serious looks disappeared.

"Casper, so good you could make it!" said

Henry joyfully. Cameron just continued to stare out at the water. After the day at his house when he had attempted kiss me, he had been a little distant. I had tried to avoid any more awkward run-ins, and tried to keep our meetings to Marrow things. Apparently, he wasn't happy about that.

"You all have a real party going on in there. Who are all these people?" I asked, pointing back at the house.

"Just some friends and other members," said Henry.

"Oh."

"Not the type of party you're used to, is it? We aren't stuffy like Kythera. We know how to have real fun without all the rules and etiquette," Henry said with a laugh.

"How long have you guys been in town to know this many people?" I came over to the railing and leaned against it, facing Henry and Cameron. Cameron finally looked my way and smiled for a second before returning his gaze to the water.

"We make fast friends around here. This town was ready for some new blood and they welcomed us quickly, didn't they!" He nudged Cameron, but didn't get much reaction out of him.

"So, what about Veronica, why did you kill *her* instead of Tyson?" I asked, trying to sound confident, like that was something normal to randomly bring up in a conversation.

But Cameron quickly looked my way, his eyes roaming up and down my body. I felt my mouth go dry. "Why would you want to talk about that?" he asked, turning around and leaning his back against the rail.

"Just curious," I said, shrugging. I could feel the heat rising in my cheeks, but I prayed it wasn't going to show on my pale skin in the dim light.

"This is a party—we try to keep things upbeat," Henry finally said. He gave Cameron a long look. I was starting to get really nervous.

The conversation stopped and I didn't know what to do, so I turned to look out at the ocean and the giant yacht now moving up and down in the large ocean waves. I was afraid to look at Cameron, who I could tell was staring at me—I was afraid that he would see the fear in my eyes.

"I'm going to go check on some of the other members and see if they're having a good time," Henry said, and walked back into the house, leaving me alone with Cameron on the deck.

"So, why are you so interested in all that junk?" he asked.

"I'm just curious. I'm just trying to understand how you think," I said, hoping he would think I wanted to get to know him better. I hated to stoop to that level and flirt, but I needed something. I was drowning.

"Why would you care how I think? Thought you weren't interested? You're supposed to still be mourning the Roman kid."

I scooted closer to him. "Maybe I'm over it

now. My life has been so much better since I left Kythera—since I met you."

That got his attention. He turned to look at me. The embers of light from the house lit up his green eyes and I knew I had his attention again. "Are you really?"

I nodded slowly, fluttering my lashes and trying to look all sexy, but I didn't have a clue what I was doing or what would actually be *sexy*.

Whatever I did must have worked because he inched toward me and laid a hand on my arm. "You want to go inside?" he asked, leaning into my ear.

"No—why does everything have to equal sex for you? I thought older guys were more mature? Most of the high school guys think about it, too, but I thought you were different."

He held his hands up in the air. "Sorry, I'm not used to a classy babe like you. Most of the girls I've been out with are like the ones at the party or the club. They're just looking for a good time. Plus, I'm sure you've been with Roman boy. He had a reputation."

"Why can't you just say Cal? And, no, we didn't. He never pressured me, either," I said, proud to know that Cal could see me as more than just a sex object.

His eyebrows shot up. "You must be something special, then. He was the teenage playboy from what I heard."

"Who told you that?"

"Veronica," he stated.

"So, you were there that night at the club? I thought you said you didn't kill her," I said, relief coursing through my veins that he had given me the opportunity to ask him about it.

He hung his head to the side. "I told you already that I didn't do it—I just planned it. Remember?"

"If you only planned it, then who actually did it?" I asked.

I felt like I was sitting on pins and needles waiting for the answer. This was what I had been waiting for all along. Once he gave me the answer, I could leave and it would all be over.

He looked at me, and then pointed toward the house. "You see the guy at the bar with black hair and with a bottle of beer in his hands?" He waited until I nodded before continuing. "He's the guy who took Veronica out into the parking lot and got rid of her."

"What's his name?"

"Michael Grover," he said.

"He's the one who killed Veronica, but you planned it?" I said, whispering in his ear.

"Yes."

"Did Henry Porter have anything to do with her or Cal's deaths?"

"Yes," he said slowly, but I could feel his body tense.

Suddenly he grabbed my body and started kissing my neck, and his hands roamed over my body. All I wanted to do was scream and run away, but his grip was too tight. He had his hands around my waist and then they were under my shirt. I wanted to stop him, but I could barely move as he let his hands travel up my stomach toward my breasts. He stopped as he felt the thin wire taped to my body.

"You're wired, aren't you?" he said, shocked.

"Yes," I said, and held my breath.

He pushed me toward the deck railing. "Why would you do that!?" he said, pushing me until my back was up against the rail.

"Because you tried to kill Cal and me," I said, my heart rate rising.

"What do you mean *tried*?" he said, as he put his hand around my neck.

"Cal's still alive," I said.

His grip on my throat tightened. I could barely get any air in and out of my lungs. He pushed me further against the rail, and my feet lifted off the deck. I tried to reach out for the railing, but couldn't put my hands on it.

He was going to kill me. I didn't know if I would suffocate before he threw me over the railing into the water, but I knew that one way or another, I was going to die. The party was still raging on behind us, and I could see all the happy people dancing and drinking, oblivious to what was going on outside. Cal had been right. I was in over my head.

"He's alive? Where is he then?" he asked, his voice strained, the anger evident in every word.

I couldn't respond because my air had been almost completely cut off. I gasped, but I couldn't pull any air into my scorching lungs. I pushed against him, putting my hands out, trying to grab him, but that only put me farther out over the rail. All the energy I was using was eating up what little air I had left. My lungs felt like they were going to explode and my whole chest burned like someone had set it on fire. The world was starting to fade and my body felt light and tingly.

"Hey!" said someone, but I couldn't tell who it was because my vision was dark and blurry. It sounded faintly like Cal, but . . .

Seconds later, my body crashed to the deck floor and air came rushing back in. I took several deep breaths, almost hyperventilating, my lungs desperate for oxygen. I coughed and struggled to look up to see what was going on around me.

Cameron fell to the ground in front of me, knocked out cold. I finally looked up to see Cal standing over him. His locked with mine and he rushed over to me.

"Are you okay?" he said, wrapping his arms around me. I was still too out of it to respond.

"Who's that?"

"Where did he come from?"

"Is that Cal?"

The party had finally taken notice of what was going on outside and they were starting to flood out onto the deck.

Cal grabbed me up into his arms, and started

walking to a set a stairs of stairs running down the outside of the house. I could hear the crowd all gasping as if they had seen a ghost. I guess technically they were seeing a ghost. It felt like the night at my house all over again as Cal started moving faster, jostling me back and forth as he ran down the dock. Even the sound of sirens in the distance had become all too familiar. I opened my eyes a little to see cops storming up the driveway, blocking anyone from leaving.

"It's over, Casper," Cal whispered into my ear.

I felt excited, but was unable to say anything. The world was still swirling—and then it went black.

Chapter

24

I STOOD QUIETLY, HOLDING CAL'S HAND as we looked out over the harbor at White Point Gardens. The normally golden water was fading to a neutral color, with navy ribbons running through it. I leaned my head on his shoulder and looked up at the sky that was almost purple and dotted with faint stars.

"So, are they all gone?" I asked, still looking out at the water.

"Yes, I think so."

It had been a month since that frightening night at Cameron's house; there was only a couple more days until we would be out of school for Christmas break. We had been planning on returning to Kentucky for Christmas, but that was before Dad had left us and I had spent a few more nights in the hospital. Cal had gotten me out of Cameron's just in time. I was amazed we both made it out of that house alive, but apparently everyone was so stunned to see Cal alive, they didn't know what to do. And it didn't hurt that the police had stormed the place as we left.

That night, Cal had decided to sneak out when he heard the plan for me to wear a wire. Tyson had wanted to stop him, but he had been determined to come get me. I guess he was my knight in shining armor after all.

"Now we can start thinking about normal things again, like going to prom or school football games. I feel like I've gotten *almost* all of my life back."

"Yeah, what's missing?" Cal asked.

"Dad and Wendy," I said.

Tyson had done as he had promised and signed her over after Cameron and Henry were arrested. Their faces had been all over the papers. One journalist started digging into Marrow, revealing its members and their shady businesses. Within a few days, the members and the pins were gone. And, of course, Kythera's name had been kept out of everything.

My dad had yet to come home, though. Mother still refused to tell him the truth about what she was doing with Mr. Gray, because she said her work wasn't done. They hadn't found a way out yet. Things couldn't be fixed with Dad yet—but at least I could see Wendy and she was legally mine.

"You want to go out to the Hunt Club tomorrow after school?" he asked.

"You want to go?" I said with a laugh, tilting my head so that I could look up at him.

"I'm not letting you out of my sight after everything that's happened." He kissed me on the forehead just the way I liked.

"Come on, you've got to give me some credit."

"True, you did a pretty good job until you were almost strangled." He smirked and I let go of him, faking shock.

"Well, someone almost took you out in the hospital and you couldn't do anything about it," I countered.

"Yeah, but I was in a coma. They wouldn't have stood a chance if I was awake," he said with a wink, and started to remove his shirt.

"What are you doing?" I asked, as he threw it on the ground.

"Going for a swim." He started walking toward the railing near the water.

"You're kidding, right? It's freezing out! And what about sharks?" I asked, but still following him—as always.

"Live a little, why don't you? If we can survive everything we've been through, then I think we can survive a cold swim in the harbor." He turned back around to look at me. His chiseled chest was breathtaking as ever, even with the bright red scar from his open heart surgery that drew a straight line down the middle. Ironically, his scar ran right through the "K" of the Kythera tattoo on his chest. Maybe it was an omen that we would get out eventually.

I knew one thing: that scar was a constant reminder of what we had been through and what we both had survived.

Cal turned back around, and jumped over the rail into the water. Droplets of cold water splashed up on me as I leaned over the rail to look at him. I looked at the water only a few feet below, air bubbles coming up through the golden waters. Cal surfaced and motioned for me to get in. I looked around the park to see if anyone was watching.

"Get in, and quit worrying about who sees you," he commanded.

I pulled my shoes off, took a deep breath, and jumped over the rail into the water in all my clothes. The water was freezing, my skin tingling all over as I swam to the surface. I let out a noise that was half a scream, half a laugh.

Cal pulled me close and gave me a big, wet kiss. "Wasn't this fun?"

"Maybe once my skin goes numb," I said, my teeth chattering.

He pulled into him and kissed me again. The coldness instantly went away. The minute he let me go, I couldn't help but violently shiver. Cal started splashing me and, of course, I had to let him have it. We continued throwing water at each other until we couldn't take the cold anymore.

Cal swam back toward the rail and pulled himself up out of the water, back over to the boardwalk. He leaned over, reaching his hand down to help me up. He pulled me out of the water, but he pulled so hard that, as I climbed over the rail, I fell into him really hard and he took a couple of steps back to keep from falling.

"Oh! Are you all right?" I asked, still crushed against him. Ever since his surgery, I had been afraid I was going to do something to hurt him and then I would lose him forever.

He laughed, and I was mesmerized by his gorgeous face. "I'm better than all right as long as you're here with me." He reached out and tucked my wet hair behind my ears, his visible breath curling like silvery mist around my face.

I shivered in my wet clothes. He pulled my face to his and our lips met. I kissed him eagerly, not wanting to let go, even though my wet shirt was plastered to my freezing back. The longer we stood there, kissing in the cold, the hotter my skin got. I wanted to take my shirt off—but then I remembered we were in a public park. No one was around to see us, but a random dog walker or something could come by at any second.

Finally, I pulled away for a second, my face hovering above his. "I love you," I said, my breath crystallizing in the cool, dark air.

He put his hands on my cheeks. "I love you, too. I don't know what I would do without you."

"You'd be lost," I said with a laugh. "Let's get inside before we freeze." I started moving slowly toward the street.

He reached for my hand as we walked across

the park to my house. Even though I was freezing, I felt more alive than I had in months. We were so close to being free that I could feel it in my bones. A weight was lifted off my shoulders with Marrow gone—and although getting out of Kythera was still my ultimate goal, I wasn't in such a hurry anymore. I was having too much fun knowing that I wasn't a target to focus on getting out. I needed time to breathe and enjoy some happy moments with Cal before plunging into our next move.

Next semester, I would turn my focus to getting out of the K for good.

———◄◆►———

I didn't dread school anymore. For the first time since the move, I felt like a normal teenager. My biggest problem went back to being a pop quiz Ms. Epling surprised us with this morning.

Cal was back in school, which would have been easy to explain if we were all actors on a soap opera, but to everyday students it was a hard to explain how he had never died. The Roman family had released a statement about the fact that someone had attempted to murder Cal so they needed to put him in a "witness protection program" of sorts, which was pretty much the truth. They just didn't mention Kythera or Marrow. But the gossip around school was way more entertaining. There was the rumor that he was an undercover spy and that he had to pretend to be dead since his cover was blown.

My favorite rumor was that as he was about to be buried, he had popped out of the casket and yelled, "Surprise!" Then where did they think he had been since the funeral? That one made me laugh pretty hard.

"You want to go riding this afternoon?" asked Dev, breaking into my thoughts. I hadn't even noticed him standing next to me while I pulled my calculus book out of my locker.

I shut the door and looked at him. He was smiling from ear to ear. He had been really surprised, like everyone else, to find out Cal was alive. In a way, I think Dev was upset that Cal was back, because he knew that I wouldn't be running to him anytime soon. But we had quickly become friends again and things weren't so awkward.

"I would, but I'm going to the Hunt Club to see Wendy. I haven't been able to spend as much time with her as I want since everything that's happened."

Brandon hadn't thought it was safe to spend a lot of time alone out there until they were sure that most of Marrow had left. I was too vulnerable out by myself on the fields. He had said so every time I went out to see her, and he made me stay near the barn.

Once he finally gave me the okay to spend time with Wendy, that was when he had packed up his things and left. I did get a hug before he went—and he promised to keep in touch, which

I was sure was him just being polite. I would probably never see him again, once he took on some other clients somewhere else.

"I understand. Maybe I should come out there and ride with you? We've started boarding a couple of horses out there so we can ride the trails," he said, readjusting his backpack on his shoulder.

"That sounds great. See you out there," I said, closing my locker.

He nodded and walked down the hall. Seconds later, Cal appeared by my side.

"Ready to go to lunch?"

"Sure."

In the cafeteria, we sat down at our usual table with Marcus, Charlotte, Sarah, and Alex, who was more like himself since the arrest. He hadn't been able to do anything to Cameron, Henry, or Michael, who were all responsible for Veronica's death, but he took pleasure in knowing that most likely they all would be in jail for a very long time.

"Hey, do you two want to ride with Marcus and me in a limo to prom?" Charlotte asked—before we even had time to sit down with our trays of food!

"Isn't it a little early to be thinking about prom? It's not even Christmas yet," I said, putting my food down on the table and taking a seat.

"No, it's never too early to start planning. I'm going to go prom dress shopping this weekend. Okay, so I'm just mapping out the stores to see who has the best selection. And if I can't find anything, my parents said I could take a group of girls to New York City to shop. You should come along!" she said, clapping her hands together.

"I'll think about it." I had been on a couple of shopping trips with Charlotte and I wasn't much of a shopper. She had dragged me into every store and made me try on tons of clothes. I couldn't imagine a whole weekend of shopping with her.

"So, what about the limo?" she asked, not skipping a beat.

I deferred to Cal. "I've got a surprise for Casper, so . . . thanks, but no thanks."

"Okay, but you have to tell me what you are up to, Cal Roman," Charlotte said playfully.

"Wait, she gets to know and I don't? And you've already got something planned?" I said, irritated that he was trying to surprise me *again*.

"Yes," he said.

I rolled my eyes. "You're never going to stop with the surprises, are you?"

"No."

Marcus sat down, but he didn't look that happy. "What's wrong?" I asked.

Charlotte's happy demeanor quickly disappeared. She patted Marcus on the shoulder.

"Mom moved out last night," he said, staring at his plate of food. He didn't make eye contact with anyone.

"Oh, sorry," I said, and I felt a heavy weight settle back in my stomach. I hated not being able to tell Marcus the truth. He looked so miserable.

"Yeah, me, too," he said, moving the carrots on his plate around in a circle.

"It'll be okay, man, just have faith. It will all work out. You'll see," Cal offered.

Marcus nodded. "Thanks. I hope so."

Everyone looked at each other, clueless what to say next.

"Let's all celebrate tonight with dinner at the Thoroughbred Club in honor of our number-one horse-riding queen," suggested Sarah, trying to make the mood light again.

"I would love to, but I have a date at the Hunt Club with Wendy," I said.

"And, apparently, I have one with Lightning," Cal added, putting his arm around the back of my chair.

"Good luck with that," said Marcus, some of the darkness lifting from his face.

The bell rang and lunch was over. Everyone scattered to their classes. I gave a Cal a quick kiss before heading off to P.E.

"Meet you after school?" he said, pulling his backpack onto his shoulder.

"Yep," I said. As he walked out of the room, I grabbed my own backpack. Out of the corners of my eyes, I couldn't help but notice Dev was staring at me, and he didn't look happy. I figured it was because I was obviously still with Cal and happier than ever. He had probably thought I would come running to him when everything was over with Marrow, but Cal had ruined his plan.

From the intense look on his face, he was wishing Cal wasn't around—or maybe he was wishing I wasn't still around. A chill ran up my spine.

I looked at him and waved. He waved back and the serious look on his face disappeared instantly. Maybe he had been concentrating on something else altogether, like a test, or he was having a bad day or something. It was pretty obnoxious of me to think it had anything to do with me.

Maybe I was reading too much into things.

Chapter

25

A S WE STARTED OUT ON the trail, I kept Wendy at a steady pace so Cal could keep up with us. He was doing better this time around, and Lightning had only bucked him once. I looked back at Cal, who was holding so tightly to the reins that his knuckles were turning white.

I shook my head, it was so obvious he wasn't meant to be a horsemen or a cowboy. I laughed to myself. Besides, he would look ridiculous in a cowboy hat.

"How's it going back there?" I called to him.

He looked up and tried to smile, but then Lightning shook his head and Cal's face went pale. "Fine," he said, and returned all his concentration to making sure he didn't end up on the ground.

"You can leave me behind—I'll be fine. I know you like to run—and isn't Dev coming out here to ride with you?" he said, his voice controlled and even. He was afraid to show any emotion that might startle his temperamental horse.

"You sure?"

"Yes," he said.

With that, I gave Wendy a little nudge, and we started picking up speed. She kept getting faster and faster, without any suggestions from me. She loved to run as much as I loved being along for the ride. Even though Wendy had never run a race in her life, the instinct to go as hard as she could was there.

After a good few minutes, I tightened up the reins and we started to slow down. I loved to run and feel the wind against my face, but I also liked to go slow and take time to just stare at the beautiful fields, listen to the birds, and take in the quiet.

I finally brought Wendy to a complete stop in the middle of the field and just looked around. There wasn't a cloud in the sky, and it was an impossible blue. The leaves were still green, but were thinning, and a few trees were tinted with crimson and orange.

I could hear the fast-paced pounding of hooves. I looked around, knowing it was definitely not Cal. Finally, a white horse emerged, Dev firmly in control on its back.

I waved at him, happy to have someone out here to run with. He came to a stop near me.

"Hey! I ran into Cal and he said you were out this way. He isn't much for horse-riding, is he?" he said with a laugh.

"No, but I'm glad he's willing to try for me. With some help, I think he'll get the hang of it."

"I still don't understand what you see in him. I mean, *we* obviously have a lot more in common," he said, surprising me.

"You really want to go there right now? I thought we got past all of that. I can't explain it, but he gets me. And I know that sounds like a stupid line, but he does. He's the first person I've ever really connected with beyond the horses. We just have a connection," I said, looking straight at him.

I wanted Dev as a friend, but if he couldn't get that we could only be friends, then there was no point in us hanging out together. I liked Dev, and if there had never been a Cal, then I could see myself dating him—but there was Cal and there was no competition.

"He has a couple of girlfriends every year. He'll find someone else eventually. Why not go out with someone who isn't going to dump you at the end of the semester?" His face was serious; all the joking had gone away.

"Why can't you just take no? I really want to be friends, but if we're going to have this conversation every time, then we can't." Wendy started to get restless, so I patted her on her neck.

"Why can't you just see the truth? I'm better

for you than him. I know you have feelings for me. Remember the day in my driveway? It felt real, and I know it did for you. Why can't you just admit that?"

I squeezed my eyes shut, and breathed deeply. "Listen, I would be lying if I said I didn't have some feelings for you, but I also thought I would never see Cal again, that he didn't like me anymore. Don't you see? I only saw myself with you if Cal was out of the picture." I was starting to get agitated.

"I hate to hear that, because you leave me no choice, then," he said, a cruel sneer crossing his lips.

I was totally confused as to what he was talking about. Then he pulled something out of his shirt pocket and threw it to me. I caught the little gold pin in my hand. My stomach dropped and dread filled my chest.

I hadn't put it together this whole time. He was one of them.

Shouldn't I have figured it out sooner?

All the pieces started to make sense. I had brought him to the club the night Veronica had been killed, and he had disappeared after I had gone out on the dance floor with Charlotte.

"You're the one who killed Veronica," I said quietly, the realization making me sick.

"Yeah, and you didn't have a clue. You're not as smart as you think you are. Prince Cal came at just the right time so I could get away without you even noticing."

"You knew he was there that night?"

"I saw him dancing with you on the floor. I have to admit, I got a little jealous, but still I had to take advantage of the situation. Veronica was more than willing to go outside with me—she was such a flirt and she wanted anything she thought you had. She wasn't your number one fan," said Dev.

"Wait, what about when you went back with me to the club? You knew Cameron and he knew you."

"We had it all set up. I would play the nice guy, so you wouldn't suspect anything."

"Why didn't you kill me when you had the chance before? Why tell me all this now?"

"Because we really did want you to be part of Marrow. We've been watching you since you got here."

"That's how you knew about the Calla lilies."

"I saw Cal leaving them on your doorstep all the time. He's such the romantic. I should've killed him then; maybe you would have fallen in love with me and you wouldn't have tried to get rid of us. But now there's no use for you."

"But I thought Marrow was gone? Why fight for something that doesn't exist anymore?"

He shook his head slowly, a sinister grin on his lips. "Who says we're all gone? We'll never be gone."

Wendy was getting even more restless. She was picking up the tension in the air. I knew then that I needed to turn and run. With one quick movement, I had Wendy turned in the opposite direction and she started running as fast as she could. My heart was beating so fast—I could feel it pounding in my chest, keeping time with the thud of Wendy's hooves against the ground.

I looked back quickly to see Dev chasing after me. He wasn't too far behind; he was a good rider. A few seconds later, his horse was inching up beside me and, without any encouragement, Wendy went faster. I was surprised and didn't know what to do but to hold on. She was in control and I was just her passenger. Now she was flying and the wind was roaring in my ears. We pulled away from Dev and I felt better—until I saw the familiar stone wall up ahead.

Oh no, I thought. I was terrified to jump and Wendy was just as afraid as I was. It was okay if the rider was terrified—but if the horse was too afraid to make the jump, it could be a disaster. That was what had happened to me at the Adequan Championships. Hot Stuff had locked up at the rails of a jump and he had stopped so suddenly that I had been thrown off. I could still remember hitting the ground with a sickening thud, and the pain in my arm was so intense that I passed out.

Fear filled my thoughts. Wendy would probably stop short of the wall and the momentum would throw me over her neck and onto the ground—or the wall itself. I didn't know if I could survive that kind of fall; not many people could.

I looked from side to side to see if there was another way except over the wall, but there wasn't. I tried to slow Wendy down, but she wasn't listening. She was too determined to beat Dev and his horse—and they were starting to fall back. Dev was an experienced rider, but I didn't know if he knew anything about jumping.

They caught back up with us, and Wendy faltered a step as Dev bumped his horse into us. I slid half off the saddle, my right foot losing the stirrup. I held on tightly, and tried to get back upright, but Wendy was not going to slow down. Finally, I was able to get my foot back into the stirrup and sit squarely in the saddle. I looked back to see Dev was now several links behind us. I turned my attention back to the front just in time to see the wall only a few feet away.

I held on tightly, shutting my eyes and praying I could somehow have a strong enough hold on her to keep from being thrown over. My heart was beating so fast, I was becoming lightheaded. Maybe that was a good thing. Maybe I would faint before I fell.

I gritted my teeth and squeezed my legs tightly against Wendy as I felt us leave the ground. It felt like we were flying, soaring in the air like a bird. Then we hit the ground hard, jarring me to the point that my eyes popped open. I looked behind me and we were already several feet from the wall. Wendy had jumped it without even thinking twice about it.

I kept looking back as Dev came up to the wall, but his horse wasn't ready to jump. It came to a halt and threw him to the ground. His body hit the ground with a thud, disappearing behind the wall. I finally pulled the reins hard enough that Wendy stopped. I turned around, galloping back toward the wall, unsure of where he had fallen exactly. I edged Wendy to the wall, hoping he wasn't waiting to jump up and get me from the other side.

As I stood up in the saddle, I found him lying motionlessly in the tall grass. He was sprawled across the ground inches from the wall. He wasn't moving and the top of his head was covered in bright red blood. His deep brown eyes were open and glassy.

I jumped down from Wendy, and crossed over the wall to help him. I put my hand on him and could feel that he wasn't breathing. I looked around for my phone, but it had fallen out of my pocket somewhere in the field. Even if I could call for help, it was obvious that he was already gone. I felt sick, but I couldn't bring myself to take my hand off his arm. He had seemed like such a nice guy, with what appeared to be this perfect family that I had to admit I'd been jealous of. *Oh*, his family. What would they say when they found out? I knew he had been trying to hurt me, and that he hadn't been the nice guy he'd been pretending to be, but he was still a person and I hated to see someone else die.

I stood up at the sound of another horse and knew it had to be Cal; it was not moving at a very fast pace.

"Casper!" he called out, jumping down from Lightning and running the rest of the way over to me. He hugged me fiercely. "Are you all right? I thought you fell off your horse when I couldn't see you. And Dev . . ." he said, letting go of me and looking at Dev's lifeless body.

I nodded my head. "Yes, I'm fine but Dev's gone. He was one of them, Cal. He wanted to kill me."

Our eyes met and I could see the shock on his face. He hadn't suspected it either. "He was a member of Marrow?"

"Yes, and he said they're not all gone."

Cal didn't say anything; he just kept staring down at Dev.

"They won't ever be gone, will they?" I asked, knowing already what the answer would be.

Cal's face was like stone. "No, they won't. And even if Marrow is gone, there will always be some other group trying to come after us. It will never be over until we get out of Kythera for good."

I bent down and picked up the gold pin that was lying near Dev. I must have dropped it when we jumped over the wall. It was ironic that had it had landed near him, since Marrow had a habit of leaving them near bodies.

"We'll just have to find a way out, then," I said, putting the pin in my pocket.

I turned to look at Wendy, who was standing at the wall looking at us. I went to her and placed my face on her cheek.

"You're such a good girl, Wendy. Thank you for protecting me," I whispered, and kissed her nose.

She shook her head up and down, as if she understood the incredible thing she had done. I knew she was a horse and didn't really understand what was going on beyond the fact that another horse was trying to outrun her, but part of me thought she had known what was at stake. She'd known she had to run to save my life, and she'd taken the jump without thinking twice—over a wall that not too long ago I couldn't even get her near.

"I've got cell reception so I'm calling 911," said Cal, his phone up to his ear.

I nodded, but turned my attention back to Wendy. I put my hands around her neck, giving her a hug.

"I love you, Wendy," I said. I could hear her familiar heartbeat in my ear, and her steady breathing that always calmed me. After everything we had been through, I was even more determined to get back to the horses that I loved. They were part of my family and I couldn't leave them behind.

We made it back to the house several hours later—after the ambulance arrived and the police questioned us about what had happened to Dev. It would be written as a riding accident, which was true, but no one would know he was a part of Marrow.

Cal and I walked into the front foyer of my house, and my mother ran toward us and hugged us both. "Are you two all right?"

"Yes, we are," I said, my face tucked into her shoulder.

She released us and took a step back. Mr. Gray walked into the foyer. Even though I knew the truth about their relationship, I couldn't help but feel a little bit angry. He was the reason my dad wasn't here right now.

"What did Dev say to you?" he asked me.

"That Marrow wasn't gone and that they never would be gone."

Mr. Gray and my mother shared a knowing look. Mr. Gray stepped toward us with something in his hands. He handed it to Cal, and I leaned over to see what it was. It was a black and white photo of a man and woman sitting, very properly, on an ornate couch. A pretty little girl with black curls and a frilly white dress on was perched on the man's lap. The man was wearing a tuxedo, and the woman was wearing a floor-length beaded gown. A giant painting hung behind them, and it was obvious even in black and white that it was the same painting hanging over the mantel in the front room and in Cal's house. It was the Kythera painting.

"Who are these people?" I asked, my eyes focusing on the pretty woman, her dark hair pulled up in a neat bun. She was wearing a giant glittery diamond necklace around her neck.

"That's the Roman family, my dad's grandparents," Cal whispered, still focused on the photo.

"No, Cal, that's your mother's family. The little girl is your maternal grandmother," said Mr. Gray.

I looked at the photo again, noticing a tiny black spot on the little girl's leg. I leaned over Cal and rubbed the photo to see if it was a speck of something stuck to it, but it didn't come off.

"What's that on her leg?" I asked, still staring at the photo.

"A Kythera tattoo. We had to have the photo blown up to see it, but it's definitely the same tattoo," said Mr. Gray.

"That can't be," he said, looking up at Mr. Gray

"We think this photo is the answer to getting out of Kythera," my mother said.

Cal flipped the photo over and looked at the date. It said 1925. But that wasn't all that was written on the photo. There was a phrase that I couldn't understand.

It read, *Laissez les bons temps rouler.*

"What does it mean?" I asked.

Cal looked up at me. "It means we're going on a trip."

Cal handed the photo to me and walked into

the other room. I flipped over the photo and read the phrase over and over again. It looked French, but I couldn't be sure.

"*Laissez les bons temps rouler*,'" I read once more. Whatever it meant, I was ready for what it would bring . . . even if it *might* be a "prince's" revolt.

Acknowledgments

I cannot believe I've finished the second book in Casper's adventures already. Time has truly flown, but I couldn't have done it without love and support from the following individuals:

First and foremost I want to thank my parents, who've not only continued to support me, but have turned into an invaluable part of my marketing team. They have a definite future in PR. Once again, I couldn't have done it without my first readers and dear friends, Karey and Alicia. My editor, Anna Genoese, who always does an amazing job and keeps me sane. The great team at Streetlight Graphics, who once again helped put it all together and created the beautiful cover. To my husband, Michael Tyler, who's always supportive of my dreams. And thank you to everyone who enjoyed The Kings of Charleston and wanted to continue the journey with the sequel, All the Kings Men. Your support means so much to me.

About the Author

Kat H. Clayton is originally from Kentucky and attended Eastern Kentucky University. She now resides in South Georgia with her husband, Michael Tyler, Frank, the cat and Lil, the dog. For more information on Kat H. Clayton please visit: www.kathclayton.com.

Connet with Kat H. Clayton online:
Facebook: Facebook.com/kathclaytonwriter
Twitter: Twitter.com/KatHClayton
Email: kathclayton27@hotmail.com

Coming Soon from

Kat H. Clayton

The Kingdom's Revolt (Fall 2013)

Other Titles by Kat H. Clayton

The Kings of Charleston (Volume One)

Made in the USA
Charleston, SC
13 May 2013